Ink

ISABELLE ROWAN

Published by
Dreamspinner Press
382 NE 191st Street #88329
Miami, FL 33179-3899, USA
http://www.dreamspinnerpress.com/

This is a work of fiction. Names, characters, places, and incidents either are the product of the author's imagination or are used fictitiously, and any resemblance to actual persons, living or dead, business establishments, events, or locales is entirely coincidental.

Ink
Copyright © 2011 by Isabelle Rowan

Cover Art by Anne Cain   annecain.art@gmail.com
Cover Design by Mara McKennen

All rights reserved. No part of this book may be reproduced or transmitted in any form or by any means, electronic or mechanical, including photocopying, recording, or by any information storage and retrieval system without the written permission of the Publisher, except where permitted by law. To request permission and all other inquiries, contact Dreamspinner Press, 382 NE 191st Street #88329, Miami, FL 33179-3899, USA
http://www.dreamspinnerpress.com/

ISBN: 978-1-61372-253-4

Printed in the United States of America
First Edition
December 2011

eBook edition available
eBook ISBN: 978-1-61372-254-1

Life is too short for fear and regret… even for a vampire.
Provehito in altum.

Chapter
O N E

ANOTHER fractured line streaked above the cityscape, followed almost immediately by low, drawn-out rumbling. The air crackled with electricity. He could smell the first drops of rain as they hit the hot asphalt road and turned to steam. The humidity suppressed the noise and subdued the normally exuberant inhabitants of Chapel Street.

Dominic knew the street well; he had watched it change over many years. These days the geography of the street housed two very distinct cultures. Closer to South Yarra, Chapel was all trendy, upmarket boutiques and sushi bars, where pretty young things with glitter sprayed on their skin and too-high shoes hobbled their way into clubs and cocktail bars. Dominic always found the rundown Windsor end infinitely more interesting. Café culture had only begun to intrude, and you could still see storefronts with bondage corsets and adornments for the multipierced sitting comfortably next door to white orthopedic shoes for lawn bowlers.

A tramcar rattled past and gave its warning "ding" to an errant pedestrian; Dominic looked up to watch its progress. Tonight, as on many other nights, he sat at the outdoor table of a small café, where he could see the passing parade of people coming out of the tattoo parlor with their small patches of cling wrap taped to arms or ankles. Even when it wasn't visible, Dominic could smell the newly broken skin. It sent a wave of hunger through him, but he ignored it. Not tonight; tonight was for other pleasures.

He paid for his coffee, which, as usual, sat untouched, and walked to the painted windows of the little shop across the street. Nothing could be seen from the outside. The entire shop front was a montage of demonic creatures and skeletal dragons, the name Ink taking up an entire glass panel. Dominic pushed open the door. Inside a man flicked through a photo album while another checked out the designs on the wall. Both glanced at him but quickly looked away.

Dominic stood quietly at the counter until a woman sporting a kaleidoscope of color work on her arms and a head of startling crimson hair came out from the back room. She smiled at him and asked, "Can I help you?"

"I have an appointment," Dominic answered quietly.

She frowned, sensing something slightly off kilter about this man, but reached for the appointment book. "I don't think so. It's almost closing. Scott is with someone, and I'm sure Michael is finished for the night." She opened the book and checked under each name to affirm what she'd just said.

"Look again," Dominic said in a deceptively soft voice and pointed to a blank time slot. "There's my name."

This time she could clearly see the name printed under Michael's, although the moment she looked away, she'd forgotten what it said. "Oh, I'm sorry. I'll get Michael for you," she mumbled, confused, and called out to the back room, "Mikey, you have a customer."

A young man with dark curls and equally dark eyes walked through the curtained doorway with an almost sheepish grin and said, "Hey, sorry, I thought I was done for the night. Come through." He turned and bid Dominic to follow him.

The back room had obviously been part of a previous owner's home at some stage in the distant past. A high picture rail that would once have displayed much-loved family portraits barely managed to cling to the crumbling plaster, and the disused fireplace now housed an odd collection of movie action figures and battered metal lunchboxes. The walls of the room were painted a dark purple, although they were all but hidden by screen-printed posters advertising obscure industrial bands. The two workspaces, however, were a sharp contrast to the carefully composed chaos of the décor; the bench tops and ink trays were immaculately organized and clean.

Michael walked to the second workstation and sat on the small vinyl swivel stool. He indicated for Dominic to sit in what looked a lot like a leather dentist's chair and smelled like it had just been wiped with antiseptic. Michael usually made small talk at that point to put customers, particularly first-timers, at ease, but there was something about the man that stopped him. Instead, he asked quietly, "What exactly is it you want?"

Dominic almost laughed at the question. *What is it I want?* But he answered, simply, "A design on my left arm." Almost as an afterthought, he turned his face, stared directly at Michael, and added, "I'll let *you* decide what."

The vampire knew this scenario well: along with the spoken word went an echo in Michael's subconscious that left him more than a little shaken. Dominic's pale gray eyes locked him in place, trapping Michael's breath until his chest ached.

They may have sat like that for a mere second, but to Michael it felt an age before he was released to look down at the location of the intended tattoo. "No, man. I mean, are you sure? Um, maybe something tribal would look good. You know, black work?" His eyes flicked briefly up to Dominic's before he swiveled the stool around to the workbench where he could focus his attention on preparing his tattoo gun.

Dominic watched as Michael's fingers fumbled with the elastic band. It took him several attempts to get it correctly placed, and then he slotted the needle into the tattoo gun. His chest rose with a deliberately deep breath, deep enough to calm his nerves a little but not enough to hide that he was rattled.

Michael's reactions were familiar to Dominic because he'd grown accustomed to the discomfort of others when forced to share his space. He looked at the other workstation, where a teenage girl's young skin was being broken by a man with long dreadlocks, some blond, some blue, and one with a bronze key sewn to its end. Even from that distance, Dominic could smell the girl's blood, and his senses twitched at the sharp tang the ink added to the normally rich, earthy smell. He wondered absently how it would taste if he were to slide his tongue over the newly tattooed shoulder, red and black staining his mouth. He felt the hunger rise, but denying it felt good.

The sudden touch of Michael's fingers through the linen of Dominic's shirtsleeve pulled his attention back to the young tattooist.

"I'll get you to roll up your sleeve or slide your arm out, and you can show me how big you want the design," Michael said, beginning to feel more at ease as he slid into his comfort zone of routine.

Dominic carefully unbuttoned his shirt and slipped it down to fall on the back of the chair, then waited for Michael to begin. It had been a long time since Dominic had felt nervous, and it surprised him that he could still feel the flutter of anticipation. He watched Michael closely, not willing to let any part of the experience escape unnoticed. So intent was his focus on the movement of Michael's hands that he was startled when the fingers actually made contact with his bare skin. Over the years, his heightened senses of sight and smell had become part of Dominic's nocturnal life, but he had almost forgotten voluntary touch. Generally people avoided any form of physical contact; it was as if a primal survival instinct made them cringe away when he was close.

He closed his eyes. It was such a simple touch, fingertips marking out the boundaries of the proposed tattoo, but it sent a deep shiver through Dominic's long-neglected body and sparked a different hunger. Michael felt Dominic shudder and shrugged it off, understanding that clients were often more nervous than they looked. He laid his palm flat on Dominic's arm, spread his fingers, and asked, "How about this for size? It would be from the tip of my thumb to the end of my little finger?"

Dominic didn't look. He merely nodded and said softly, "Whatever you want."

Michael frowned. "Okay, man. It's your arm, I guess."

When there was no response, Michael shook his head, picked up the black marker pen, and began to sketch out a design directly onto Dominic's arm.

The cool tip of the marker skittered over Dominic's skin. With eyes still closed, he felt every slide and stop it made. He tried to *see* the image as it was drawn, through touch alone, but was constantly distracted by the heat of Michael's hand and the puff of his breath as he leaned in to check his work. Dominic opened his eyes and looked down at Michael. The young tattooist was totally engrossed in his work. A slight frown of concentration creased his brow, and he chewed lightly on his bottom lip. While he drew the gently curving lines, his thumb stroked absently over the sensitive skin of Dominic's arm.

It had been so long since Dominic had been this close to someone other than prey that the rush of sensations threatened to overwhelm him. The warmth radiating from Michael's unblemished olive skin. The faint smell of his shampoo. Cigarette smoke and sweat. Human smells without the sharpness of fear.

Suddenly the hair on the back of Michael's neck prickled, and he looked up to meet Dominic's gaze. As Michael stared into the pale eyes, the vampire felt the long fingers wrapped around the cool skin of his arm tighten their grip. It was only then that Dominic broke the connection and looked down at the design coming to life on his arm, and Michael was able to murmur, "Is this the kind of thing you want?"

Dominic's voice was quiet and tinged with a sadness that didn't go unnoticed as he said, "That is what I want."

Michael sat and looked at Dominic for a lot longer than he intended, then he gave himself a mental shake and turned to the workbench. He finished setting up the gun and pulled on a pair of fine latex gloves. Dominic smiled at the care the young man was taking. *Unnecessary. I would catch nothing and pass nothing on to you.*

"The outline usually hurts a bit, but your skin soon gets numb," Michael said while he gently placed a steadying hand on Dominic's arm.

The first touch of the needle bit the surface of Dominic's flesh. Dominic watched the point of the gun glide along a section of the hand-drawn outline. The excess black ink bubbled out the edge. The pain was minimal, but it was enough to remind Dominic of things long absent.

Michael lifted the needle and wiped away the ink to check his progress. He glanced up and asked, "You doing okay?"

Dominic considered the question seriously and answered, "Yes, I'm okay, thank you."

It surprised Michael at how carefully Dominic had answered what was a standard question. He blushed a little when he realized he was smiling at Dominic's response and dipped his head to get on with the tattoo.

Normally, Michael chattered in a continuous stream while he worked, partly to distract the client, but mainly because it was his nature to talk. With Dominic, however, he barely spoke. There was something about the man that silenced him. Michael was too aware of the pale smoothness of Dominic's skin, the rise and fall of his chest, and the way his eyes held you locked in place.

With a mental shake, Michael told himself to stay focused on the task. After all, it was just another inking, one of many he'd done that day. But when Scott finished with his client and headed over to watch, Michael realized he was actually irritated by Scott's close proximity to *his* client. Although it was normal practice for the two friends to check out each other's artwork, tonight Michael did not want him there. He clenched his teeth and tried to push away the feeling that Scott was somehow intruding on something intimate.

When he finished the outline, Michael stopped and looked up. "Listen, man, I'm gonna be a while yet. You head off, and tell Abby I'll lock up when we're done."

Scott frowned. That wasn't the usual way they operated. It wasn't safe to be on your own with an unknown client that late, and something about the guy made his skin crawl. "Nah, it's fine, mate. I can hang around until you're done. Abbs and I have nothing planned tonight, just TV then bed."

Michael was about to argue when Dominic said in a barely audible voice, "He told you to go."

Something about the voice, rather than the words, convinced Scott that it was indeed time to go home. "Okay, I'll see you tomorrow, Michael," he conceded, but he refused to take his eyes off Dominic until he was out the door.

Michael was also watching Dominic. There was something about him he couldn't quite define. Clients usually fell into very distinct categories, but this one was different.

Once Scott had gone, Dominic gave Michael a small smile that instantly sent a flood of heat through the young tattooist's chest and down to his belly. "Um, yeah… the outline is done…. It looks good," Michael stammered as he began to gently wipe the excess ink and smudges of blood from Dominic's arm. "Filling it in will feel a bit different." He glanced up and smiled but quickly dropped his eyes back to the skin. As he ran his gloved fingers over the raised and reddened outline, the burn in his belly spread, and he felt his cock twitch within the confines of his jeans.

Dominic could smell the change in Michael and closed his eyes. *This can't happen with him. Why am I doing this to myself?* But he knew. He *was* genuinely curious about the outcome of a tattoo on his inhuman skin, but the main reasons were his fascination with the tattooist and the desire to be touched again. It had been so long.

The pain of the coloring process was less sharp. It was more like a dull and insistent burn on his skin, yet it was no less intense. Dominic let his head fall back against the seat, allowing the smell of the ink and his blood to blend with the human scents while he listened to the steady hum of the gun. He told himself to enjoy the experience—and his time with Michael—but remain detached. This must not become more than it was. Dominic knew that, even though he walked among its people, he was no longer part of *this* world.

Michael had to force himself to concentrate, and although he took the necessary care, he frequently stole glances at Dominic. Knowing the man's eyes were shut, Michael would take extra time wiping and cleaning the area so his gaze could flick to Dominic's face and body. He could tell Dominic was older than he, but other than that, he could only guess Dominic was maybe early-to-mid thirties. His clothes were pretty conservative, bordering on old-fashioned, and he had no visible piercings. In fact, he could have been one of those people who would simply blend into a crowd unnoticed. Except for those eyes.

A trickle of sweat ran down Michael's back as he filled in a swirl near the top of Dominic's shoulder. He swapped the already soaked tissue for a new one and wiped away the last traces of ink from the unmarked surrounding skin. Though Michael was loath to admit it, the tattoo was finished. The problem was, he didn't want it to end, and despite the fact it was well past their usual closing time, he didn't want this man to leave. But Michael knew he could only drag it on for so long. He sighed and said, "It's done."

Dominic opened his eyes and looked first at Michael and then the fresh artwork. Melancholy seemed to hang in the air of the small purple room when he said, "You do beautiful work. Thank you."

"Um, that's okay," Michael mumbled, suddenly more than a little flustered by the man's attention. "Here I'll, ah… I'll put some of this on and get it patched up." He fumbled under the counter until he found the tube of antiseptic cream and carefully smeared a thick layer over the raw inking. He held up the roll of cling wrap and taped on a square, ensuring it was completely covered while explaining, "There, that will keep it clean and protected. Try to leave it on for a couple of hours, okay?"

Dominic smiled at the way Michael had begun to babble and said simply, "Thank you. How much do I owe you?"

Just another fucking job, remember, just another inking. Dominic "heard" Michael's thought clearly and cursed himself for unsettling the beautiful young man. The cost was disclosed, and they walked together to the front desk. Dominic handed over the money, thanked Michael again without making any more eye contact, and headed for the door.

A surge of panic instantly rose in Michael at the thought of Dominic leaving, and he quickly followed him. "Hey, um, I'm heading out for a drink if, ah, if you'd like to join me? Nothing special; I'm just going to the pub around the corner." Michael had had no intention of going anywhere after work, but he needed just a little longer.

Dominic stopped and looked back at him, immense sadness evident in his eyes. He reached out to Michael and gently stroked his cheek before walking alone through the door.

Chapter
T W O

THE sun was already high in the sky and streaming through Michael's window when he began to stir. Actually, opening his eyes was still too big a task with a full-blown hangover threatening to kick in, so he lay with them closed and tried to gather together the little threads of disparate consciousness. He'd dreamed about someone; his touch was still on Michael's skin. He tried hopelessly to cling to the image, but it faded quickly, leaving him with just an impression of gentle fingers and pale blue eyes. Or were they gray?

Michael groaned and turned onto his side. He peered cautiously at the clock. *Fuck, how can it be midday already?* He rubbed his hand over tired eyes and stared at the peeling paint on the far wall for a few more minutes before hauling himself upright onto the edge of the bed. Michael had ended up grabbing a bottle of vodka on the way home from work, and he vaguely remembered drinking almost half of it before hitting bed. Why he'd bought the bottle, he *couldn't* remember. He sat, forearms resting on his thighs, and frowned. He was never a morning person, but that morning there was something different, something on the fringes of his thoughts that he just couldn't get hold of. It was like clutching at that shadow you see in your peripheral vision, but you turn to look and there's nothing there. He shook his head and instantly regretted the action when a flood of nausea rose from his belly. Michael stood up with a lot more care and wandered into the bathroom.

His reflection grimaced back from the soap-spattered mirror. It definitely didn't look ready to face another day. Michael ran his hand over the patches of stubble and decided shaving simply wasn't going to happen. His frown deepened when something distracted him in the mirror. It was nothing that actually existed in the reversed image of the bathroom, but a recollection of another reflection in another mirror. He screwed up his face and turned away in disgust to have his shower.

Michael took his time getting to work because generally people who wanted tattoos didn't venture into Ink until late. He stretched his arms high above his head, enjoying the sound of his spine clicking into place, and wandered toward Chapel Street. The rain of the night before had cleared the air, and the gentle heat of the sun warmed the backs of his shoulders and helped to dispel the clouds that had settled in his thoughts.

By the time he'd made it into the secondhand music store, picked up a Nine Inch Nails CD, and flicked through some comics in Alternate Visions, Michael had all but forgotten the presence of the man in his dream.

Abby was already unlocking the door of Ink when he arrived. She looked up at him and grinned. "Hey, gorgeous, been spending your hard-earned money?"

"Come on, Abbs, how could I resist?" He smiled and flashed the CD. She rolled her eyes at him, muttered, "Old school," and pushed the door open.

The moment Michael walked into the store, the feeling of anticipation and then loss returned. His inability to pin down *why* he felt this way niggled deep in his gut, as if something important was just out of his reach. With a final shake of his head, Michael went over to his customer book to see what he had on that day while Abby checked the register. She uttered a confused sound, pulled Michael's book across the counter, and compared it to Scott's. Michael watched her count the money again and asked, "What's up? Has Scott been raiding the till again?"

Abby pursed her lips and gave him a confused look. "No, quite the opposite. There seems to be $150 more than there should be."

Michael turned the book back toward him and cast his eyes over last night's clients; again, something didn't seem right. How could there be money in the register but nothing in the book? Both tattooists knew Abby would have their guts for garters if they messed with her recordkeeping. "Don't question good fortune I guess?" Michael suggested.

"Nice that it's in our favor for once." Abby smiled and put the extra money under the money tray where Scott wouldn't find it. "Okay, now get that cute arse of yours into the back room and make me more money."

Michael chuckled and leaned over to give her a kiss. "Only because I love you," he said, with a grin. They had been friends since he'd first appeared in the shop, and he *did* love her. Abby and Scott were the closest thing Michael had to family since leaving home, and she was the only person he could actually talk to about stuff that really mattered.

Grabbing his list of clients, Michael walked into the back room and sat at his workstation. There it was again, something on the edge of his memory. Michael could feel its teasing prickle. He ran his hand over the worn leather of the chair in front of him. It was as if his fingertips were looking for something to lock onto, and although there were little fragments of touch, smell, a *feeling*, nothing really came together, nothing tangible. Michael huffed a sigh and leaned back against the workbench.

"Hey, Mikey boy, rough night?" Scott threw the curtain back and flopped into the chair in front of him.

"Nah, man… well at least I don't think so." Michael pulled a face and laughed at his own confusion. "It's all a bit foggy."

"Sounds more like one of my nights." Scott grinned, but Michael knew Abby had kept a tight rein on Scott's habits since they became a couple. "All I know is that you were still working on someone when I left."

Michael rubbed his fingers over his stubble, listening to the light scrape as he tried to remember his last client. It was a woman getting a star on her forearm, but Scott was still there when she left. "Are you sure?"

"Yeah, some guy…. Shit, for the life of me I can't remember what he looked like." Scott hit his palm against his forehead. "Fuck! I hate that! I was working on a girl's shoulder tat, and her boyfriend was being a pain in the arse, breathing down my neck in case I did something 'inappropriate'. I can see them clearly, but your guy just grays out. Maybe Abby's right, and I'm smoking too fucking much."

"Maybe the weed under your workbench isn't such a good idea after all." Michael laughed and slapped Scott across the shoulder. "Come on, you wanker, get off my chair so we can set up for the day."

DOMINIC didn't sit at the café that night. He avoided the Windsor end of Chapel Street completely because he knew it was dangerous for him there, dangerous to be around Michael so soon after their last contact. The young tattooist brought back too many memories and human needs that he knew couldn't be fulfilled. But *other* needs had to be met. Tonight he would have to feed closer to the upmarket end of Chapel, even though he usually preferred to avoid the clubbers and their chemical cocktails.

Slowly, but purposefully, he made his way along the crowded street, ignoring the averted eyes and wide berth given him by late-night shoppers and the last of the café dwellers. Dominic reached his destination a little before eleven.

A long queue of youths waited to enter the already over-full club. There was the usual mix of colored dreadlocks, screen-printed T-shirts, and pale-skinned Goths sporting oversized silver crucifixes that could no more save them from his attention than the garlic that adorned the pizza slices they'd consumed for dinner.

It's all myth and legend, children.

Dominic walked past the doorman, who suddenly found a chip in his fingernail a lot more interesting than the fair-haired man with the unnerving eyes.

Most of the club was as dark as the music pounding through the speakers. Dominic scanned it carefully. He'd been there before and knew the layout. The bar was always crowded and noisy, the best-lit area, and therefore to be avoided. The dance floor changed as the night progressed, with waves of the drunk, stoned, or simply enthusiastic each taking their turn. Dominic always watched this with predatory interest, waiting for someone to drift toward the exit unseen by all but one. Frequently, Dominic's prey found him. While most listened to their primal instincts and avoided him, some were attracted to the very fears that kept the others away. These were more dangerous because they could sense what he was and wanted what he was always unwilling to give them.

He moved toward a small table at the back, and its occupants quickly decided they needed to be elsewhere. From his vantage point, Dominic could wait and watch for one to break away from the herd, too drunk or newly heartbroken to realize his intent.

SCOTT was already well on the way to being drunk by the time they entered the club, and he leaned heavily on Michael, who joked with Abby. "Shit, man, how can someone so skinny be so fucking heavy?" Michael groaned and pushed him off. "Keep an eye on him, Abbs. I'm going to check out who's here."

Abby gave Michael an indulgent smile. After a year with Scott, she was very used to ensuring his safety when he'd had a few too many. "Yeah, sweetheart, I'll keep him out of trouble. You go have some fun and find someone to make your heart sing." She winked and turned to Scott. "Come on, you, let's find a quiet place where you can tell me how much you love me."

Michael moved away, a broad grin on his face, knowing it was very true—as much as Scott might deny it, he loved Abby with all his heart.

Michael generally didn't frequent the clubs on Chapel, but Hunters had one night a week that the usual clubbers shunned: *Hard and Heavy*. The music was industrial, and the drugs of choice tended to be more alcohol and weed than pills and poppers. It usually meant a drunken, sweaty night that often led to an equally sweaty hookup. The music roared in his ears, and he felt his breastbone vibrate as he squeezed past one of the speaker columns to get closer to the bar.

DOMINIC wasn't sure what made him turn his head, but he quickly focused his attention on a figure in a dark red T-shirt pushing his way through to the bar. He watched Michael call out his order and then lift the pot of beer to his lips. He seemed at home among the clamor of sweaty bodies and "inadvertent" touches. Others were drawn to Michael as he flashed them a welcoming look and genuine smile. *Warmth and light*, Dominic mused and watched the ease with which Michael laughed and shared himself with the others. The intensity of Dominic's gaze grew, and soon it was as if the other inhabitants of the club had faded out around Michael, leaving only the flash of red and a glow that seemed to emanate from the young tattooist.

Despite the crush of bodies that threatened to overload his senses, Dominic could recognize Michael's scent and hear the elevated pump of his heartbeat. Dominic knew that couldn't happen among so many heartbeats and was just a residual sensation from the previous night, but it felt real, and the temptation of the lithe body was *very* real.

It surprised Dominic how difficult it was to witness Michael laughing and drinking with newfound friends. His ever-present loneliness, usually ignored, took hold, and Dominic knew he needed to leave the club and seek his quarry among the street dwellers.

But someone else had already seen Dominic.

When he stood to leave, a young man who Dominic assumed had entered the club on a fake ID approached him. The teenager was typical of the young Goths the place attracted: pale skin, blue-black hair, eyeliner smeared by sweat.

Another one who wears despair as a fashion accessory, Dominic sighed.

He stood in front of Dominic and made to place a tentative hand on the vampire's chest but instantly thought better of it. He stepped closer. Dominic recognized the need in the boy's look—he'd seen it so many times before—and the hunger rose.

MICHAEL drained his glass, turned away from the bar, and scanned the rest of the room. For no discernible reason, his scrutiny fell on a man standing very still in front of a teenager. The club lost focus for a split second. *I know him*, Michael thought, although he couldn't give him a name or reference point. It was just a memory of a touch and a look. Michael ignored the shoves of those trying to take his place at the bar and stood transfixed, watching the man and the young Goth head out the rear exit. He had no idea why, but Michael needed to follow. It was hard going trying to cross the already manic dance floor. Dancers pressed in, surrounding him with the acrid smell of the hot bodies that blocked his progress. Michael normally enjoyed the frenetic energy of the near mosh on the tiny dance floor, but tonight he felt panicked when his path was blocked and he could no longer see the man.

IN THE narrow trash-filled alley, the humidity of the night was oppressive. The teenager reeked of sweat-soaked velvet and patchouli oil, but above all that, Dominic picked up the red scent of blood. He raised his hand as if to caress the boy's smudged cheek, but moved it quickly to grasp a handful of hair and jerk it back to expose the pale throat.

Dominic watched the tiny pulse point, needing to simply close his lips over it and drink, but he wanted to wait, to smell the boy's desire a little longer. It made it easier to pretend there was some possibility of a connection other than nourishment. A small moan brought him back to the moment, and with an acknowledgement of the wide, pleading eyes, Dominic bent the boy's head further back to expose more of his vulnerable throat. The delicate skin punctured so easily, and the first warmth of the blood hit Dominic's tongue. He paused and licked the tiny wound, savoring the coppery sparks. The young man under his mouth whimpered at the pause, and Dominic gently stroked his hand over the boy's black hair, soothing him before returning to the "kiss."

THE exit door was slightly ajar when Michael finally reached the outlying tables. He pushed it open and stepped out into the dark rear alley. As the door closed behind him, the noise from the club dimmed until it was just a steady, muffled bass beat. His eyes took a few seconds to adjust and focus on the figures near the dumpster. The man was there. Michael could make out his back and shoulders, his head bent over the youth firmly held in his grasp. Absently, Michael lifted his fingers to his mouth, living the witnessed kiss through his own touch. He stopped and let them drift to his cheek. In that instant, he knew—the man had touched him there. He didn't know where or when, but he knew the man's touch.

Michael watched the figure straighten, his face now partially in view. Their eyes met, and a chill hit Michael deep in his belly when the silent command came. *Go home, Michael.*

Chapter
T H R E E

DUSK during the Melbourne summer was a haze of orange that would have rivaled any in the world except for its brevity. The twilight of Europe lingered.

The small room faced west, which allowed the glow of nightly renewal and avoided the first penetrating rays of morning, permitting an extra few precious minutes of sanctuary before the airless heat behind heavy curtains became a necessity.

As the room darkened, the figure in the bed stirred.

There was no dirt-filled coffin or abundance of black velvet and dried roses such as typified the lair of a fictional vampire. The room was ordinary, although obviously furnished from a vanished era. Clothes lay over chairs rather than finding their way into the heavy wooden closet, and a single lace-up shoe was left discarded in the middle of the floor.

Dominic always found waking painful. He'd done it too many times, and each night seemed to hold the same offering of possibilities meant for others and his inevitable loneliness. He rolled onto his back, leaving the crumpled white sheet behind, and watched the reflection of the red-tinted light fade on the ceiling above the curtains. Feeding was not needed tonight, but he still needed to get out and be near those whose life sustained him.

His thoughts drifted unbidden to the tattooist, Michael. Dominic knew it was dangerous; dealings with humans had to be kept to a minimum. Still, his fingers moved to his now healed arm. The black ink had faded during the night. His unnatural body healed itself until the markings were completely gone, and Dominic's skin was once again unblemished. The touch of the young man lingered, however. He could still feel Michael's warmth and smell the blend of ink, blood, and pheromones.

Dominic closed his eyes against the memory, but that only served to intensify the image. He could feel his body stir; the tickle that fluttered deep in his belly began to spread. He stretched, trying to release some of the building tension, but the fine weave of the sheets beneath his skin only served to heighten his newly awakened sensitivity. Torn between denying the images settling in his head and reveling in the opulence of the sensations they created, Dominic allowed his hand to skate lightly across his belly. The scent of the young tattooist filled his lungs as his fingertips danced through the trail of hair below his belly button, slowly moving down. He had almost forgotten the insistent burn of an erection and moaned at the first touch of his fingers. *Michael....*

The name was no sooner given thought than Dominic stopped.

Enough! This cannot happen. He removed his hand and sat on the edge of the bed to stare down at the fingers that so recently had begun to give him pleasure. They slowly curled into a fist. Dominic looked at the floor; the glow was gone. He stood and pulled the heavy curtains apart to view the empty night outside. It had been many decades since his body felt any need other than to feed, and the reemergence of those desires frightened him. Dominic had only ever attempted to take one human lover in his long "life," and he knew he would not survive that again.

But Dominic also knew he would end up at the café opposite Ink, just as he knew he would again walk through the door of the tattoo parlor before closing time.

DOMINIC lay on his stomach as Michael's pen softly marked out a new design on his back. He understood that it would fade again before the sun rose for another day, so he could no longer blame curiosity for his presence in the parlor. The only reason for the vampire being there stood above his exposed back. Dominic could feel Michael staring at his smooth, unblemished skin, followed by a questioning touch, as if Michael were searching for marks he knew should be there.

Michael rubbed his thumb along a fresh pen mark dipping down over a shoulder blade and asked, "We've met before, haven't we?"

The question was expected. Dominic knew increased contact would leave an impression, similar to the indentations on the clean page of a writing pad left behind after the letter had been removed. He kept his face turned away and replied quietly, "No, you don't know me."

Michael didn't argue, but the answer felt wrong. There was an undeniable familiarity to the man's skin. With a shake of his head, he pulled his stool a little closer and focused on his drawing.

Dominic closed his eyes and tried to block the connection he knew was forming. Every conscious thought told him to get up and leave.

Why am I doing this to myself?

Every moment of contact with Michael was dangerous now—to both of them.

What will I do when the connection is complete and Michael knows? Am I willing to impose a death sentence on him?

He knew the effect he was having on the young man; his interest was obvious through both touch and smell.

The song of pain and addiction that had filled the room came to a crescendo, signaling the end of the CD.

The small purple room fell silent, at least to human ears.

The felt tip of the pen continued to pass over the plane of Dominic's back, short, deliberate markings morphing into long sweeping strokes. Never hurried, always considered and followed by a pause in which Dominic could hear the slight change in Michael's breathing as he contemplated the *shape* of his work.

For once, Dominic's senses were not that of the predator. Possible dangers in his surroundings faded as his mind and body were captivated by the swirl of touches. He took a deep breath and let himself drift....

The tattooist hesitated and watched his client's skin expand with the intake of breath. He laid his palm just below Dominic's shoulder blade, fingers spread, feeling the contraction of the exhale. Without fully comprehending why he needed to do it, Michael rolled down the thin latex glove and let it drop to the floor. Dominic's skin was cool despite the slight flush that seemed to rise when their skin met.

The single touch vibrated through Dominic's body, a rush of warmth and longing. It forced a memory of another time, a time before he became a hunter when Dominic's back was tanned and freckled from a European summer.

He was stretched out on the grass, the smell of crushed vegetation rich and lush in his nostrils as his companion placed playful kisses across his shoulder blades, tickling and teasing.

The air abounded with insects, and their steady hum vibrated through Dominic's sun-warmed skin. He groaned as a blade of grass appeared over his shoulder to brush against his nose.

"Are you just going to lie there and make me do all the work?" the voice whispered playfully next to his ear.

"So I am work, am I?" Dominic grinned and opened his eyes.

The sun was so bright that Dominic's eyes stung when he tried to turn his face up toward the man behind him. It created a halo of light around his lover's dark head, and the air rang with his laughter as he pushed Dominic back to the ground.

Dominic tensed and pushed the memory aside. That was the last time they had made love before... before his legion traveled to the other land, and he met.... *No! I cannot have that again. That man no longer exists.*

SCOTT finished going through his appointment book and stretched his tired muscles. He'd had a lot of customers and pulled a long shift. He glanced at Michael's book and realized that he should have finished an hour ago. Reaching over to the well-loved and battered sound system, he reduced the volume and listened. The music had stopped in the back room. There was no hum of the tattoo gun or standard conversation. He looked at Abby, who was busy wheeling in the rack of screen-printed

T-shirts and PVC "one-offs," getting ready to lock up, and asked, "Is Michael still out back?"

She paused and tried to remember, "Yeah. I think he has someone with him."

Scott shook his head and wandered through the curtained doorway to the workroom. "Hey, Mikey, you okay in here?"

He stopped abruptly as soon as he entered the room. Something was wrong about the whole situation. He watched Michael's fingers trace his design, repeating caresses over certain spots. Scott's discomfort rose as he watched; the scene was too intimate and he was intruding.

He looked into the mirror opposite and saw the eyes of the man watching him. A shiver passed down his spine, and his skin literally crawled. He wanted to tell Michael to stop, to tell the man to go, but Michael broke the silence with a quiet, "I'll lock up, Scott. Everything is alright here."

Michael wanted to add that he was safe with Dominic, but for some reason he wasn't willing to speak the name out loud. Despite the power Dominic radiated, Michael felt an unreasonable, but overwhelming, urge to protect him. He felt a connection to the man under his hand, a connection that blinded him to the fact that Dominic's name had *never* been spoken aloud.

Scott's gaze never left those eyes in the mirror until he heard the voice give a command he couldn't deny. *Listen to him.* Scott blinked and saw that the man's eyes were now closed. He shuffled a little toward the door, where he hesitated and said in a confused voice, "See you in the morning, mate. Stay safe." Scott turned and left, the curtain swinging behind him.

Barely aware that his friend had been in the room, a remnant of an image flitted briefly through Michael's subconscious, leaving him hard and confused over a lingering scent of grass. He looked down at his fingers and frowned at their naked coarseness against the pale skin beneath them as they followed both his pen marks and lines yet to be drawn.

Michael slowly removed his hand and straightened up, unsure of what had just happened. He rubbed the offending hand absently over the soft skin between the hem of his T-shirt and the belted waistband of his jeans.

Dominic watched the reflected image of Michael as he wiped off the lingering sensation of Dominic's touch. He then saw the tattooist's fingers pass over the small inking of a sun just below Michael's bellybutton—*warmth and light*—and a new melancholy settled over him. Like the beautiful tattooist, these were things eternally denied him.

At that point, he knew he had to leave.

With a single fluid movement, Dominic eased himself off the bench and reached for his shirt.

Confused, Michael mumbled, "But, we're not done. I… ah, just lost my train of thought for a minute." His hand moved quickly down to cover his fairly obvious arousal, and with a blush, he said in a very flustered voice, "Shit, I'm sorry, man. This doesn't usually happen. I…."

With a sad smile, Dominic stepped closer and slid his hand slowly under the frayed edge of the tattooist's T-shirt. He kept his eyes on Michael's and gently caressed the warm black sun, feeling how the flesh trembled under his light touch. "I have to go, Michael," he murmured and then stilled his fingers.

The young tattooist dropped his gaze to Dominic's pale hand and wanted more, needed more. "Please don't go," he whispered.

A longing so strong it imitated physical pain hit Dominic. *Maybe just tonight….* The hope passed through his thoughts, but he knew the other man's safety had to come first.

He shook his head and said in a barely audible voice, "I have to go."

Dominic reluctantly pulled his hand away, let it drop to his side, and took a step back. Michael could read the sadness in his eyes and was all but engulfed by the waves of loneliness emanating from the man in front of him. He lifted his hand and gently brushed his fingers down Dominic's cheek. It was a small and simple touch, but one that almost broke Dominic's heart.

Not a word was spoken when Dominic turned and walked out of the workroom, but Michael heard them nonetheless. *Thank you.*

Chapter
F O U R

MICHAEL knew he was waiting for Dominic. He'd been waiting for almost three weeks. Each night around closing time, the same anxious anticipation started to build in his belly. He would become distracted and begin watching the door, looking up each time it opened. Clients who requested late evening bookings were all declined because he knew he needed to keep that time free for "the man"... for Dominic.

Tonight, like every other lately, Michael hovered around the workroom until Scott had had enough. He put down the tattoo gun he'd been attempting to clean, watched Michael's incessant pacing for a few more seconds, then finally groaned, "For fuck's sake, Michael, what is your problem lately?"

Michael stopped. He stood and looked at his hands to see if there was any way he could explain how he felt. In the end he knew he couldn't. What could he say? *I met this guy who I'd met before, except I don't know if I had. He talks to me in my head. Fuck, I'm hearing voices now.* Michael knew there was no way he could give Scott a reasonable answer.

It was at that moment that Abby parted the curtain and walked into the workroom. The tension hit her. She looked first at Michael, who was standing with his back to her. Michael was the most easygoing person she knew, but tonight his hunched stance was sending out waves of agitation. Abby spun around to Scott with what sounded very much like an accusation. "What happened?"

Scott looked at her with obvious frustration and huffed. "Michael is driving me fucking mad with his latest nighttime ritual."

Abby totally ignored Scott's tone because she knew this was completely out of character for Michael and, in a far gentler voice, asked, "What's up, Mikey?" She noticed Scott roll his eyes and said, with a shake of her head, "Ignore him; he's just pissed off 'cause I'm making him cut back on his weed intake."

Disgusted, Scott tried to make a show of storming into the main shop, but unfortunately for him, the drama was somewhat diminished by the impossibility of slamming a curtained doorway. Abby pulled herself up onto the bench and whispered, "Tell me, sweetie. Tell me what's wrong?"

Michael turned to face her and opened his mouth to start, closed it to reorganize his thoughts, and started again. "A man came in a few weeks ago. I've seen him a couple of times and…." Abby cocked her head and nodded to let him know she was listening. "And, I dunno." Michael stopped speaking.

"Hey, gorgeous, it's not like you to get this worked up over someone," she said gently. And it was true. Michael didn't really have relationships; he socialized a lot and got laid regularly, but he never reacted like this.

Michael gave a frustrated shrug and sat heavily in the chair with his back to her.

Abby jumped down off the bench and stood behind him, gave him a chaste kiss on his neck, and then started to knead his shoulders. She felt him relax a little into her touch and gave him a minute or two more before asking, "Have you tried to talk to him?"

Michael shook his head and said sadly, "I can't. I don't know where he is, except I know that he's not far away." He stopped and frowned. *How the fuck do I know that?*

He looked up over his shoulder at Abby and said, "This is gonna sound really strange, Abbs, but I can *feel* him, you know, here." He illustrated the point by turning to face her and pressing his hand to his chest.

Abby sighed and kissed him lightly on the forehead. She put her arms around him and held him while she thought that through. Finally, she asked, "Can you use that, Michael? To find him, I mean?"

He pulled gently out of her embrace and, with a hesitant smile, asked, "So you don't think I'm going mad?"

"Oh I don't doubt that you're quite mad, but hey, seriously, stranger things have happened."

She sat next to him and put on her best organizer voice. "Okay, I think you should finish early and go for a walk. Listen to the 'feeling' and see if it gets stronger anywhere. How does that sound?"

He reached up and held her hand. "Sounds about as nuts as I do at the moment. Thank you for not laughing at me, Abby," he murmured. "I was really starting to think I was losing it."

ABBY was right; there were areas where the feeling was stronger. Each night Michael tried a different section of Chapel Street and the surrounding areas. At times the frustration of sensing Dominic was palpable: a breath on his skin, a faint smell or sound of a sigh. It was as if he could almost reach out and touch him, but he wasn't there. Other times it was like an afterthought, something on the edge of his consciousness that kept slipping out of his grasp.

One area was very strong. Michael spent several nights sitting at the café near Ink—one table in particular. He had asked the waitress if she remembered serving a quiet, elegant man with sad gray eyes. She thought about it carefully and said, "There was a man, maybe…. No, I don't know. I see so many people here. Sorry." Michael thanked her anyway and wondered how many nights Dominic had sat there watching the store. *Did he watch me? Choose me? Or was it simply a coincidence that he was my client? It wasn't a coincidence. No way.*

Michael sighed, drained his tea, and left a little more than the correct amount of money on the table.

THE South Yarra end of Chapel always grated on Dominic's nerves; the noise and pretension irritated him. But it wasn't safe in Windsor while his connection to Michael was so strong.

Another late-model car boomed past with its "techno" thumping at an ear-bleeding level. Dominic winced at the cacophony and tried to find refuge at the back of a small bar. Quickly, the noise of the street faded, replaced by laid-back jazz and the intimate quiet of couples at nearby tables who, in the dim light and dark furniture, felt secure in the privacy of each other's company. Dominic leaned against the back wall and closed his eyes. He'd fed the night before so hadn't really needed to venture out, but the solitude of his home had become oppressive. Dominic needed to sit among whispered words and shared heartbeats and, even for a moment, pretend he belonged with them. However, once more his thoughts strayed to the young tattooist. He knew it would happen, and that was why he had carefully avoided prolonged human contact, taking only what he needed and no more. Up until the night he saw Michael.

Dominic listened to the steady bass of the music and considered the possibility that to survive a little longer, he had needed *more* than the physical nourishment of blood. But Dominic knew the thought was merely an attempt to justify his actions because his truth was too painful to acknowledge. Michael's touch, his smell, his essence stayed with Dominic, but rather than being pleasurable, it tickled and scratched at him, reminding him of what he could no longer have.

Suddenly, it all felt too real, and Dominic's stomach clenched at the mental caress of Michael's presence. He squeezed his eyes tighter, trying to block it out, when he heard a soft voice say, "Dominic?"

MICHAEL had decided to reject logical thought about search patterns and likely locations and just follow the pull in his subconscious. He'd walked street after street, occasionally backtracking when he felt it, or more to the point, when he felt *him*. By the time Michael reached a dimly lit bar patronized by the more affluent denizens of Chapel Street, the sensation was so strong that he hesitated by the doorway for several minutes, earning curious glances from patrons.

He's in there….

Michael peered through the moody lighting and tried to make out a face of which he only had the vaguest recollection. The features were hazy in his mind, but he didn't doubt he would know him when he saw him. Michael's gaze flicked over the couples too into each other to even notice him and stepped further into the bar.

The back of the room was engulfed in shadow, and he could only see faces illuminated by the red candle bowls on the tables. None of them were Dominic.

He's in there….

Michael slowly wound his way through the tables. His agitated pulse pounded in his ears as he neared the back of the room. And then he saw him, a solitary figure in the gloom of the back corner. Dominic's eyes were closed, and Michael almost backed away. Only almost, because he knew he couldn't leave after all his time searching. He took a deep breath and murmured the name that had been haunting him, "Dominic."

Dominic sighed. *Don't do this, Michael.*

The silent message was strong, and Dominic was surprised when the young tattooist stood his ground and said, "I've been looking for you."

It was a simple statement, but one Dominic did not expect. Sensing the honesty of the words, he opened his eyes, looked at Michael, and asked quietly, "Why?"

Confusion flitted over Michael's face, and he faltered for a moment before saying the only thing he knew to be true. "Because I needed to see you."

No, I can't let this happen to him. Dominic shook his head sadly and murmured in a soft but commanding voice, "Just go home, Michael. I cannot let this happen to you."

Before he realized what he was doing, Michael started to turn toward the door. This time, however, he didn't take more than a single step before he stopped and looked at Dominic, his face a mixture of confusion and accusation. "You've done that to me before, haven't you?"

When Dominic didn't answer Michael pleaded, "Please don't send me away."

Michael stood a little awkwardly for several minutes trying to read some expression on Dominic's face and then sighed. "Do you want a drink? I think I need one." Dominic shook his head, but a faint smile curled the corners of his lips when Michael said, "I'll get two because something tells me I might need them both."

Watching Michael make his way to the bar, Dominic knew he could quickly and quietly slip through the tables of lovers and out into the street. Michael might feel something on the very edge of his senses, but it would be too late for him to follow. The only problem was, this time Dominic wanted to stay, wanted to talk with Michael and enjoy his company. If only just for one night. At least, that's what he tried to tell himself.

The conversation started slowly, full of awkward silences and embarrassed smiles, but Michael persisted. He talked about his job, the people he worked with, even tales of childhood adventures—anything to keep this man in front of him. Finally, Michael seemed to run out of things to say and tried to encourage some words from Dominic.

Watching and listening was easy, but Dominic found it difficult to fall into the pattern of normal conversation. He couldn't remember when he last simply talked to someone for more than a few stilted sentences. Michael tried to ease the way as much as he could and asked questions about the normalities of daily life, but when Dominic didn't or couldn't answer, Michael just shrugged and moved on to something he could. Even though he wanted to know about Dominic, ultimately all he needed was to be close to him. What was said didn't matter.

Dominic soon found himself smiling, a broad, genuine smile that led to a soft laugh. Again he silenced the little voice that niggled and warned how dangerous this was, how intoxicating it was to be around Michael.

By the time the bar closed, Michael had drained both glasses and followed them with a few more. All the other couples had gradually dragged their eyes from each other long enough to make their way to other, more intimate, destinations, leaving the two men alone in their corner. The bar staff shuffled chairs around them as a not-so-subtle hint but were finally forced to point out that their shifts were over, and they had homes to return to. Dominic and Michael were ushered quietly to the door, and it was locked behind them by a barman who kept his eyes firmly on Michael and carefully avoided both physical and visual contact with Dominic.

Other than the distant rev of a hoon driver in a club car park, Chapel Street was quiet. They stood and watched a tram rattle by, its brightly lit interior housing inner city dwellers heading home to see out the remains of the night. Dominic watched it run by, sparking the overhead lines when it crossed a junction, and he said quietly, "You need to go home now, Michael."

Michael's gaze left the retreating tram and settled on his feet. Dominic could feel a silent plea radiate between them: *Not yet... please, not yet.* So it was no surprise when Michael looked up and asked hopefully, "I live close by; walk with me, please?" As much as he knew he shouldn't, Dominic didn't refuse. Michael slipped his hand into Dominic's and began to walk.

Everything screamed to Dominic how wrong it was to be with the man any longer than he had already, but the gentle touch threw him. Instead, he found himself focusing on the warmth of the young man's palm against his own rather than the inherent death sentence of the intimacy. Yet despite all he knew, Dominic wanted this so much, and his body ached with the knowledge that the soft touch would have to end before it could be taken further.

They crossed a small park amid the high rise apartment blocks, and Michael led them to a picnic table where he stopped and shrugged. "Just a little while longer, please? I know there has to be something we didn't get a chance to talk about."

You are a fool to put yourself through this, Dominic thought, but his warning went unheeded. Instead, he smiled and sat, his elbows resting on the graffiti-carved table, while Michael sat cross-legged right in the middle, still talking and asking questions until he knew he no longer had to.

They sat quietly, finally accepting that the silences didn't need to be filled. Michael watched Dominic closely and listened, not for physical sounds, but the warm echo of thoughts he now knew were present since that first night, that first touch. "How can you put thoughts in my head?" he asked softly and was not surprised when Dominic didn't answer. "Okay, then at least tell me why you wanted me to leave?"

Dominic looked at him, his expression sad. *How can I explain to you that I* will *kill you, Michael?* He shook his head and turned to watch the gentle sway of eucalypt leaves in the graying light. Dominic's voice was barely louder than his thoughts when he whispered, "Because I'm bad for you, bad for us."

He heard the rustle of Michael's clothes and the faint creak of the table but still did not expect the warmth of fingertips down his cheek and the voice near his ear saying, "I don't believe that."

Dominic knew he could have stopped what happened, but he could not resist the soft press of Michael's lips, his warm breath tinged with alcohol. When Dominic didn't pull away, Michael deepened the kiss, his hand slowly moving over the cool skin of the vampire's face. Dominic didn't move, let Michael touch him, taste him. The kiss lasted mere seconds before Michael reluctantly released Dominic's lips and eased back. The loss of Michael's touch hurt all the more for having had that moment. Emptiness filled Dominic with the understanding that the kiss dare not be repeated.

The sadness on Dominic's face was not what Michael expected, and it surprised him how vulnerable Dominic looked in the growing dawn. He reached to take Dominic's hand and smiled. "You know we just spent the whole night together."

Dominic frowned and looked down at their joined hands in the gentle, pink first light.

It was morning.

His expression was stricken as he looked into Michael's eyes. *You've destroyed me, Michael.*

Dominic had felt the warnings of approaching dawn but systematically shut each of them down, so great was his need to be with Michael. But now he felt the heat, the burn of his skin, and the searing pain in his eyes as the light intensified over the surrounding buildings. Dominic fought to protect his companion and sever their link, but it was already too late. Above his own pain he was forced to witness

Michael flinch away in terror, clutching both his heart and mind as the white noise invaded his thoughts. Michael lifted a trembling hand to his face and uttered, "Dominic...? What's happening?"

Dominic couldn't answer. He stood up and began a stumbling run across the park, only to fall to his knees before reaching the relative safety of the nearby buildings.

Confused, Michael jumped off the table and ran to him. "Dominic, what is it? What's wrong?" he cried, now in a state of panic as he watched Dominic's desperate crawl across the brown summer grass. He heard a quiet grunt of pain but no words, although it was becoming evident that something was terribly wrong. An angry discoloration on Dominic's exposed skin was spreading; small lesions formed and broke the fair skin. Michael began to understand that the pain and fear he was feeling were Dominic's. He *knew* the urgent need to find sanctuary in darkness.

Michael quickly pulled off his jacket and draped it over Dominic's head before hooking his arm around Dominic's waist. He half ran and half dragged the stricken vampire to the alcove of the nearest doorway. "We'll be okay, Dominic," he gasped breathlessly, not really believing his own words as they huddled in the concrete doorway and watched the shade recede with the rising sun.

Their tiny sanctuary shrank rapidly as the shadow line crept toward their feet. Michael knew he had mere minutes to get Dominic out of there and somewhere safe.

"Fuck. We're gonna have to make a run for it," he muttered, more to himself than Dominic, and tried to remain calm enough to calculate the risk of getting to his apartment. "My flat isn't too far; I know we can get there." Michael knew that wasn't true, and their chance of making it to the haven of his home was minimal at best, but it was all he could think to do to keep Dominic safe, and as their shade receded, he was rapidly running out of options.

Dominic clung to Michael. Even though the growing sunlight was not yet touching his skin, he could feel it steadily approaching, like a predator stalking, waiting for him to fall again when his daylight-enforced lethargy stole his ability to run. His fingers tightened on the worn fabric of Michael's shirt, and he gave a slight shake of his head, and Michael knew their destination. They needed to get to the vampire's home.

With gritted teeth, Michael made sure Dominic was firmly in his grasp and bolted out of the alcove. The pain he felt was instant and searing, even though his human skin remained flawless in the morning light. Michael faltered in his run; he couldn't do this without help. Hefting Dominic a little higher in his hold, Michael muttered hoarsely, "Come on, Dominic. Help me or we won't make it." The pain instantly eased, and Michael knew Dominic was concentrating on blocking as much of it as he could. He listening to the labored breathing for a few more seconds, then took the opportunity to pick up their pace.

Michael never questioned how he knew the way to Dominic's home and didn't stop until they rounded a corner and the rays of the rising sun fell behind a row of terrace houses. He slumped onto a low brick wall and assessed their surroundings. "Almost there," he whispered, more than a little afraid at the growing harshness of Dominic's breathing.

Dominic barely registered the words, leaning against Michael and moving only when he was pulled to his feet again. Their progress along the old, tree-lined street was slow, each step taking its toll on both men. Michael didn't look up from the footpath, concentrating only on keeping Dominic moving. He murmured constant encouragements, his voice taking on an edge of urgency whenever he felt Dominic's "presence" slipping. Finally, he pushed open a small rusted gate and led them carefully along a narrow path to a covered veranda. The deep shade was cool, and Michael eased Dominic to the floor, his breathing reduced to a pained wheeze.

Crouching beside him, Michael placed a gentle hand on his arm. "I need to get you inside, Dominic." When Dominic didn't respond, Michael tried to listen without his ears. He soon understood that someone like Dominic didn't need to lock his door because no one would willingly enter his home.

He stood quickly and opened the door before helping Dominic to his feet. "Come on, Dominic. You'll be safe in here." Michael didn't know why, but he knew it to be true.

Dominic leaned heavily on him as they made their way up the stairs. Each step took an epic effort of will, and Dominic only succeeded by drawing on Michael's remaining strength.

When they reached the first floor landing, Michael headed unwaveringly to Dominic's bedroom and helped him to the edge of the bed before double-checking that the heavy curtains were firmly closed.

He carefully sat on the bed next to Dominic. In the darkened room, the panic and pain that had invaded Michael's mind slowly began to subside, and his own thoughts gradually resurfaced. He looked at the man sitting next to him and frowned. Dominic's thoughts were now closed to him, and Michael was left feeling lost and more than a little frightened. Dominic was barely able to sit upright, and he struggled to breathe through lips that were cracked and peeling.

"Maybe I should get a doctor or call an ambulance?" Michael asked quietly, wanting to reach over to touch Dominic, but confronted with the man's obvious injuries, he was afraid of hurting him even more.

It was now a mammoth effort to move, but Dominic managed to shake his head and whisper a firm, "No."

Exasperated, Michael rubbed his hands over his eyes and asked in a voice full of fear, "What can I do to help? I have to do something."

Your blood, Michael... that would help, passed unbidden through Dominic's mind, but he refused to acknowledge it. "Go home, Michael," Dominic muttered without looking at him. "I need to sleep."

Michael stood up, but only moved as far as the chair near the window. He sat quietly, never allowing his eyes to leave the man on the bed. He'd heard that command before, but this time it was said in a human voice, a voice that could not control his actions. It was Michael's turn. With a rough sigh, he said, "No." He stood up again and began to unfasten the small pearl buttons of Dominic's shirt, a little surprised that he met no resistance. He eased the soiled fabric carefully over Dominic's shoulders and down his arms, revealing skin that was raw and blistered even though it had not come into direct contact with the morning light. His fingers hovered over the broken skin, but he knew better than to touch.

"I can't feel it anymore," Michael whispered, understanding that the pain must be unbearable. Dominic's eyes flicked briefly at Michael before exhaustion closed them.

Dominic didn't resist when Michael squatted to unlace the old-fashioned leather shoes and remove his socks, nor when given the softly spoken direction to lie down on the white sheet.

"You'll be okay," Michael whispered as he pulled the top sheet over Dominic's now trembling body.

He sat in the armchair near the bed and watched while Dominic gradually settled into a fitful sleep. For the first time in his short life, Michael felt very alone. It was hard to admit, but it frightened him, feeling only his own thoughts and needs.

For what may have been an hour, Michael chewed on the frayed skin around his fingernails while he watched over Dominic. Gradually the shivering eased and Dominic became still. Michael moved from the chair to the edge of the bed where he could see the steady rise and fall of Dominic's chest and the gentle ruffle of the sheet where it rested near slightly parted lips.

Relief began to replace fear, and exhaustion finally overtook the adrenaline that had kept him going. He rubbed a weary hand over his face and realized for the first time how close to tears he felt. "Just tired," he muttered, trying unsuccessfully to convince himself, and pulled the edge of the sheet a little higher over Dominic's shoulder. He crawled onto the bed beside Dominic, careful not to touch, and lay watching him through heavy-lidded eyes. "I'll just rest here for a few minutes," he whispered.

THE heat of early afternoon buzzed through Michael's head as he fought to wake up through the oppressive drowsiness of the hot, airless bedroom. A small trickle of sweat made its way down his temple, and he frowned in an attempt to shake off the vagueness clouding his thoughts. The reality of the morning broke through, and he was startled into full wakefulness, only to *feel* the soothing stroke of Dominic's presence.

He rolled over onto his back and lay there listening, listening both to the soft breathing beside him and the gentle hum of Dominic tickling the edges of his mind. There was no conscious thought, simply an *awareness* of the sleeping man.

Michael exhaled slowly and carefully sat up. The sheet was clammy beneath him, and he rubbed his hand through his sweat-dampened hair. It wasn't the first time he'd woken during the day to find himself in another man's bed, but this was very different. He turned to check the still form beside him and gently eased himself off the bed. Aching muscles complained as Michael stood up. He hadn't noticed any of the strain placed on his body that morning; all he'd felt was Dominic's pain. Michael glanced at the closed curtains and wished he could open the window to let some air in, but he knew the risk was too great to Dominic.

"What are you, Dominic?" he murmured softly and readjusted the top sheet before turning to find the bathroom.

The house was silent other than the soft pad of Michael's feet along the wooden floor of the hallway. Framed pictures lined the wall, mainly sketches with the occasional black and white photograph—people and places, observances rather than intimate portraits of the subjects. Michael looked at each one in turn before grimacing at the pressure of his bladder and hurrying to where he knew the bathroom would be.

The cold water washed over his hands while Michael looked around the small bathroom. There were no toiletries visible, and the only thing that adorned the marble vanity was a clear glass vase containing five bright daffodils. Frowning, Michael ran a still wet finger over a yellow petal, wondering if Dominic had picked them in the dark of night. The image saddened him, and he quickly cupped his hands under the streaming water and splashed it over his face. He straightened and closed his eyes while the cool water ran down his face and throat to soak the neckband of his T-shirt. Michael sighed and looked at himself in the mirror, wondering, not for the first time, what the hell he was doing there. But the thought had barely passed when he glanced again at the daffodils and needed to get back to the bedroom.

Dominic hadn't moved and still lay with his back to the door, but Michael instantly felt more settled back in the room. He sat on the bed and carefully pulled the sheet back to see that the lesions on Dominic's skin had cleared and only faint discolorations remained. His fingers hovered over Dominic's arm. There was a physical memory there that Michael couldn't quite grasp; he *knew* that skin. Slowly Michael's fingertips touched the now cool skin and images of tattoo designs filled his head. He smiled and leaned over to press his lips softly against Dominic's shoulder before stretching out and letting his eyes close again.

THE last remnants of the orange sunset had faded when Dominic woke to the scent of human. He looked at the sleeping man, who was totally unaware of his present danger. It hurt Dominic to see him, face passive and lips slightly parted in the bliss of sound sleep. *Innocence I can never again experience.* Dominic lifted his fingers to Michael's face, but stopped short of touching him. *This can never happen again.*

The need to feed gripped Dominic, and that meant he must get as far from Michael as possible.

Michael murmured softly when Dominic slid off the bed, but didn't wake. Dominic dressed quickly as he tried to block the allure of Michael's warm blood and the hunger that compelled him. He stood well away from the bed and sent a direct and urgent message for Michael to wake up and leave.

Chapter
F I V E

"GIVE me a break, Abby," Michael moaned and shook his head.

"Well, what other explanation is there?" she retorted and slapped his thigh, indicating that he needed to shuffle a little further down the counter to give her room for the account books. Michael hopped off the counter and leaned against it, keeping his back to her.

"Well?" she pushed.

"Look, he is *not* Lestat, and I'm not part of a fucking Anne Rice novel," Michael growled and folded his arms.

"Sounds more like a Louis actually," Abby said with an indulgent smile and rubbed her hand over his back, well aware of the tension there.

Michael sighed and turned around to face her. "I dunno, Abbs; there has to be a logical explanation. There are diseases that make you allergic to sunlight, yeah?"

"Maybe?" She shrugged but wasn't convinced, and she pushed Michael's hair back to touch his forehead. "But what about what's in here? Can you feel him?"

Michael looked down at his recently bitten fingernails and nodded. He lifted his hand to his chest and said quietly, "And here." Abby gave him a curious look, so he continued, "I can feel it when he wakes up and if he's close. It's like when you know someone is going to call you and then they do, but more. Heaps more."

"So do you know what he's thinking?" she asked, trying to understand exactly what Michael was saying.

Michael sat and thought about that until he eventually shook his head. "Only if he wants me to; otherwise, it's just a sense of him, and now, today, I can vaguely sense him even though I know he's not awake yet. It's getting stronger, and I can tell he's sad."

"Sad? What's he sad about?"

Michael shrugged. There was a melancholy surrounding Dominic's thoughts that he couldn't adequately explain because he didn't really understand it himself. "About me, I think." He looked up at Abby and frowned as he tried to piece together what was mostly just a general feeling. "He's so lonely, Abby. I know that, but he's frightened too. Frightened of what will happen to me."

"What will happen to you?" Abby repeated, real concern entering her voice for the first time since they began talking about Michael's new relationship—if that's what it was. "Are you in danger, Michael? Is he something to worry about? I mean, would he hurt you?" She struggled for the right words, not wanting to come out and ask *Is he going to bite you and suck your blood?"*

But Michael was quick to reassure her. "No. No, he wants to protect me, I think. Although, bloody hell, Abbs, I really don't know *what* I think anymore." He shrugged with a smile that was almost a grimace.

Abby returned a real smile as she wrapped her arm around him and said in a matter-of-fact voice, "If that's the case, I think you need to find him again and figure this out. Stop fretting about what might or might not be happening and go do something about it. Courage, Michael. You need to chase your dreams if they're ever going to become reality."

"Yeah, I know." Michael nodded but frowned. "You're not serious about him being a vampire, though, are you?"

Abby simply grinned at him and stated, "There are more things in heaven and earth, Horatio, than are dreamt of in your philosophy."

MICHAEL.... Images of the tattooist swam through Dominic's first waking thoughts. He rolled onto his back but kept his eyes closed and groaned. Michael's scent remained in the room. It surrounded him, even though he'd taken great care to wash the bed linens and had flung his pillow out the door in frustration when images of Michael continued to dance through his mind. Those long-denied thoughts plagued him in his waking hours and invaded his dreams during daylight hours.

It had been a few nights since Michael shared his bed, and not one had gone by that Dominic did not run his fingers over the empty space beside him before settling to attempt sleep. Logic screamed at him that every thought about the tattooist brought them closer to Michael's destruction. Every dream signed Michael's death sentence, but the lure of his light and warmth dragged Dominic back to human desires he was sure he had killed. Stirrings of lust brought with them memories of the bewilderment in the eyes of humans in the moments before they suffered the cruel death of a vampire lover.

"I can't do this," he moaned into the empty room and pressed the heels of his hands into his eyes, but the red lights flashing behind his lids danced with the blood rushing through his ears. He hungered for more than blood.

Dominic's hand rested lightly on his belly, and with only the barest movement of his fingertips, it began.

MICHAEL gently wiped the excess blood and ink from the raw skin around a fresh tattoo. "Almost done," he said softly to the young man in the chair, who was desperately trying to look calm in front of his friends while his gray pallor betrayed his real feelings. The needle wove its way down the final sweep of the design, and gradually, the last of the bare skin disappeared beneath the vivid pigment. Michael put the gun on the bench and crouched to check his work.

He's awake. The thought came unbidden to Michael's mind, but he knew it to be true. Michael frowned and tried to focus on the skin in front of him.

"Is it finished?"

For a second, the question was meaningless, and Michael struggled to make sense of the voice. He glanced up at the mirror and caught the impatient look in the eyes of his client.

"Um… yeah, all done," he said and nodded as he straightened and reached for clean tissues to wipe the surrounding skin. *Focus, Michael.* He mentally kicked himself and smeared a thick coating of antiseptic cream on the fresh wound before covering it with cling wrap.

Taking a step backward, he quickly turned away and started fiddling with the tattoo gun. "Just head out the front and settle up with Abby. She'll give you the sheet of instructions for aftercare, okay?" Michael mumbled, trying to fight the distraction of the images that suddenly flooded his thoughts.

"Okay…," the guy drawled, a little put out at the abruptness of his dismissal. But as they left, Michael could hear one of the client's friends chuckling about how the tattooist had a boner for him.

Michael fell back against the bench and pulled off his gloves to run now trembling fingers through his hair.

DOMINIC took his time and began to reacquaint himself with a body that had become an enemy over the decades. Slowly, his fingers followed the line of his flesh and muscle, sliding over the slight protrusion of his hip bone down to the crease of his thigh. His head fell back against the pillow, and he let out a shaky breath between parted lips.

The texture of his pubic hair was a confusion of silky and coarse under his fingers as they moved to the base of his erection. He held his breath at the surprising heat in his palm and gently cupped the underside of his cock. With a slow exhale, Dominic allowed his hand to travel the length of the hardened flesh. The ridges of veins were familiar from his youth and brought back memories of the summer sun and sensual touches. The power of the image startled him, and he quickly withdrew his hand. *Don't do this to yourself.* But the thought had barely formed before he knew it was all right. Michael was with him but safely away from his touch.

Dominic cautiously moved his hand to the head of his cock and traced the slit with a fingertip, sliding softly over a drop of moisture and wondering briefly how long had it been since he'd felt that. He lifted his hand to his lips and tentatively touched the tip of his tongue to taste himself. He returned his hand to his needy flesh and touched Michael's mind.

FINGERS roamed unseen over Michael's body, and he sat silently with his eyes closed. *You're not here... not here...*, he tried to reason with himself, but the thought lacked conviction against the pleasure of the touch. He pressed hard against his crotch, pushing the buttoned fly down on his aching cock. *This can't be happening.*

Michael's heart hammered against his chest as he opened his eyes and looked around the empty workroom. There was no doubt he was alone, but Dominic enveloped his senses, and it felt *so* damned right. Michael knew he could stop it. Dominic would hear his thoughts and stop if he asked. But Michael didn't want it to stop.

Ignoring the debris of ink and bloodstained tissues, Michael walked away from his workstation. The sound of Abby chatting to his clients reached the periphery of his hearing, but none of it broke through the echo of Dominic's faltering breath. Closing the bathroom door behind him, Michael "heard" the whisper of his name, and he leaned his forehead against the peeling paintwork of the door and whimpered. A small trail of sweat trickled through his hairline, making its way down his neck and beneath the frayed collar of his T-shirt. Despite the heat, he shivered.

A hard-to-find breath forced its way between his lips, and Michael slid shaking fingers along the brass studs of his fly, flipping each open as they passed. He flattened his other palm against the door and stifled his moans against the damp skin on the back of his hand as he took hold of himself.

Dominic, please, Michael mouthed, his mind reeling at the dual assault of touch and smell. His hand moved with the other's. Both close. Both needing. And when he reached his release, the spill of come over his fingers went almost unnoticed, so great was the wave that both shook and cradled him. But the warmth of what Michael could only identify as love was suddenly overwhelmed and overtaken by immense grief. Shaken, Michael slumped against the door and again moaned Dominic's name, but this time he was met with silence.

Tears of hurt and frustration prickled Michael's eyes as he slammed his fist against the door. Michael pushed back and gulped a few breaths of air. His gaze wandered around the room, where it took in but rejected his surroundings. He shook his head.

"Mikey? What's wrong?" Abby asked in a surprised voice when Michael came storming through the shop. Without stopping he muttered, "I have to see him."

"Well, yeah, you do," Abby murmured and watched her friend disappear through the front door, hoping like hell she was wrong about Dominic, and he was just a secretive man with a strange skin disorder.

Michael had no idea what he wanted to do or say when he got to Dominic's house, but he knew he needed answers.

By the time he left the growing bustle of Chapel Street, Michael's walk had become a jog that evolved into a run when he rounded the corner of Dominic's street. But the house was in darkness, and as he stood almost bouncing on the balls of his feet, Michael was suddenly at a loss.

Michael strained to sense Dominic, but there was nothing. Not knowing what else to do, he sat on the concrete step leading up to the veranda and looked at the small border of daffodils running down the drive. He thought about Dominic crouching in the moonlight planting the bulbs, tending the small garden, and then picking the flowers, never to see their true yellow under the artificial light of his house.

They are *my sun, Michael.*

The words resonated around and through Michael's thoughts. Jumping to his feet, he looked up at the house to see Dominic in the now illuminated bedroom window. They stood and watched each other for what may have been minutes, and then Michael murmured softly, "Dominic. *Please?*"

Longing and sorrow wrapped around Dominic's heart. He slowly shook his head and walked away.

A sudden fury filled Michael. He tore one of the golden heads from the flowerbed and shouted at the empty window, "Don't you fucking do this to me, Dominic!"

The crushed yellow petals hit the nearby fence and fell to the shadowy garden bed. Michael watched them fall and clenched his fist in frustration. "I won't be dismissed like that, Dominic."

Michael turned and paced the length of the veranda, fuming both at the man in the house and himself for needing him so much. Another fruitless glance up at the window and Michael's anger rose. He slammed his fist against his thigh and stormed into the house. Without letting thought or logic break through emotion, Michael bounded up the stairs two at a time toward the darkened bedroom.

Leaning against the wall next to the window, Dominic felt each angry breath and heard each footfall as Michael grew closer. *I'm sorry, Michael,* his mind whispered, so softly that its intent would only curl around the anger of the young tattooist without penetrating.

Dominic's cool fingertips passed over the shredded flesh of his wrist; the blood had stopped flowing, and the finer tears were already beginning to knit. *This is all I have to offer you, and I can't do that.* Dominic sighed and closed his eyes, listening to Michael's approach. He knew he could drive Michael from the house even before he reached the bedroom, but Dominic understood Michael needed the confrontation. Perhaps then he would understand.

It was only when he reached the top of the staircase that Michael realized his progress had not been slowed and the bedroom door was open. He frowned and stared into the darkened room. It was several seconds until his eyes adjusted to the gloom. Gradually, he made out the back of a silent figure hunched miserably near the window, and Michael felt his fury drain.

"What have you done to me, Dominic?" he whispered to the back in the shadows. The question instantly brought back waves of pain and regret.

"I'm sorry, Michael. So sorry," Dominic mumbled against the faded wallpaper, purposely using his physical voice.

Michael wanted to be angry, wanted to rage and yell, but all he felt was pain. "It hurts, Dominic," he whispered. "And I don't know if it's my hurt or yours, but that doesn't matter, does it?"

He quietly crossed the bedroom floor and reached out until his hand rested on the back of Dominic's shoulder. The tension was instant under his touch, and he heard a quiet "Don't...."

But Michael wouldn't listen to the words anymore. What he'd felt was stronger than any refusal or denial, so he stepped closer and leaned against Dominic's back.

Dominic turned his face just enough to feel Michael's breath against the cool skin of his cheek. It warmed him, and he closed his eyes, living through each puff of air. The breath faltered and lips touched him tentatively.

"No, Michael," Dominic whispered, his near-silent voice heavy with sorrow.

Michael stopped the kiss but rested against Dominic, their cheeks touching. "I don't know what to do."

Dominic winced and despair engulfed them both. *We can't do this. I will hurt you.*

Michael sighed and shook his head, not questioning the voice he heard clearly in his mind. "I'm already hurting, Dominic. It only stops hurting when I'm with you," Michael replied and slid his arm slowly around Dominic to caress and hold him.

I never meant this to happen, and you'll forget in time, Dominic lied, knowing what he had done to the young man was unforgivable.

"I don't want to forget you. I can't forget you."

"Do you know what I am, Michael? Do you understand what I can do to you?" Dominic murmured, loathing the truth behind the question.

When there was no answer other than a sense of frustration and confusion, Dominic lifted his damaged, bloodied wrist and held it for Michael to see. "I did this as I came, Michael, and I would do it to you. I would do that and a lot more."

Michael tentatively touched the healing flesh, feeling it cool beneath his fingertips. "Abby said you were like Louis," he whispered, keeping his eyes down even when he felt Dominic's confusion. *Vampire.* He couldn't say the word, but the thought was out and Dominic heard it.

"I feed on blood and can kill. I *have* killed, many times, and those I loved died by my touch." Dominic's voice held all the misery of centuries alone, but Michael shook his head. "You won't do that to me."

"It is part of me," Dominic whispered. "Your flesh would be torn like mine, but you wouldn't heal."

"You won't hurt me," Michael said again, as if trying to convince both Dominic and himself.

Dominic stared at the fingers still resting on his broken skin and closed his eyes against the sight, only to see images of his past lover ripped and bleeding. He forced the memory away and pronounced, "I would kill you, Michael. Do not doubt that."

Michael only had the barest sense of Dominic's vision and felt the love he had lost. He made to tighten his arms around Dominic but was abruptly pushed away with a desperate cry. "This can't happen again. Get away from me."

Dominic stood with arms outstretched as if holding an unspeakable terror at bay. When Michael made a move toward him, Dominic sent the clear message: *Do not touch me, Michael.* The burst of energy in Michael's mind blinded him for an instant before it seared through all conscious thought.

Michael staggered backward, clutching his head. Dominic watched what he was inflicting on the man he had drawn into his world. He wanted to stop, wanted to reach for the human, but that couldn't happen, could *never* happen. *Get out. Get away from me.*

PAIN, overwhelming pain, filled Michael's head as he ran down the silent street, stumbling over his own feet in his haste. *Run, Michael.* As much as he wanted to stop, to argue, he couldn't. The fear was urgent, primal, and couldn't be overcome by either logic or love.

When he finally reached Chapel Street, it began to release its grip, and Michael slumped, exhausted and shaking, against a poster-plastered light pole. He slid awkwardly down to squat, his tearstained face buried in his hands.

A couple enjoying a late night drink at an outdoor café watched him warily before exchanging glances and getting up to see if they could help.

"You okay, mate? Need a hand?" came the well-meaning questions and a hand on Michael's shoulder.

"Don't fucking touch me," Michael spat at them and pulled away as if the touch burned him. "I'm okay. I'm okay." His voice faded as he stood shakily to prove his point to them.

Though unconvinced, the man indicated for his partner to return to their table as he said quietly, "I don't know what your problem is, mate, but you obviously need help."

Michael blinked away the last of his tears and nodded, then backed away to turn toward the relative safety of Ink.

DOMINIC felt each step as Michael fled, but still he raged, driving him further away to where he belonged. *Please stay away*, he begged as Michael reached those of his own kind, but as much as he hoped it would be enough to dissuade the human from returning, he knew Michael would come back. Their bond was too strong now. The damage was done and could not be undone.

He stared out the window at the now empty street and understood what he needed to do.

Forgive me, Michael, but I have to keep you safe. Dominic wasn't sure if the message would penetrate the fog of panic and despair in Michael's mind, but the intent would surface later.

Dominic paced his room alone. The hunger gnawed at his belly, but he would not leave to feed. *Never again.*

THE sky paled. Dominic fought the lethargy of sleep daylight brought and moved to sit in the high-backed chair near his bed.

He was ready.

Dominic watched the light slowly creep toward him across the floor. Even though it stopped a good six inches from his bare toes, he could feel the radiant heat begin to scorch his skin. For a moment, he contemplated ending it quickly—simply walking naked out into the tiny unkempt garden, with only the daffodils to witness his fiery demise. He'd heard of it happening before. Although vampires rarely sought each other's company, he knew of another and his screams in the sun when he had suffered enough.

But Dominic did not want a fast end to his unnatural life. The slow degeneration of old age and the gradual inevitability of death were denied to him, but this was close. His body would become frail as it began to suffer the ravages of starvation, and eventually, he would slip into death.

Soon, echoed Dominic's silent plea.

Chapter
S I X

I will stay with you through nightfall, quiet kisses I will take
I will never forget you, but I'll be gone before you wake....

"THAT was an old, classic Goth outing from the now defunct Soul Collectors, and now for the latest Melbourne weather...."

Michael had heard the song many times on the radio, but today it caught him off guard. When Abby walked through to the back room, she found Michael at his workstation with tears tumbling down his face.

She calmly moved beside him and, without saying a word, enveloped him in her arms.

"I can't feel him anymore, Abbs," Michael said, so softly she had to strain to hear. "It's been ages since he sent me away, and... and tonight he faded completely. I kept waiting to sense him waking up when it got dark, and he's not there."

"Maybe the connection is cut? You know, because he wanted you to go?" Abby suggested as she eased back a little to shrug.

Michael shook his head. "It's not like that. Okay, yeah, I know he was blocking his thoughts from me, but I could tell something was wrong. He felt wrong and now...." As much as Michael wanted to believe that Dominic was simply blocking everything from him, he knew it wasn't true. "I don't even know him, don't know anything about him, but he is... was... part of me, and I don't think he *could* block me anymore." Dropping his face to Abby's shoulder, Michael mumbled miserably, "I should have tried to go back."

"Maybe he won't stop you now," Abby offered as she gently rubbed her hand over Michael's back, shooting a warning look at Scott, who had started to come in, then thought better of it and retreated to the front of the store.

"I don't know," Michael whispered and sat back to drum his agitated fingers against his chest. "It's like he's not there anymore. He's not there and it's empty now."

"Okay, sweetheart, you're gonna tie yourself up in knots over this until you know for sure," Abby said in a determined voice and sat up straight, pushing Michael's hair back off his face. "Scott can close up, so go now, but promise me one thing? Be careful, and you better let me know what happens, okay?"

THE house was like any other house on the old street. There was nothing to make it stand out from the rest. Nothing to mark it as the home of a vampire. Nothing that was Dominic.

Michael sat for a long time on the steps of the porch, digging his heel into the dirt of the overgrown garden bed. He knew he could go into the house any time he wanted because there was nothing to stop him; the sense of dread and warning was gone.

It was just a house.

The sun had been down for a long time, but Michael was still alone, and it was a loneliness he could never have imagined. It ate at him, leaving him lost in his despair.

"I can't do this, Dominic," he whispered to the small moon-paled flowers peeping out through the weeds near his feet. "I don't want to be alone."

Michael stood, kicked the dirt off his shoe, and stepped up to the door. He was so scared he would find the house empty, but he'd already put it off too long.

As before, the front door was unlocked, and it opened with the faintest creak. Michael stood in the silent foyer and listened, both with and without his ears.

Nothing.

His fingers touched the old-fashioned hall stand and worked their way to the coat that hung on the brass hook. They closed around the sleeve, and he leaned into it, smelling the faint scent of Dominic. With the near-threadbare wool still pressed against his cheek, Michael turned to look at the stairs leading up to Dominic's bedroom. He knew he needed to go, but then it would be final. Dominic would be gone, and Michael doubted he could cope with the emptiness of the room.

You have to know for sure, sweetheart. Abby's words rang in his mind, and Michael knew she was right. He would never have peace if he didn't know. Reluctantly, he let the fabric fall back against the stand and walked to the stairs.

Each footfall sounded with a dull thump as he climbed the stairs and made his way to the door.

It was open.

The bedroom was bathed in the silver-blue light of the moon, which flooded in from the open curtains. Michael stood and stared. The breath left his body at the sight of the naked form on the bed.

"Dominic?" he whispered.

No response.

"Dominic, please?" Michael said a little louder, panic beginning to take hold when his words simply fell flat in the stifling room.

Slowly he moved to the edge of the bed. Dominic was very still, and Michael had no sense of him actually being there. "What did you do?" he asked before his trembling fingers touched the chill of Dominic's back. The unresponsive skin was as smooth and cool as porcelain beneath his fingertips. Michael quickly withdrew them.

He sat on the edge of the bed. The cold of the body crept through him despite the summer heat and the distance across the empty side of the bed.

"I don't know how to be without you anymore, Dominic. I don't think I *can* be without you," he said, even though Dominic could no longer hear him.

Gently, so as not to jostle Dominic too much, Michael turned and crawled over the mattress. He curled up against Dominic's back as if to warm him.

He had no plan, no logical steps to be taken. Michael simply knew he couldn't leave. Not yet.

Michael stayed with Dominic throughout the night, rising to close the curtains when the sun's rays entered the room. "Keep you safe, Dominic... like last time."

Although Michael knew what Dominic had done was very different from the burns he had suffered, part of him wouldn't believe the vampire was gone. It was only when the demands of his bladder forced Michael to the bathroom that he moved away from Dominic.

"I won't be long. I won't leave you alone," he whispered.

Michael spent the rest of the day drifting in and out of a fitful doze, waking to talk to Dominic or run soothing hands over his cold body.

It was late afternoon when Michael finally slept—and dreamed.

"You can't be here, Michael," Dominic whispered as they sat together in the grass, the sun caressing their faces.

"I can't go," Michael countered and reached out to hold Dominic's hand, enjoying the warm pressure of his palm. "Haven't you figured it out yet? We have to be together."

Reality slowly replaced the dream, and Michael fought to stay in the bright field where the sun warmed Dominic's face, but the darkened room bled through and pushed the other image away.

"No... please," Michael moaned, his face pressed into the soft strands of Dominic's hair.

Then he heard it.

What he'd assumed was an echo of his dream became more. A whisper touched his mind, so faint it was barely there. But it *was* there.

Michael's pulse pounded loudly in his ears and frustrated him as he struggled to hear a sound that faded even before he heard it. He sat up and looked down at Dominic's seemingly lifeless body. Michael leaned closer and stroked the fine tendrils of hair from Dominic's face. He murmured, "Don't go. You can't leave me."

Michael clambered off the bed and moved around it to squat in front of Dominic. The face was passive, almost peaceful in its "sleep," but the wordless whisper still crept over the edges of Michael's awareness.

Almost bouncing on his heels, Michael ran through desperate scenarios. *Blood....*

Adrenaline pumped through Michael as he stood and began to pace. "You need my blood. You're a vampire and you need blood. I can do that," he muttered.

With clenched hands, Michael nodded and repeated what was becoming his own little mantra: "I can do that." Quickly, he ran to the bathroom to scramble through drawers and cupboards, looking for scissors, razor blades, even safety pins with which to puncture his skin.

Nothing.

"Fuck!" Michael cursed and stared at himself in the mirror. His eyes fell to the retro button badge pinned to his T-shirt, and he fumbled to unfasten it. The old pin was slightly crooked and a little rusted, but still sharp. Michael took a breath and stuck it into the pad of his finger. "Shit, shit, shit," he cursed, and he squeezed it to watch the bead of blood form a slow trickle.

Not enough, but I've gotta try. He glanced from the pinprick toward the door.

With one hand, Michael carefully drew the sheet up over Dominic and tucked it in at his waist. He dragged the chair a little closer and gave his bloody fingertip another hard squeeze before reaching out. Dominic's lips parted easily, and Michael smeared the small trace of blood just inside. He frowned at the thin transparent smear. *Not nearly enough.*

The kitchen offered no solutions, and Michael knew time was running out. The faint echoes he'd felt earlier were leaving him.

Michael forced away tears of frustration and fear as he lifted his finger to his own lips, tasting the trace of copper. He knew he'd have to leave, if only for a little while.

"I won't be long," he said to the empty kitchen and raced out the door.

The pharmacy was only a street away, but Michael ran so hard he incurred a look of suspicion from the sales assistant when he skidded to a breathless halt. It took him a second or two to collect himself enough to ask, "Razor blades, please... or sharp scissors?"

Instead of meeting his request, she glanced over to the pharmacist behind the prescription counter, indicating that the man in front of her could be a problem.

"Can I help you?" the older man asked as he walked toward Michael.

"I just need something sharp like razor blades or scissors... for work," Michael requested again, trying to mask his growing agitation at the delay. "And maybe some sticking plasters... just in case I slip and accidently cut myself," he added as an afterthought, hoping it would settle their concerns.

The man nodded, and the young assistant directed Michael to the items. Thanking her quickly, Michael shoved some money into her hand and took off out the door.

THE blade hovered over vulnerable skin until Michael's frustration boiled over. "Just fucking do it, you coward," he derided himself and swiped the steely edge across his palm. The pain was instant, and Michael dropped the blade with a mental curse at all the TV shows he'd seen in which the actor merely grimaced before the fake blood gushed out. But as the flash behind his eyes eased, he looked down to see the growing well of blood pooling in his cupped palm.

The line of blood poured into Dominic's unresponsive mouth, only to trickle straight out to stain the pillowcase. "Come on, Dominic, please," Michael pleaded. He tried to catch the blood but only succeeded in spreading it over the pale skin around Dominic's lips. His panic started to rise, but he stopped it short. "Okay, stop it," he muttered to himself. "That won't help. He needs you to do this, so get it done."

Carefully, Michael took the corner of the sheet and wiped Dominic's face clean, then moved up the bed and sat at the pillow. With some effort, Michael managed to move Dominic's dead weight to cradle his head gently in his lap. This time the blood stayed, and Michael stroked back Dominic's hair while he clenched his fist, squeezing out as much blood as he could.

Feel it, Dominic. Feel it running down your throat, bringing you back to me....

Chapter
S E V E N

DOMINIC watched Michael sleep.

It was night and hunger ate at him, but lethargy born of his weakness kept Dominic in the bed. Waking had been difficult. It had slowly crept into his consciousness that the pain of every new breath was real. It hurt to come back. It hurt to sense Michael's gentle soul as he lay beside him, knowing the young man's blood had been given to the one who would ultimately take his life.

Dominic gently touched Michael's chest and felt the rise and fall of his contented breathing. *Why didn't you let me go?* But Dominic knew the answer to his silent question. It was for the same reason he had chosen Michael's life over his own.

He gently lifted Michael's hand and examined the tortured palm and fingers; touching the sticking plasters over some of the deeper cuts and shaking his head. *Do you really understand what you have done, Michael?* The young man moaned softly in his sleep and closed his fingers around Dominic's. Michael sighed, and a smile curled the edges of his sleeping lips. Watching him, Dominic's thoughts were sad, but maybe, just maybe, they held an undertone of impossible hope that he hadn't felt in what seemed like an eternity.

Settling back against Michael's warm body, Dominic closed his eyes, too exhausted to acknowledge the hunger that heightened the smell of Michael's blood and urged him to take more. Gradually, he drifted off into sleep, not meaning to eavesdrop on Michael's dreams, but unable to resist their humanity.

DOMINIC was still asleep when Michael awoke. Slowly, he opened his eyes and allowed his vision to adjust to the darkened room. Even before he could see, Michael could *feel* Dominic there with him. Carefully, he searched for Dominic's hand, let go in sleep, and wrapped it in his own. It wasn't warm like his, but at least the vicious cold of the night before was gone. Michael gave it a soft kiss and whispered, "I know you just woke up, Dominic." Michael turned and smiled into the pale eyes that watched him. "We're gonna be okay."

Dominic's gaze lacked Michael's optimism. He tried to repress a futility practiced over many years alone and stated softly, "Maybe."

Michael frowned. *I can tell what you're thinking, Dominic. It's strong now. Your thoughts are strong and clear, so you can't hide anything from me anymore.*

I know. Dominic's thoughts mirrored the sadness in his eyes. *I should never have let this happen.*

"*You* didn't," Michael said out loud, his words bouncing around the otherwise silent room. "This was *my* choice, my decision, *my* free will."

Do you have *"free will" after what I've done to you?*

Angered by the question, Michael sat up to glare down at Dominic. "Of course I do!" He swung his legs over the side of the bed and stood up. For the first time, he noticed the throb from the multitude of cuts on his hands.

"I could have let you die," he fumed, not exactly sure why he was so angry. "The connection was gone. *You* were gone. I could have stayed away like you told me to do. Then I'd have just gone to a club, got drunk, and fucked someone, but I *chose* to come here. Do you understand that I chose to come back to *you*?"

"You should have let me go, Michael," Dominic murmured stubbornly, not lifting his head from the pillow. "I did this to keep you safe."

Michael simply stared at Dominic, his fury and frustration at the statement making words difficult. "Keep me safe?" he eventually spat out. "Did you *ever* really consider what *I* actually wanted?"

"Would you really know?" Dominic asked quietly.

Michael was stunned by Dominic's lack of awareness. He slammed his injured hand against his thigh, almost enjoying the bolt of pain that jarred his entire arm. Grunting out an exasperated breath, Michael resisted the urge to tell Dominic to go fuck himself and stormed out of the room.

Muttering angrily to himself, Michael watched the stream of pee hit the inside wall of the toilet bowl. "I am *not* doing anything I don't want to," he growled as he hit the flush button. *And I know you can hear me, Dominic!*

I can hear you.

The gentle tone of the thought seemed to wrap around him as he peeled off the sticking plasters and washed his hands. The cut on his palm was still raw, and the skin separated, allowing a small trickle of blood to seep from the injury.

I didn't just do this for you, Dominic. I did this for us.

The thought was almost a plea, and Dominic closed his eyes against it. *Come back to the bedroom and let me see your hand, Michael.*

Michael stared at his reflection for a moment, trying to see past the dark circles under his eyes to find the strength of conviction he'd had the night before. "I'm tired, Dominic," Michael muttered and wandered back through to the bedroom.

He stood silently at the bottom of the bed, his shirt crumpled and spotted with the brown spatters of dried blood. His hand ached as it hung by his side.

I'm so sorry, Michael, Dominic sighed and held out his hand for the young man to join him. *But there is no way we can be together.*

"Why not?" Michael countered and paced a few steps, passively refusing to either return to the bed or leave the room until he got an answer.

"Tell me this," Dominic inquired, quietly but with the barest hint of hardness to his voice. "Could you walk away now?"

Michael went to give an instant and angry response but stopped himself. He thought about the question, about leaving this house, leaving Dominic. It was pain and emptiness he felt, but not the mindless compulsion Dominic was implying. He walked over to sit on Dominic's side of the bed. "I think I could if I had to," Michael said softly and reached out with his damaged hand, only to stop short of actually touching Dominic.

"Then maybe you should." It was said, and Dominic knew it was for the best, but his heart constricted a little with each word. He took Michael's hand in his own and turned it over to see the razor cut, reopened on his bloodied palm. "You should not have to do this."

Gazing miserably at the mess of his hand, Michael whispered, "Give me a *real* reason why you deserved to die for me, Dominic? If you can do that, I'll go."

Dominic sighed and leaned forward to gently run his tongue over the injured palm. Michael shivered slightly and frowned, not understanding the action until he saw the wound begin to knit. Slowly, the edges drew together until only a red line remained. Within seconds it faded, and all traces of the cut were gone. Michael looked up to meet Dominic's sad eyes.

"I'm not human, Michael," Dominic said in a voice that mourned the man he had been. "This is what I do. Not to heal victims because I feel for them, but to protect myself."

With his hand still resting in Dominic's, Michael screwed up his face in frustration. He shook his head, confused. "I don't understand." *I want to understand.*

Dominic's lips did not move, but the misery in his thoughts was clear. *I feed on humans, and while I feed, we merge. Their thoughts and memories are mine; mine, in turn, become theirs—if I allow it. Even when I don't, some slip through.*

It was hard to hold Dominic's gaze when it held so much sorrow, but Michael had too many questions that he needed to have answered. "Does it last? After, I mean?"

Dominic nodded. *It would last, but I heal their wounds and can make them forget. It keeps them safe and keeps me safe.*

Michael's frown deepened as he let the concept sink in, and he turned his hand, pressing his palm to Dominic's. "Do *you* forget?"

Dominic gently pulled his hand from Michael's grasp and whispered, "I don't forget.... I never forget. I still remember the fear and suffering every victim brings to me. Many come willingly and offer themselves to me in their loneliness and despair. A few beg to become what I am, and that is something I always deny them. I can't forget."

"You wouldn't have to go through that anymore," Michael stated, already suffering the loss of Dominic's touch. "You *already* have my blood in you. I can feed you, Dominic. It would be okay, and you wouldn't have to get blood from others." Although his heart hammered as he offered himself, Michael knew it was a way they could be together.

"No," Dominic said simply, but the twitch of a muscle gave away how tightly his jaw was clenched.

Michael met the refusal with determination of his own. "You will be safe, Dominic. I'm not arguing with you about this. I need you to be safe."

Slowly Dominic reached his hand toward the young tattooist so the tips of his fingers gently brushed down the lightly stubbled cheek. "You don't know what you're offering, Michael."

"Don't patronize me, Dominic," Michael growled half under his breath before looking up to match Dominic's eyes in an unrelenting stare. "I know *exactly* what I'm offering."

The attitude in both his voice and expression made it clear to Dominic that Michael was not going to back down. He shook his head.

"Do this, Dominic," Michael said firmly, then took Dominic's hand in his and drew the fingers down over his throat.

Dominic could both feel and hear the pulse rushing beneath his fingers. His breath quickened. He wanted it, but could he really feed from Michael? A hundred arguments ran through Dominic's thoughts, each one more logical than the last, and every one of them should have stopped his final thought: *We could be together.*

Slowly, Dominic slid his hand around to cup the back of Michael's head and lowered his face carefully and reverently to the beating pulse.

As brave as Michael had been when he offered his blood, he trembled when the soft breath touched his throat. It tickled, warm against his skin, until soft lips formed a gentle kiss that drew an involuntary shiver. He waited for the pain of penetration, only to feel the cool touch of Dominic's tongue. Michael moaned, his fingers twining lightly in Dominic's hair. *Do it, Dominic.*

Michael was willing, but Dominic could smell his fear. His arms gently encircled his prey… *Michael…* and held him tightly as the sharp tips of his fangs pierced the vulnerable skin of Michael's throat.

Even though he knew the bite was coming, the primal instinct to survive took hold, and Michael fought against Dominic's arms.

But Dominic had tasted blood.

Michael's blood was sweet as it flowed over Dominic's tongue, but sweeter still were the images it brought. *Sun… laughter… light.* The essence of each thought and memory flooded through Dominic as he drank, swallowing each and wanting more. The two men joined in the images and lived them together beneath the summer sun and away from the dark room.

Then through the blaze came a warning: *Stop.*

The agony of letting go was greater than the starvation he'd so recently suffered, but Dominic knew it had to be done.

Michael clutched blindly when Dominic pulled away. He was dazed by the rush of images and emotions still pervading his thoughts and whimpered, "Dominic, don't leave me alone."

Grasping his wrists, Dominic dragged Michael against him. *I'll make it stop, make it go away.* He raked his fingers through the mess of dark hair and whispered the same words aloud, "I'll make it stop."

But as he moved his lips over the weeping wound, Michael held a weak hand to Dominic's cheek. "Don't, Dominic. Please don't take that from me."

"I can't leave you with that, Michael," Dominic murmured, knowing that as he had shared Michael's memories, Michael had shared a fraction of his. Even a fraction meant the damage of several centuries' worth of darkness.

Michael shook his head and settled against Dominic's chest. "They're yours. I want to remember *with* you."

That Michael was willing to hold on to even a fragment of Dominic's memories was like sharing his loneliness, and perhaps chipping some of it away. He rested his head against Michael's hair and heard the quiet whisper, "You have to know I love you, Dominic."

Dominic nodded and closed his eyes, failing to stop his tears. "Please forgive me for that, Michael."

Chapter
E I G H T

MICHAEL fought through the layers of consciousness, each one peeling back dreams until he reached something that felt no more real. "I'm in bed with a vampire," he whispered. It sounded even more absurd when spoken out loud. With a small chuckle of disbelief, Michael turned his face to look at the vampire in question. *I'm in bed with Dominic….*

He lay and watched Dominic for several minutes, noticing the soft flutter of lashes and movement beneath the lids. *Dream good dreams now, Dominic.*

With an almost chaste kiss to the sleeper's cheek, Michael swung his legs over the edge of the mattress. It was day, late in the day, judging from the faint orange glow to the stripe of light beneath the heavy curtain. Rising, he checked the seal of the curtains, logically knowing it was safe, but needing to make sure before he left.

Pulling on his low-slung jeans and dirty T-shirt, Michael leaned over Dominic and told him, "I'm coming back, Dominic. I just need to get something to eat." He knew there wouldn't be an answer, but he also knew Dominic would remember the message.

The world of Chapel Street seemed to have tilted a little since Michael was last there. *Can it only be a couple of days?* He looked into the faces of each passerby, and what he saw no longer held any meaning to him. *I don't belong with them anymore.*

The smell of a burger bar distracted him. The juices of his belly rebelled and growled loudly. With a grimace of hunger-induced nausea, Michael ordered a burger with the lot, then reached over the counter to grab a handful of ketchup packets. He grinned at the teenage girl who was on the verge of telling him off, then ripped the packet open to squeeze its contents into his mouth.

"Gross." She giggled but shook her head and handed the order through the open hatch to the kitchen.

By the time Michael reached Ink, the hamburger was just a faint grease smear around his lips, which he wiped off with the hem of his T-shirt.

The tattoo parlor was still closed, but peering through the gaps in the painted window, Michael could just make out Abby going through the bookings to get things ready for the evening trade. Rummaging through pockets filled with coins and sticking plasters, Michael located his keys and let himself in with a quiet, "Hey, Abbs."

"Where the hell have you been?" she berated, but she pulled him into a bear hug before he could answer. "You were with *him*, weren't you? Oh man, I'm glad to see you. I was so scared. I kept thinking.... Oh, never mind what I was thinking."

"I'm okay," Michael mumbled, still trapped in her arms.

Finally, she released him and shrugged. "I know you said you were going to him, and when you didn't come back...." She shrugged again.

Michael had the decency to look sheepish when he said, "I'm sorry, Abby. He was letting himself die. I couldn't let that happen, so I had to stay with him. I had to bring him back."

Abby frowned and shook her head, asking nervously, "What do you mean 'bring him back'?" She looked at his soiled T-shirt and picked at the brown stains around the collar, her expression one of worry.

Hoisting himself onto the countertop, Michael patted the spot beside him and waited for her to get settled before he told her almost all that had happened. Abby's expression changed with each part of the tale, sometimes understanding and others shaking her head in disbelief.

When Michael eventually fell silent, Abby looked at him and held his hand. "I know I said to listen to your heart and go to him... to Dominic... but you can't keep him going with your blood. Fuck, I can't believe we're even having this conversation."

Michael looked down at their clasped hand. His voice was very quiet but determined. "I need to feed him, Abby. I love him."

"I'm scared for you, sweetie," Abby murmured softly, but Michael simply shook his head. "He doesn't need to feed every day. I'll be okay. He won't hurt me."

Although Abby wasn't convinced, she could see in his eyes when Michael looked up at her that there was no further room for argument. Michael knew his mind, and she wasn't going to try to change it. Instead, she whispered, "Just be safe, okay?"

With a nod and a grin, Michael lifted their hands to give hers a kiss. "Okay."

Sliding off the counter, he glanced toward the back shelf and asked, "You wouldn't have anything to eat back there, would you? Vampire maintenance is fucking hungry work."

BENDING over a client, wearing one of the store's new T-shirts, Michael's brow furrowed in concentration. The fresh line of black left behind bubbles of blood that slowly combined to form a small trickle. He lifted the gun and watched it. There was a hint of memory previously blocked to him.

Michael smiled. *You're awake.*

I'm awake.

The memory grew.

Pale skin, broken by his needle. Those gray eyes watching him wipe blood and ink from a growing tattoo. Michael felt the cool of Dominic's skin beneath his latex-covered fingers. A rush of heat at a remembered blush....

Michael turned away from the young woman in the chair on the pretense of getting a drink. *Stop it, Dominic. You're getting me hard,*

Michael grumbled in a thought tinged with the elation of sharing a joke with a lover.

In a silent room several streets away, Dominic lay on the bed and laughed.

I heard that. Michael grinned.

MICHAEL bounded up the stairs two at a time to find Dominic sitting at the old-fashioned dresser looking at himself in the mirror, illuminated only by the bright light of the moon.

"Do you have any idea how old I am?" Dominic asked, glancing up to meet Michael's eyes. "Yet I don't grow old. I still look the same as I did the night I was turned."

Moving closer, Michael stood behind the chair and looked at the Dominic in the glass. "I thought vampires didn't have a reflection?" he asked, focusing on the pale blue eyes.

"Myth and legend," Dominic murmured and reached forward to touch the cold features of his face.

Michael smiled gently and pushed the hand from the glass to climb between Dominic and his reflection. Perched on the edge of the dresser, Michael cupped Dominic's face in his palms. A small shiver ran through the vampire at the voluntary touch. Michael dipped his head to capture Dominic's soft lips, and each time Dominic tried to speak, Michael grinned and kissed him again.

"You should know by now I'm not letting you go there." Michael rested his forehead against Dominic's before sliding off the dresser and onto his lap. The touching was tentative at first, as if neither was sure how to continue, but the kisses deepened and silent moans were passed between them.

Michael clutched at the hem of his T-shirt and dragged it over his head while grinding his crotch against Dominic, reveling in the feel of hardening beneath him. Slowly, he slipped his hand between them and pressed against Dominic through the fabric of his trousers. Dominic's forehead fell onto Michael's shoulder as he canted his hips up into the hand. He could hear the hoarseness of his breath; it seemed deafening in the quiet of the room.

"Need you, Dominic," Michael whispered.

Dominic gulped a mouthful of air and moaned. It had been so long since he'd been touched in that way. Yet, along with the lust coursing through his body was the red haze. As his desire grew, so did his need to consume.

"Stop," he gasped and quickly repeated the word with greater desperation. "Stop… we can't do this."

"We can," Michael murmured, nuzzling Dominic's neck, his hand still moving over the aching flesh.

No!

Michael stumbled and almost fell as he pushed back from Dominic's thighs. The "voice" forced him away, forced him to break all contact.

"Dominic?" he whispered as the echo cleared from his thoughts, but Dominic was already standing by the window, his back to Michael.

"Dominic, please?" Michael tried again, still unable to move from his place a room's length away.

"I warned you, Michael. I warned you that this is what I am." Dominic's voice was quiet but cold. It held a certainty of the way things had to be between them. Or more to the point, what couldn't happen between them.

Michael shook his head. "I know, but—"

"You don't know!" Dominic shouted and turned toward Michael. "Look at me! Look at what I am." His face did not have the grotesque physical transformation of a fictional vampire, but the predator was there. Dominic's eyes held a sickly luminous glow, and sharp points had replaced human teeth. Hunger, *inhuman* hunger, faced Michael.

"You see why we cannot do this," Dominic said. The anger had seeped from him to be replaced by shame for what he was. "Believe me when I say I *will* tear you apart, only to see and despair at what I have done when it is over."

"There *has* to be a way. You don't understand; I can't *not* touch you."

"There is no way, Michael."

Michael sat in the now vacant chair at the dresser. Their combined pain threatened to overwhelm him, but ultimately, he knew there *was* a way they could be together. Michael took a breath and requested as calmly as he was able, "Make me like you, then." The words hung in the room, tempting and terrifying.

Dominic began to speak, but Michael quickly held up his hand. "I couldn't live without you. Know *that* before you argue," Michael stated with clenched-jaw defiance in the face of Dominic's resistance.

They stared at each other in the silent room as if neither could break through the invisible barrier they'd erected, until Michael stood and slowly crossed the room to stand in front of Dominic. His fingers barely touching the fair hair, he murmured, "I *will* die without this."

"You will die *with* it."

Michael shrugged as if it were a minor consideration. "But we'll be together."

The truth of what both said was undeniable. Dominic grasped at the possibility as if it were a tiny bubble of air when his lungs were burning. He looked at Michael and took a shallow breath. "You would come to resent me, Michael. It is a long time to never see the sun."

Michael moved closer. *It's a long time to be alone.*

So alone.

You have me now, and we don't have to be alone again.

The words resonated deeply. No matter how hard Dominic wanted to deny them, he knew he couldn't. He had Michael and Michael had him. With a small nod, Dominic allowed himself to be led to his bed. They lay looking at each other a long time. Finally, Dominic stroked Michael's lips with his fingertips. *You will have fangs like mine.*

I'll wake at moonrise with you.

The primary emotion Dominic felt emanating from Michael was determination, despite the young man's mortal fear, fear that still pervaded the space between them until Dominic's lips replaced his fingers. *We'll wake together or not at all.*

Gradually, Dominic's kiss moved over Michael's jawline. When the points of his fangs pierced the skin of his throat, Michael was ready.

The first taste of blood was as sweet as before. It contained so much hope and promise of love that soon the savagery of the act diminished. Memories and hidden thoughts flowed between them. Their embrace tightened. Dominic held the rapidly weakening Michael in his arms.

Dominic? The thought was small and so lost.

Let it go, Michael. We're almost there.

The brief flash of panic dissolved as Michael's awareness became distant. The room was gone, and he was cold. Colder than he'd ever felt.

I'm still with you, Michael. You can find me, but you have to try.

In the dark of dying, Michael searched for Dominic, barely feeling the warmth seeping through his lips.

Take me into you, Michael.

Copper slid down Michael's throat, slowly, at first, but he clung to the taste of Dominic and began to draw at the blood.

Dominic's eyes were closed when Michael finally started to feed. "That's it," he whispered. "Take all you need."

Chapter
N I N E

AM I alive?

Only as much as I am.

Michael didn't move, but the press of the humid air in the still room was palpable against his bare skin. He frowned, a little confused at its touch until slow awareness dawned that all his body's responses had changed. No, not changed so much as heightened. The dusty smell of the old curtains tickled his nose. He easily heard the hum and flutter of a moth's wings against the windowpane, the rustle of the pages of an unread store catalogue catching an occasional warm breeze in the letter box far below. All this before he opened his eyes.

Was it like this for you?

Some….

Carefully Michael cracked open his eyes and saw the smile he could already feel. "Hey," he said, his voice sounding dry and cracked.

Dominic smiled and asked the impossible question: "How do you feel?"

Letting out a long, slow breath, Michael shook his head, "Like me, but not. It's like I know who I am, but my head is full of other stuff too."

"A lot of other stuff," Dominic acknowledged quietly.

Like the man with the green eyes? The image was very strong in Michael's mind, yet he didn't feel it could be spoken aloud in their room. *I saw him in your memories when you fed me.*

He took my life.

But he gave you a new one.

It was Dominic's turn to frown. Those memories were always of anger and regret, remembered in terms of taking, not giving. He was not someone Dominic wanted in their shared thoughts. Dominic looked at Michael, who simply smiled and said, "You would have died long before I was born without that new life."

There were no words, but Dominic released a long-held sigh, and Michael's smile grew. His hand moved up to Dominic's face, taking in so many sensations at once. *So new; you feel so new to me.*

Dominic smiled and whispered, "You feel the same."

But Michael shook his head. "You, you're... I dunno... *more*." He laughed and watched his fingers reach up to touch Dominic's eyelashes as if he'd never really seen them before. "You are so much more."

"More." Dominic grinned, remembering well the initial rush of information that had previously just poked at the edges of his consciousness. Silently, he lay and let Michael explore his skin, only responding when the touches became more intimate by closing his hand over Michael's.

"It's okay now, Dominic," Michael murmured, lifting both hands to Dominic's lips, all the while watching the reluctant hope in those pale eyes. "You won't hurt me now." *We can be together.* Words of reassurance were spoken between gentle kisses until there was no room left for them.

Slowly, Michael ran his hand down the length of Dominic's body. Each finger left a fine trail through the hair of his belly as they followed it down. A small sound escaped Dominic's lips when the hand closed around his cock, but he knew that this time it was all right.

Michael traced the veins and ridges beneath the silken skin of Dominic's erection, his mind reeling at the mingling of Dominic's need with his own.

He glanced up briefly before shuffling down the bed to slide the tip of his tongue over the single drop of fluid forming at the slit. The pre-come was sharp against Michael's changed taste buds, and he frowned at the near feral hunger it aroused.

With his fingers fisted in the sheet, Dominic watched Michael and recognized his confusion. Releasing the tortured sheet, he held his hand out and murmured, "It's something you can't deny now, Michael. The hunger will also be with you."

Crawling back up the bed, Michael let himself be wrapped in Dominic's arms, their tongues finding each other between needle-sharp fangs.

The hunger will take us, Dominic warned silently, under their increasingly urgent breaths, as he rolled them over to settle between Michael's thighs. *You can't fight it. It is part of our nature.*

A faint hint of fear passed through Michael, but he could feel the change in himself. He needed Dominic and *all* that brought with it. With his thighs hooked over Dominic's hips, Michael whispered, "I... ah... I don't have anything with me."

Dominic paused and looked down at Michael with a questioning smile.

"Condoms and stuff," Michael explained.

Dominic's smile broadened. *"We* don't need anything." The words were soft, as was the brief kiss that followed. Dominic licked a broad swipe across his palm and slid it along his cock. *Human disease won't touch us*—he nudged the head against Michael's puckered entrance and began the slow push in—*and our bodies need only each other.*

Michael moaned as Dominic entered him, but not in pain. He arched up while pressing hard against Dominic with his crossed feet. He'd had many partners in his short life, but nothing compared to the intensity of joining both physically and spiritually. He clung to

Dominic as if he were a tiny thread of reality in a swirl of sensations that threatened to swallow him whole.

They moved together, rising and falling, snatches of thoughts, memories, desires, passing between them. When they came, it was with the muted gasps and the broken skin of vampire need. But it was also with a love that Dominic believed had died with his humanity.

The night was spent in embraces; time enough to feed when they were sated with each other. They slept in the summer-warmed room behind heavy curtains, sharing dreams until the strip of light beneath the window faded.

MICHAEL woke first, hunger niggling but not yet urgent. His fingertips traced lightly around a nipple, and then he flattened his palm on Dominic's chest, where his bite marks were now healed. He frowned, slightly surprised at the slow rhythm he felt.

More myth and legend, my love.

Michael grinned at the silent voice and looked up at Dominic.

Our hearts still beat. They beat more slowly, but they do beat.

The sound of Michael's laugh echoed around the room, his joy lingering after the sound stopped, and Michael dipped his head to kiss Dominic's chest. Dominic watched, a little bemused, and ran his fingers through Michael's dark hair, enjoying the freedom felt in the long-denied intimacy of simple touch. He closed his eyes to let it wash over him, but beyond the gentle caresses, Dominic could feel Michael's fledgling hunger. Giving the soft hair a light tug, he whispered, "I will hunt tonight. That is something you can learn later."

Michael nodded and eased back, understanding that was a new reality he still had to face.

ALONE in the room, Michael stood naked in front of the mirror. *I don't look changed?* The thought was a private one that would not reach

Dominic while he hunted. He knew all communication was blocked. Dominic had blocked him with a warning that he wasn't yet ready to cope with the need of his prey as they begged to be taken. Although he tried to hide it from Dominic, both knew the act of taking another's blood worried Michael.

He sighed. His hand moved over his lightly rumbling belly, stopping when it came to the small inked sun. Michael looked away from the reflection and focused on his colored skin. *Dominic's faded.* Closer inspection proved that the tattoo was just as dark and clear as the day it was inked. Swirling a finger around the circumference of the sun, Michael hatched a plan.

He knew he'd have to be quick so he'd be back when Dominic returned.

CHAPEL STREET felt forever changed. The tramcar still rattled along the tracks, and friends still chatted over espressos in the street cafés, but Michael knew it would never be the same for him. The coffee aroma tickled his nose in the way it had before, but the warm, earthy scent of the humans overtook it. Michael looked at a nearby couple, who glanced briefly at him before making a point of turning away. Snatches of thoughts or emotions fluttered through Michael's mind when they passed him, but they were like the faint hues that surrounded them: something he thought was there, but wasn't yet sure. *Do they see it in me? Have I changed that much?* Michael wondered and looked down at his hands, half expecting to see a marked pallor, or talons rather than the long, slender fingers now totally healed of his self-inflicted cuts.

He moved away from the café, startled when a bunch of revheads honked their horn to announce the size of their engine. Michael frowned. Hoons were a staple on Chapel at weekends, yet their noise grated on his nerves. More than that, it jarred his body, setting his nerves on edge. He glared at the retreating headlights with bloody thoughts of what he'd do if he caught up with them.

Where the fuck did that come from? The violence of his intentions was totally alien, and Michael shook his head as if he could clear them away. *Shit. I need to get off the street.*

"Michael?" Abby frowned when her friend slipped quietly into the store. She hurried toward him but stopped short a few feet away and held up her hand to block him. "What have you done, Mikey?"

"It's okay, Abbs," he said and tried to step forward, only to see her step away. "I won't hurt you. You know that."

"I know. *Logically*, I know, but...." She shook her head, not able to describe the pull of her survival instincts. "It's strong in you, Mikey. I can feel it."

"It's still me, Abbs," Michael tried again. "No matter what, it's still me, and I can be with him now."

"Oh, sweetheart," she murmured, fought every impulse to run, and closed the gap between them.

Sinking into her hug, he tried to block the sound and smell of her blood as it coursed through her body. He fought desperately to deny his hunger and sent her a silent thought: *I'll never hurt you, Abbs. Never.*

DOMINIC'S fear was a white noise in his head by the time Michael had convinced him he was safe and almost back to the house. *I'm here. I'm safe, Dominic. You blocked me, so I couldn't let you know....*

"See, I'm—" Michael stopped in the door of the bedroom and stared. Dominic radiated power that shimmered around him like a halo.

Where were you, Michael?

But Michael shook his head, still staring at his lover. "Is *that* because you're angry?" When he saw the confused look, Michael moved forward to take one of Dominic's hands. "You're so hot, and you're, I dunno, kinda glowing, like there's a heat haze around you."

"I've fed more than usual," Dominic muttered, still agitated.

"Is... is the person okay?" Michael asked, not sure if he wanted an honest answer.

He will be.

"Good," Michael whispered and stepped closer to watch his fingers penetrate the light around Dominic's face. That was when he noticed the smell. Warm, earthy…. Michael moaned and nuzzled against Dominic, dropping his bag to the floor.

It's the scent of prey, Michael. Dominic gently rubbed the back of Michael's neck. *Slow down your need. You must learn to control it or it will take you.*

Michael fought to hear the advice over the red haze and clutched at Dominic.

Take it slow. Gently, Dominic moved Michael's face, positioning the trembling lips over the vein. *Slowly, now; don't rush it.* Dominic resisted the instinct to tense beneath the urgent, inexperienced bite and cradled Michael with soothing caresses as his blood passed between them.

Warmth flooded Michael's body, and gradually, he became aware of more than his hunger. Dominic's thoughts and touches mingled with nourishment, completely open and honest. All-encompassing love bathed them both as Michael eased back from Dominic's broken skin. Dominic moved them to the bed, where they lay quietly, giving Michael time to settle back to himself.

"I've had an idea," Michael eventually said aloud as he ran his thumb over the healing puncture wounds.

"Should I be worried?" Dominic smiled, not quite willing to move yet.

"Nah." Michael grinned and sat up to raise the hem of his T-shirt. "I still have my tattoo. See, it's still there. Even though yours disappeared by morning, mine's still there."

Dominic nodded and looked at the little sun.

"So," Michael began as he slipped from the bed to fiddle in the bag he'd retrieved from the store. "I want to try something."

With a small shrug, Dominic watched Michael set up his tattoo gun and ink. "It will fade again," he said a little sadly.

"Maybe not." Michael grinned cryptically and spread open the fly of Dominic's pants. "Are you willing to try something with me?"

"I'm willing," Dominic agreed and settled against his pillow while Michael etched out an outline on the white skin of Dominic's hip.

It didn't take long before the final traces of ink and blood were wiped clear to reveal the image of a small, Celtic-knotted crescent moon. Dominic started to speak, but Michael held up his hand. "Not done yet." He put the gun down and leaned over the raw tattoo. With a cheeky smile, Michael ran the flat of his tongue over the design, making sure to cover it all. His eyes sparkled with delight as the healing process began. "Look, Dominic. Look. Maybe it will be there when we wake up, now."

Hoisting himself onto his elbow, Dominic looked from the small black moon to Michael's black-ink-stained lips and tongue. The sight was both ludicrous and beautiful. Dominic reached down to pull Michael up next to him.

Even if my tiny moon fades, I'll awaken to my sun.

They slept as dawn approached, too wrapped up in each other to sense the presence of another in the street. Waiting just out of the beam of the street light, a figure with green eyes felt them.

Chapter
T E N

THE tip of his pink tongue traced the curve of the moon. Night had fallen outside the heavily curtained bedroom, but he easily made out the black of the ink, standing out starkly against pale skin. Michael grinned.

Behind closed eyes, Dominic dreamed of being touched. It was a dream that had haunted Dominic for decades. Unseen fingers caressing neglected skin, eliciting longings that he'd locked away an age ago. He moaned lightly and tried to lean into the touch, needing to feel the spark as the fingers found new places, but the more he tried, the more they drew back. Dominic fought to hold it, but it was beyond him, and gradually, it seeped completely away—first the color, then the images, leaving only a hint of touch.

The faint traffic noises from a distant street intruded, but the warm tickle on his hip bone remained.

Good morning. Michael smiled, sensing the change as Dominic woke. *Or should that be, good evening?*

Dominic stretched and reached down to find Michael's fingers and twine them with his. He wanted that moment to last forever, as *they* would. The smooth skin of another's fingers slipping against his own, the strength of bone and tendon gripping and reassuring him that that was no dream. A simple touch that most would take for granted, but it held Dominic's life.

It's still there.

The soft voice penetrated Dominic's thoughts, and he frowned. He slowly opened his eyes and met dark brown eyes that showed him more joy than he'd felt since the sun warmed his skin. "What's still there?" he muttered.

The tattoo. Michael smiled and kissed the interlocking Celtic design. *And we can talk in here now, remember?* He tapped his head, still amazed by their shared thoughts.

Dominic shook his head and hoisted himself up on his elbows. "That can't be," he said, looking down at the black moon.

"Told you I was good." Michael laughed and kissed it again before crawling up the bed. "Now… what else can I do? Being one of the undead and all?"

"Is that how you see us?" Dominic asked, not offended, but curious at how Michael was dealing with his new reality.

A small giggle and Michael nipped at Dominic's shoulder. "You know, I don't feel dead, or undead even. Actually I feel fucking amazing!" He rolled over onto his back and laughed. "Can you feel your fingernails?" Michael wiggled his fingers in the air above them.

Dominic watched their dance and smiled at his lover. "Yes, I can feel my fingernails."

Michael laughed again. "And your hair? When someone touches your hair? Not the nerves on your scalp, but the hair itself. I didn't notice yesterday—too many other things to think about—but fuck, Dom, it is as if my whole body is awake."

"You learn to shut a lot of it out," Dominic explained, understanding that there were times when his vampire body could overwhelm him.

Michael turned his face and gave Dominic a cheeky, yet slightly lascivious, grin. "I might not want to shut them out, and anyway, *you* don't always shut them out."

It was Dominic's turn to laugh, and the sound was still strange to him. "No, not always."

"So tell what else we can do. Can we fly?" Michael asked as he sat up and crossed his legs.

"We can't fly unless we turn into a bat first," Dominic said, as seriously as he could muster.

"Fuck! Can we really do that?" Michael exclaimed, wide-eyed.

Dominic's laughter echoed around the room, resulting in a sharp slap on the thigh from Michael. "You know, this is a conversation we should have had before you convinced me to turn you," he said, looking up at the young vampire.

Michael shrugged. "I knew what I was getting into. I saw what happened to you."

Dominic nodded and stretched his arm down to take Michael's hand. "Then you saw some of what it is to be a vampire. What else do you need to know? Ask me anything."

There was so much Michael wanted to know, many things that were still niggling thoughts without actual words. He sat quietly for a few moments, then asked—silently because somehow it seemed wrong to say it out loud—*How often do we have to feed?*

You will need blood every night for a while, Michael. Dominic felt the grip on his hand tighten. He knew Michael was hungry and would have had it gnawing at him since he woke. *The need is strong when you are young, and that's when many of the newly turned lose their way.*

Lose their way how? Michael's concern was clear, but so was his knowledge that Dominic would not let anything happen to him.

Their desire could overtake them. But then, they were not obstinate tattooists. Dominic smiled and sat up to touch his lover's face with gentle fingers. "Feed from me," he whispered.

Before he even realized it was happening, the points of Michael's fangs pricked his bottom lip. He swallowed and moved quickly to Dominic's side. "I can't keep feeding from you," he murmured as his lips caressed the skin of Dominic's throat.

"You can, Michael." Dominic's fingers threaded through Michael's hair, holding him close, waiting for his bite. *You can feed from me for as long as you need to.*

Michael's bite was still unpracticed, and Dominic repressed a wince when his skin was torn in the young vampire's rush to find his nourishment. *Take it slowly. There's no hurry; we have all night together.* Dominic sent the thought while he gently released Michael's hair and let his finger play with the fine down at the nape of his neck. Gradually the pull on his blood eased and as it did, the confusion of bloodlust dissipated until Dominic felt their real connection form.

Images of sunshine returned, more specific this time: late afternoon sun when the sting was gone, and its warmth matched its glow as it began to sink toward the sea. There was soft sand beneath his feet. The fine grains tickled as each step pushed them up between his toes. The sun played over Dominic's bare shoulders, not searing his flesh, but warming him to his core. Dominic watched the golden light caught in the gentle ripples of the tide and breathed in the scent of fresh seaweed still trapped in the shallows.

He exhaled a long sigh. *Thank you, Michael.*

With an almost overwhelming effort, Michael stopped drawing on the rich blood and lay quietly against Dominic. When he stirred, it was with another question. "Will you stay with me the first time?"

Even though it wasn't stated, Dominic knew which "first" Michael was referring to. "Of course," he whispered. "I can find some... your first... for you."

"No," Michael muttered softly. "I'm a predator now, aren't I? I need to deal with that."

"You don't have to face that yet," Dominic said sadly. *I don't want you to have to face that at all.*

But it's what I am now, Dominic. I'm like you, and that can't be that bad. Michael rolled back and gave Dominic a smile. "I fell in love with you after all."

MICHAEL spun around on the footpath and stared at the young man who'd just walked past them and made sure to meet Michael's eyes. "Did you feel that?" he asked Dominic, his eyes wide at another new sensation. "Fuck! It was like he was oozing... oh, I dunno... lust?"

Dominic raised his eyebrows, amused at Michael's reaction to the attention. "You'll feel a lot of things from humans. Some of it good and some pretty bad."

Michael shook his head and stared at the next couple to pass them, trying to pick something up from them, but all that happened was a quick side step away from the strange young man. It was then Michael noticed most of the people they passed kept their distance, or as much as the path allowed. He felt another slight twinge of interest from an older man leaning against a shop doorway, but it was fleeting and disappeared as quickly as it came.

"Is it their thoughts I'm reading?" Michael asked, trying to separate and clarify the mess in his head.

"Not thoughts, exactly," Dominic attempted to explain. "I believe it is something less conscious, and many don't know they are sending. Perhaps we simply scent a change in their physiology when they're around us? Their subconscious reacts to the presence of a predator?"

"So you're saying it's just a chemical reaction, nothing more?" Michael asked, not at all convinced. He had sensed a little of it on his walk to get the tattoo gun, but it wasn't as strong then, and perhaps his body was still changing.

Dominic shrugged. "It's something like that. A primal response."

"Pfft." Michael tossed his hair and made a sound of total disdain, which forced Dominic to turn and give him a quizzical look.

"Don't sell us... well, *them*... short. Humans are more than that," Michael said firmly. "That little Goth guy who walked past before? Sure there was a biological response—wow, was there a biological response—but it was more than that. He knew exactly what he was doing. Get past the hard-on, and you could feel him. I mean *really* feel him."

Dominic smiled and tugged at a dark curl that had that fallen over Michael's face. "You are young. You will learn to block it."

"But that's just it; I don't want to block it. It's like their soul touches mine, even if it's just for an instant." The words were no sooner out than Michael saw darkness pass over Dominic's eyes. "Why would you want to block that?" he asked.

"Perhaps we should go home, Michael?" Dominic asked quietly. "I can feed you tonight."

"Why? What's wrong?" Michael wanted to know, confused by the sudden change of topic.

Dominic moved Michael off the path and against the side of a power pole. It wasn't done with force, just a gentle guide away from the human traffic, even though their smell still bathed both vampires.

"I worry for you," Dominic said seriously. "You still view the world as a human despite the burden I have given you."

Michael just smiled and whispered, "It's no burden because I have you. Anyway, you don't have to worry about me. I know what I am, and I know what I was, and believe me, the two aren't all that different."

Dominic was about to argue, but he could already see there was no point. Michael was a fledgling and needed to feel all the changes for himself. "I still think we should go home and try this on another night," he suggested.

"Not a chance." Michael laughed and slipped out from the pole, taking Dominic's hand. "The night is young and it's 'Hard and Heavy Night' at Hunters. And fuck, I want to feel *that*."

APPROACHING Hunters filled Michael with his usual sense of anticipation, but he wasn't quite prepared for the onslaught of heat and sound when they walked past the queue and into the club. It hit him with the force of a sledgehammer, and he stopped dead in his tracks just inside the doorway. Dominic waited at his side; he'd expected that.

Michael stood and looked at the same bar and same people he'd enjoyed for almost a year, but *nothing* was even close to being the same. The crowd jostling to get their drinks had merged into one seething mass of heat and blood to the young vampire's senses. Michael closed his eyes to shut them out, ignoring the stench of sour sweat and beer and mentally searching for Dominic. Gradually, the other's thoughts enclosed his, setting up temporary walls and teaching him the barriers he needed to put in place.

Find your safe level, Michael. The words penetrated, and gradually, Michael was able to distinguish individual sounds within the confusion of noise. Voices laughing and calling for drinks, the deep thrum of a driving bass line, and the song of a lead guitar. He took a cautious breath and opened his eyes. The mass of flesh had become individual people again, many with faces Michael recognized. Turning to Dominic, he said with a slight grimace, "Did I smell like that when I was in here?"

Dominic simply raised his eyebrows and began to walk through the club to a quieter area of tables.

"Oh, come on, I *know* I didn't smell like *that*," Michael persisted, glancing at a very drunk young man stumbling against a group of girls on the dance floor.

"No," Dominic chuckled, watching as the girls pushed him away with a few choice expletives. "You were not like him."

Michael chose a seat where he could see most of the surrounding area and leaned in to Dominic to ask with some apprehension, "So what now? Do I have to pick someone?"

"You rarely have to choose," Dominic explained, scanning those at the nearby tables. "Usually, they will find you."

"Is that what happened that night? You know, the night when I saw you out the back in the alley with the young guy?"

Dominic nodded. "He came to me wanting what I gave you. Many of them will ask for that, but you can't give it to them."

Michael sat quietly and pushed the empty glasses left by the previous occupants to the other side of the table. It made sense to him that some would want this: the romantic notion of sensual immortality, the deep and moody vampire wandering around in the moonlight looking for a lost love. He stopped what he was doing and looked up at Dominic with a giggle, then held up his hand and shook his head, not willing to tell his lover the connections he'd just made. "I know, you told me he would just remember a good night making out with a hot guy," Michael said, getting his mind off the clichés. "But will he still feel you in the back of his mind like I did?"

"Well, I'm sure I didn't word it that way. There may be a residual memory, but nothing more than a feeling like waking after a dream."

"So now we just wait, right?"

"We wait," Dominic repeated, surprised that he was enjoying Michael's twitchy impatience. "It won't take long; we are already being watched. Sit quietly and feel for them."

It was so hard not to turn and look, but Michael did what he was told and calmed his thoughts to take in those around him. He could sense the interest. Initially, it was no more than he felt when he was human, then something else clicked into place and another part of him took over. It started as an insidious feeling creeping through his thoughts, and Michael's immediate response was to deny it, but it radiated out and the changes took him. Michael's vampire instincts honed in on those whose interest in him was not merely passing. He felt their heat, knew their proximity, and began to distinguish their individual heartbeats.

Control it, Michael, Dominic insisted, knowing all too well how the bloodlust could overtake human thought.

Michael heard Dominic, but the adrenaline of the hunt was already pumping through his body. His fangs tore tiny channels inside his lips as he clenched his jaw, feeling a human—his prey—approach him.

"Hey, man." The voice was next to him, and Michael rose quickly to face the human eye to eye, but what met him filled him with instant panic.

"You okay?" Scott asked in a drunken slur, unable to comprehend what was wrong with his friend. "You look like you need a drink, mate." He grinned and gave Michael's shoulder a shake.

Dominic moved rapidly to Michael's side as his lover stared at the hand on him. He recognized the man with the dreadlocks from the tattoo parlor and inwardly cursed the vagaries of fate. This man must not be Michael's first. The predator was strong in the fledgling vampire. Dominic could sense its fight for dominance over Michael's human conscience, and it was winning.

You know this man, Michael. Dominic sent the message and moved still closer, ready to intervene if it became necessary. *He is a friend.* He touched Michael's shoulder lightly, distraction rather than restraint. Dominic's own sire had not done this for him. Instead, he had reveled in the bloodbaths that resulted from Dominic's uncontrolled desires. "I will not let you go through that," he whispered, then looked directly at the confused human in front of them, thankful for his penchant for assorted stimulants. "Your friends are waiting for you, Scott. You need to join them."

Scott nodded, then smiled. "Yeah, cool. Catchya later, Mikey." He turned and made his stumbling way back to the bar without noticing that Michael had never once spoken to him.

"I will take you home," Dominic said softly, his lips almost touching Michael's ear. But Michael shook his head and uttered with some difficulty, "I need to be on my own for a while. Just to think. Need to think."

Dominic frowned. "I'm not sure that's—"

"I need to think," Michael interrupted quickly and turned to look at Dominic. "Please. It's… it's not what I expected."

Dominic stroked Michael's hair. He totally understood the pain in Michael's eyes at the realization of what he had become. "You can't stay here."

With a heavy sigh, Michael agreed. "Definitely not here. You stay. You've already fed me tonight and need to, well… need one of them."

Even though Dominic knew that was true, he was still reluctant to allow Michael to leave alone.

"I'll go home. I just have to get away from all of this." Michael's hand moved toward the throng on the dance floor as if it were pushing through molasses. His body was not his own, even though his senses were more aware than they'd ever been, and he heard and felt the beat of each heart in the club. The hearts of people he'd once shared drinks with. Mates who'd joked about his lack of rhythm on the dance floor and bad taste in partners. Michael had shared many of their beds, but that night in the crowded club, he feared for their safety.

Keep the connection open, Michael, Dominic murmured softly in his mind while brushing his fingertips lightly down the worn fabric of Michael's T-shirt. *I want you to feel when I taste one of these, and when I release them. After, I will come home to you.*

The words reassured Michael, but it wasn't until he was in the relative quiet of Chapel Street that he felt the predator begin to recede.

Those on a different kind of hunt pushed past Michael. He could "feel" many of them, but he distracted himself by putting each sensation into a mental box and locking it. It helped. By the time he reached the Windsor end of Chapel, Michael was able to refine the often nonsensical buzz into individual sensations.

Finally, Michael stopped on a quiet corner and leaned against a lamppost plastered with posters showing upcoming gigs and recently missing persons. A tram rattled past, sending a bright shower of sparks from the intersection of its power lines above. Watching the drops of light fall and fade, Michael realized that if he concentrated, he could hear the electric current as it traveled through the lines. He smiled. It was a mundane thing to notice, but right then he decided he liked mundane.

What had happened at the club had scared him. It was a reality he hadn't even considered, and it was only once he was away from the mass of bodies that he regained some control. Michael rubbed a still shaky hand over his face and glanced around. There were very few people on the street at that end, and those who were there were too wrapped up in their nightly rituals to even notice him. *Better.* He filled his lungs with the night air, only to grimace at the exhaust fumes of a passing car.

Dominic was still there at the edge of his consciousness. Even though they were not in direct contact, Michael could feel him as he sat at the corner table of the club, watching the dance floor. Michael sensed Dominic's concentration on a single human and tried to turn his own attention away from the club. It was only then that Michael noticed another presence.

No distinct thoughts reached him, at least none he could discern. He was simply aware of being watched. Michael quickly looked up and down the street, but could not locate the source. For all intents and purposes, he was alone.

Michael closed his eyes and concentrated. One by one, he managed to block all the sounds and sensations surrounding him. All but one, and it was close. Michael knew at that moment that they weren't the unfocused thoughts of a human. The presence was aware of him, and it *was* watching.

Michael's gut turned to ice. He needed to run, but where? He couldn't pinpoint the direction of the presence, and for all he knew, he could run straight toward it.

"Ink," Michael muttered quietly to himself, but he cast a furtive look up the street, startled by the sound of his own voice. He moved quickly across the road, not even checking for oncoming cars, until he was directly outside the elaborately painted windows of the tattoo parlor. It was well after closing time, so Michael knew the glass door would be locked. He shoved his hand into his pocket and fumbled for his key. Coins clattered noisily onto the footpath in his increasingly desperate search; he knew it had to be in there somewhere. "Fuck," he cursed, trying to resist the urge to look over his shoulder, knowing that whatever was watching him was getting closer.

"Michael?" The door opened a crack, and Abby's face appeared. "I thought I saw—"

That was all she managed to get out before Michael pushed the door open and shoved her back into the shop. Once inside, he slammed the door shut, locking it quickly behind them.

Michael stood facing the door. He peered out between the painted teeth of the elaborate dragon that adorned the front of the shop only to jerk back when he felt a hand drop onto his shoulder.

"What's going on, gorgeous?" Abby asked, pressing close against Michael in an attempt to see over his shoulder and catch what he was looking for. "Is someone out there?" She raised herself onto tiptoes but couldn't make out much more than their reflections.

Michael dropped his head against the glass with a light *thunk*.

"I thought there was," he whispered, not sure if he was still scared or just feeling a little foolish. "I thought I felt someone following me."

"Did you see anyone?" Abby asked, this time leaning around him to cup her hand on the glass to get a better view.

"No." Michael sighed and slipped out from between Abby and the door to guide her gently back into the shop. "I shouldn't have come here, Abbs. I'm sorry. If someone had been following, I would have brought them straight here to you."

Abby frowned. "Of course you should have come here," she scolded. "You're always welcome here. You're just lucky I decided to stay and finish some T-shirt designs, or I would have been at the club with the love of my life."

The mention of Scott twisted the knot that had already formed in Michael's gut.

"I saw him there," Michael said very quietly. "But I had to leave."

Abby was just about to make a comment, but something about Michael's tone stopped her. Instead, she asked, "Why did you have to leave, sweetheart?"

Michael turned away and wandered through to the workroom.

"Don't think you can get out of answering me that way," Abby announced and followed him. "What happened? Is it something to do with Dominic?" She'd wanted to say "that vampire," but she knew she was standing face to face with a vampire, even if it was her Michael.

"No. Yes. Fuck. Maybe?" Michael stammered and flopped down onto his tattoo chair. After picking at the towel draped over the arm, Michael looked up at her and said, "He tried to warn me."

Abby moved quickly to the stool next to the chair. "Warn you about what?"

"Dominic tried to warn how things would be different for me now. He warned me that *I* would be different."

"Different how? I mean apart from the whole blood-sucking thing." Abby winked but took his hand to show Michael that, regardless of what he'd become, she still trusted him.

"Nothing is the same."

"I need more than that, Mikey."

Michael sighed. "Everything looks sharper. It almost hurts to look at some things. And I can feel things. What people are thinking, but not exactly their thoughts. And…."

Abby gave his fingers a squeeze. "And?"

"Oh fuck, this is going to sound so stupid," Michael groaned. "I need blood to live. Dominic tried to tell me it wasn't like in the movies, but I didn't think it through to realize what it was going to be like. I didn't really think about any of it."

"You love him," Abby said, as if that answered everything.

"I thought that would be enough," Michael said, more to himself than his worried friend, and then he screwed up his face. "Shit, Abbs, did you hear what I just said? Of course it's fucking enough. I *do* love him, and this is just a phase, right? This whole bloodlust thing?"

Abby grinned. "And I thought I was the romantic? You're worse than I am, Mikey." But her grin faltered when the rest of what Michael said registered. Abby was smart, and she quickly put two and two together. "The blood thing? That's why you had to leave Hunters, and that's why it freaked you to see Scott there, right?"

Michael saw the realization in her eyes.

"Would you have hurt him, Michael? Would you have hurt Scott?" Abby glared directly into Michael's eyes when she asked, knowing that he could never lie to her, and it seemed he still couldn't.

Michael cringed under her scrutiny and whispered, "Maybe. I don't know. But I couldn't risk that I would, Abby. I wanted to when I smelled his blood because it was almost like something tried to take over, and I knew I had to get out of there. Fast."

Abby let go of him and walked away to stand at the other side of the room. When Michael started to speak again, she held up her hand to silence him. She wasn't ready to hear him yet and needed to think. They stayed like that for several long minutes, the air thick with words wanting to be given voice, but left unsaid. Finally, a question came, short and sharp. "You chose not to hurt Scott, right?"

"Right," Michael said quietly, waiting to see what came next.

"Okay," Abby mumbled before taking a breath and stating, "You felt this bloodlust, wanted a human—who happened to be Scott—but you stopped yourself from actually doing it." Another pause where Michael wasn't sure if he was required to answer and so remained silent.

"So the bloodlust is because you're hungry, or is it just a hunting thing?"

"Hungry, I guess. Dominic says we're predators, but it's not like I want to hunt humans just because of what I am now." Michael's shoulders slumped. "Problem is, I'm hungry all the time."

Abby flinched and asked, "What about now?"

"*All* the time, Abbs."

There was misery in Michael's voice that made her turn back to him. "But I know you won't hurt me, no matter how hungry you are. That is something I know for sure."

She walked back over so there were barely inches between them and reached out to hold his hands. "You might be a vampire—fuck, I cannot believe I just said that—but you still recognized your human side and left rather than hurting someone you care about. Am I right?"

Michael wasn't that easily convinced, but Abby seemed so sure, and she was right about him not wanting to hurt her. Even though the hunger gnawed at his belly, and he could feel her strong pulse vibrate through her palms, there was no urgency to feed from her.

"Is it the same for him? For Dominic?"

"I don't think so," Michael replied, adding that to the list of things he needed to ask his lover. "He seems able to control it."

"Yep, I thought so." Abby nodded and glanced around the room. "He was here, after all, and I bet this place reeks of blood when we're inking."

"Not just then," Michael admitted and pulled a face that made her laugh.

"Nice thought. So outside, before, what was it that freaked you out so much?"

Michael instantly glanced toward the front of the store. "I don't know. I didn't see anything, but I could feel it, and it was old and strong and very fucking scary."

"Something more scary than a vampire?"

Michael frowned. "There was something... I don't know... familiar about it. It was like I'd sensed it before, but not like that."

Abby gave his hands a little squeeze and shook her head. "That makes no sense, sweetie. If it was familiar, I'm sure you could deal with it." She backed up and pulled him through to the store, where they could see through the painted glass.

Michael knew Abby well, and when it came to looking after who she loved, she could be totally fearless, so it didn't surprise him when she dropped his hand and marched over to the door. A flick of the latch and she was outside.

The streetlight cast an orange hue on Chapel Street, and Abby stood alone outside Ink. There were no errant pedestrians or cars to break the silence, so she clearly heard Michael's plea. "Come back in, Abbs, please?"

But Abby drew herself up to her full height and shook out her crimson hair before calling into the still street, "I don't know who or what you are, but I'm not afraid of you."

The air around her chilled; it was watching her. Abby fought a shiver and stood her ground against the pervading sense of malice that seemed to surround her.

Michael stood in the doorway, watching her obstinate defiance of the thing that had him almost pissing in his jeans not that long ago. He took a deep breath and stepped out to join her. "You know, we could both end up as red blotches on the tram tracks doing this," Michael tried to joke, twining his fingers in hers.

"Fuck it, Michael. I might be just a human, but woe betide anything that threatens one of mine."

"Well said," Michael agreed, only to be enveloped once again in the humid air of the Melbourne night. The bubble of threat had burst with the blast of a car horn and a shouted, "Get off the fucking road, you morons."

Abby grinned and said, "You heard the man. Go home, sweetie. Big bad Abby chased away the boogieman."

Chapter
E L E V E N

SITTING on the low step of the veranda, Michael picked at a thread where his still tanned skin peeped through a rip in the worn denim at his knee. He'd already decided that the whole incident outside Ink was his overblown sense of the dramatic reacting to too much stimulation at the club. In truth, Michael hadn't totally convinced himself, but it was the easiest way to deal with it when there were so many other things in his head fighting for attention. Besides, there was no way he was going to admit to Dominic that he was experiencing the vampire equivalent of night terrors. But he looked along the quiet street, hoping his lover would appear pretty damn soon.

Slowly, Michael began to feel him. Just a hint, at first, like a tickle deep in his chest. Then the tickle grew into a flutter that radiated warmth until his fingertips tingled. To Michael, it was as if he felt Dominic's touch, but from the inside out. So different from what he'd felt outside Ink. Michael pushed that thought from his mind and concentrated on responding in kind to Dominic's presence.

Michael frowned briefly in his attempts to send images or a specific message, then looked up to see Dominic smiling at him. "You don't have to try so hard."

"Well, I couldn't tell if you were getting what I was sending," Michael explained.

Dominic stood in front of Michael and stroked either side of his dark hair, straightening curls in their path to his shoulders. "Trust that it happened, Michael. You only need to keep yourself open to me and our connection will be there."

"But we can shut it down, like tonight, right?"

"Of course," Dominic chuckled.

"Good," Michael said with a soft smile. "Because we both know it would drive you insane to have me in your head all the time."

Dominic's fine hair brushed Michael's face as he bent over him. Michael could feel the energy spark hot between them and vibrate against his skin. His laugh was light, but it still rang through the night air.

You are my sun, Michael, Dominic sent to him. *I welcome you in my mind; never forget that.*

Michael smiled at the thought. *But not all the time.*

"Not all the time," Dominic agreed, using his physical voice. "As much as I need you, Michael, it's not healthy for either of us to live in each other's heads. I could all too easily lose myself in you."

Michael nodded, even though a whisper of unease passed between them along with Dominic's words. He tilted his face up to meet Dominic's, and the heat surprised him when their lips touched. "I can smell them on you," he whispered. "I can smell *him* on you, the one who fed you."

The wording was not lost on Dominic. "We need to go inside," he whispered.

"In a minute," Michael said, wanting to stay in the night air for a little longer. "Can you tell me about him? What he was like?"

Dominic sat on the veranda one step above Michael and encouraged him to settle back into his embrace. "They play that we are real with their blue-black dyed hair, pale make-up, and smudged eyes, but for most, that's all it is: a game, a dream that takes them away from the banality of their lives."

Michael knew the type well. He hooked an arm over Dominic's thigh and asked, "When they meet the real thing, does that dream become a nightmare?"

"It could. We are, after all, creatures of nightmare, childhood tales of horror."

With a light shrug, Michael said, "I don't feel too horrific."

Dominic chuckled. "We are also creatures of romance. Books love to portray us as the mysterious visitor in the night that you invite into your bedroom and then your bed."

"I think I've seen that movie." Michael smiled absently. "Is that what they believe... the ones in the club?"

"Some of them," Dominic admitted, thinking about the eyeliner-ringed eyes that had pleaded with him earlier that night. "You feel their need to believe that right up until they are in your arms and the reality of their situation finally hits them. Most experience panic. Some fight you. But that lasts mere seconds before their skin is broken and the feeding begins."

Michael listened quietly, trying not to be distracted by that all-pervading scent of blood that surrounded Dominic like a halo.

"It is then you have a choice."

Michael looked up from his tattered jeans, where he'd returned to worrying a loose thread. "What choice?"

"Life or death. But also you can choose to let them have their fantasy."

"Let them believe you are the gentle lover who may or may not have been the vampire of their dreams," Michael murmured, and it made sense to him.

Dominic nodded and stood to hold out his hand. It was time be inside.

Chapter
T W E L V E

"DO YOU think I look any different?" Michael asked again from in front of the dresser mirror. He glanced at Dominic in the reflection of their bedroom, then back to his own image.

"Not yet," Dominic replied, watching the new vampire run curious fingertips over his face.

Michael frowned and turned. "What do you mean, not yet?"

With an amused shrug, Dominic shifted higher in the bed, propping his pillows against the old-fashioned wooden headboard. "What exactly did you expect to have changed?"

"I dunno… something, though." Facing the mirror again Michael peered into his dark eyes as if searching for signs of his new inhumanity. Dark lashes surrounded deep, but clear, brown eyes. They looked the way they had the night before and the night before that. Nothing different, simply his own eyes staring back at him. He drew back from the glass and muttered, "I'll never see them in daylight again, will I?"

"No," Dominic whispered in reply, recognizing the melancholy that signaled Michael's new reality was beginning to hit him. "You are young to this world, so sleep will claim you while the sun is above the horizon. As you age, you can fight that sleep so you can witness it from the shadows, but remember what it did to me Michael, and I am very old." A tinge of fear colored Dominic's words. The lure of the sun was strong. It was strong to those who were accustomed to its warmth, and it grew stronger still when the years of darkness mounted up. *Especially when those years were spent alone.*

But Michael smiled at him. "I knew what I was getting into when I asked you to turn me," he said and moved to the closed curtains. They glowed with the last light of a sun that had already set, and the fabric was warm to Michael's touch. "I can feel the sun, Dominic," he murmured almost absently, watching his fingers slide around a curved pattern on the heavy material. His fingers tingled, but it was the pull in his body that forced him a step back into the bedroom. Even then the band of diminishing light on the floor seemed too near Michael's bare toes. They curled, and he took another step back toward the bed.

"We want it, Michael. We never stop wanting it, but it is our death," Dominic said quietly, knowing Michael needed to feel and understand the primal fear the sun wrought on them.

Michael watched the thin strip of light fade and disappear, until only the tiny flowers on the rug remained. He stared at it for a moment longer, until the gentle touch of Dominic's hand on the back of his neck forced his eyes away. Dominic leaned over him to pull back the curtain, and together they watched the last of the day disappear.

"What else kills us?" Michael asked, keeping his eyes on the street below. "Is it like the movies?"

"Some of it is right," Dominic said. "We are drawn to the sun, but it is fire we fear the most. There can be no coming back if we burn."

Michael nodded. "What about silver and religious stuff."

"Pretty, but not deadly, and before you ask, yes, we'd die if we were beheaded. Not sure if there are any creatures who would survive that. And I'm sure a spike through the heart would work too."

"Okay, things to avoid. Hey, I don't think I want to go to Chapel Street tonight," Michael said when he saw who he assumed to be one of their neighbors make his way along the quiet road with the enthusiastic pace of one who had a big night planned. "Too many people on Chapel, and I have too many of my own thoughts in my head to deal with without the thoughts of others. I know I can block them, but not tonight okay?"

Dominic carded his fingers through Michael's hair and asked, "What can I do for you tonight?"

Michael twisted around to face him. The sadness was clear in Dominic's eyes, but with his lover's hands on him, Michael felt none of that sadness and whispered, "I have no regrets. I am what I want to be. I'm just a beginner at it and figuring it all out." He traced the strong cheekbones and cupped Dominic's face. *Please don't ever doubt what we did. I couldn't have lived my human life without you.* Michael's lips pressed lightly against Dominic's as the thought was sent, and he knew it to be the truth for both of them.

MOST of the passengers left the tram halfway along Fitzroy Street, and Michael watched the huddled mass make its way to the crowded entrance of the bar. He wrinkled his nose. "I know I've asked before, but did I really smell like that to you?"

Dominic took in the look of utter disgust distorting Michael's features and laughed. "Sometimes," he admitted. "You'll get used to it. Adrenaline and sweat are pungent, but you'll start noticing the difference in each and be able to single out the ones that...." Dominic hesitated, not wanting to say the words.

"The ones that are less distasteful?" Michael offered as an end to the sentence and grinned.

The tram bell dinged, and it rattled away from the stop. Michael watched the parade of pedestrians as they passed, and he briefly wondered if the presence from the other night near Ink was out there watching them. He blocked the thought as quickly as it formed and distracted himself with another question. "Do they taste different?" he asked, still looking outside the tram but also seeing Dominic's face reflected in the dark glass. He turned, curious about the answer.

Dominic had felt something in Michael, but it flashed by so fast he let it go and thought about the question. "Not between creeds or colors. Blood tastes the same beneath the skin, but age or illness taints it. Chemicals should be avoided."

"Don't do drugs, huh?" Michael deadpanned, but quickly saw that Dominic didn't get the joke. He smiled and teased, "So, basically I have the impossible task of finding a non-smelly, drug-free virgin?"

"They don't have to be a virgin," Dominic said seriously, but his expression slipped, and he couldn't hold back his smile. He had been alone so long, and tonight he was happy.

"This is where we get off," Dominic announced when the tram rolled to a stop.

As soon as they alighted from the tram, a new smell was added to those of cars and their human inhabitants.

"How long has it been since you've been here?" Michael asked as they made their way across four lanes of the still busy road.

Dominic looked along the boardwalk next to the sand and smiled. "Too long," he murmured and pointed to the pavilion halfway along the wooden pier. "That was newly built, and on warm summer nights, it was definitely the place to be."

"Is that where we're going tonight?" Michael asked and slipped his hand into Dominic's.

"It's quiet now," Dominic said and started them walking to the pier. "Everyone spends their nights in clubs and bars, so there won't be too many people, if any at all."

The boards creaked beneath their steps as the hum of the traffic dimmed behind them, and Michael began to hear the steady lap of the waves against the pylons and the faint sound of music. It wasn't the techno thump of a bar on the main drag, but something lighter and more melodic, as if it was not from their time. It tickled at the edge of his hearing—there but not there. When he noticed Dominic watching him, Michael asked, "Can you hear it?" Dominic nodded and led them to the pavilion.

The café had closed for the night, and all the doors were bolted shut, but they made their way to the outside tables and sat on the bench seat next to the railing.

"You asked about my past, so I thought I could share a little of it with you," Dominic said and leaned across the table to hold Michael's hands in his. "Close your eyes."

One last look at Dominic, and Michael did as he was told.

Michael listened to the music, listened as the faint tinny sound grew in depth and volume. There was the light laughter of a woman near him, followed by a man's voice. The voices faded as if they were walking away from him, but slowly, very slowly, Michael could see them. A young woman with her hair piled high under a broad-brimmed hat held in place with a large pearl hat pin. She smiled coyly as the skirt of her long white dress swished against the legs of her partner when he took her to join the other couples in their elegant dance.

A string quartet formed in Michael's mind's eye and played what he thought was a slow waltz. The dancers swirled in circles in front of him, gloved hands and neat buttoned boots completing the picture. Michael could feel himself smiling, then heard the whisper, "Dance with me, Michael."

"But it's not real," he replied and began to open his eyes, only to feel Dominic's hand gently cover and close them.

"It was real," Dominic assured him. "You are seeing what I saw. Now dance with me, please?"

Dominic's hand returned to clasp his, and Michael rose to his feet. *Trust what your mind sees, Michael.*

A couple danced past them, and Michael smelled the delicate scent of tea rose. He gave a nervous giggle and confided, "I don't know how to dance like that."

Dominic's lips were next to his ear, and he heard: "You don't have to; just follow me."

Together they circled slowly through the other dancers, their feet tapping lightly on the wooden pier as they moved with the sway of the music. The song of violins merged with the hiss of the gas lamps illuminating the couples, and Michael spun gently around in Dominic's sure hands. It was then that Michael could "see" him. Dominic's hair was shorter and combed back over a starched white collar. Dominic smiled, and the flicker of the light shone in his eyes.

"Is this how you looked back then?" Michael whispered, not wanting to disturb the other dancers.

"This is how I will always look," Dominic replied and brushed his lips over Michael's eyelid. "Time passes, but we stay the same."

"Did you dance with someone then?"

Leaning his forehead against Michael's, Dominic admitted, "I didn't dance then. I think I was waiting for you."

They danced in each other's arms until the final strain of the violin faded and became the lone cry of a seagull. Michael opened his eyes, and the dancers dissolved into memory. He leaned against Dominic and stared out across the bay to the lights of Melbourne. They shone in a way that seemed strangely alien to him. "Have you been alive a long time?" he asked, still watching the distant city.

Dominic let a dark curl slip through his fingers, not wanting to think about his centuries of hidden solitude and what went before that. "A very long time," he eventually answered.

"Well, we'll have that time and more together," Michael said and tightened his hold on his dance partner.

"The world will change around us, and you will witness a great many things."

Michael thought about that, but it still seemed too big to comprehend. "Tonight I'm just gonna think about us, okay? And maybe we can dance a bit more."

Dominic smiled. *Close your eyes, Michael.*

Chapter
THIRTEEN

"DID you check out that creep Cameron tonight?" The petite blonde giggled and stumbled drunkenly in her red stilettos. Her companion caught her and quickly linked arms. "He's a fucking stalker, Jules. How many times did he message me today?"

"I know. He's just a user. Gets what he wants then you'll never hear from him again," Julie agreed and turned them off the main street to cross the small park. It was the same route they took every Friday night, and even with the lateness of the hour, they felt as safe in the familiar surroundings as if they were discussing boyfriends past and present in their room.

Tracey stumbled again, so she stopped and kicked off her clubbing shoes, pouting at a new blister and picking up the shoes by their red ankle straps. "Anyway, like I was saying. I ended up posting on Facebook this afternoon that you'd have to be a real loser to keep messaging someone when they don't message back. Because honestly, Jules, I think I only answered about half his messages."

Julie rolled her eyes and stepped onto the path next to the tall brick perimeter wall that separated the park from the housing commission apartments.

"I think he must have read the post, though, 'cause he only texted me twice tonight."

Chattering and swinging her shoes, Tracey didn't immediately realize that they'd stopped walking, and her friend hadn't answered. She staggered to a halt and shot Julie a withering look, but her friend's attention was on the beautiful young man sitting on top of the wall watching them. His pale skin was almost translucent in the moonlight, and his long blond hair fell like silk past his shoulders. His eyes were greener than any she'd seen before.

Both girls smiled at him.

The last thing Tracey noticed was how full the man's lips were when he smiled at her, and how sharp his teeth.

Chapter
FOURTEEN

A CRYSTAL of raw sugar hit the chocolate-sprinkled foam without disturbing the surface. Another few tumbled out of the paper tube, and gradually an indentation formed in the middle and threatened to destroy the neat little row of hearts created by the skilled barista. Michael poured the rest of the sugar directly into the middle of the glass so it sank into the coffee without damaging any more of the foam. He smiled, scooped some onto his teaspoon, and stared at it. "So, I can have this, and it won't make me vomit blood or anything?"

Dominic raised his eyebrows and gave Michael a look of mock disgust. "Seriously, Michael, I really do wonder where some of your ideas come from."

"Really cool horror films." Michael grinned, then stretched out his tongue to lick a little of the sugary foam. It tasted as good as it ever had, so Michael scooped a bigger teaspoonful and made a show of sucking it off the spoon, then crunching the sugar granules. "You can't blame me, though, because I really don't know too much about all this yet." He looked at the empty bowl of the teaspoon and saw his distorted reflection looking back. He frowned and said seriously, "It occurred to me earlier that I've spent more nights with you than I have with anyone, and up until you, the thought of staying with anyone for more than one night—even for a whole night—would have terrified me. But I'm going to spend a whole lot longer than that with you and...."

"And?"

"And I can't imagine, don't want to imagine, waking up without you, but we really know very little about each other."

It was a question Dominic had been expecting for quite a while and one he'd hoped to avoid for a while longer. How could Michael comprehend all the years he'd witnessed or the monster he'd become when it all began?

The question hung unanswered for several seconds until Dominic suggested, "You first, it won't take as long."

Michael screwed up his nose and said, "Don't think I don't know what you just did, but okay, I'll fill you in on my story. Then I plan to find out yours."

Dominic just smiled.

"A short but interesting life," Michael began, knowing it actually wasn't all that interesting. "Twenty-six years ago, Trevor and Christine Chapman had a son—the most beautiful boy the hospital had ever seen." Michael giggled when he was forced to add, "Well, at least that's what my Nan told me, but as I was the first grandson after six granddaughters, I think she might have been a little biased. Anyway, my story would be a whole lot more interesting if I came from a broken home with a meth lab in the garage instead of my dad's old boat, but I grew up in the outer suburbs down by the bay with an older sister, both parents, and a dog called Bob. Boring, huh?"

"Sounds perfect," Dominic muttered honestly. "Tell me more."

"We lived near the beach, so I ended up there more than at school. It was easier because I didn't really fit in too well once I hit high school. I didn't surf or worship at the feet of the almighty football, and as cute as the footballers looked in their tight shorts, I wasn't supposed to notice that, was I? Gay kinda wasn't an option at our school, and although that wasn't the reason I left, I did wonder what would happen when I got away from my oh-so-conservative environment. But I digress. School just didn't interest me, outside of the art room. Then I decided to take a few drawings in to the local tattooist, and I was hooked. I moved away from home, went to the big city where I did my apprenticeship in a job I love, and the rest, as they say, is history."

"History," Dominic repeated sadly. "Then you met me, and I took you from a life you loved. You were not one of those who begged to leave their bloodless life. You were happy at Ink."

"Oh come on. You know that is bullshit," Michael retorted quickly, angered at the implication that he had no part in the decision and that Dominic took complete responsibility in turning him. "Yeah, I was happy at Ink, still can be, but you did not *take* me away from anything. So can you quit the dark, broody shit because I made the decision, not you, and I pushed for the turn, not because I hated my life, but because I found someone who would make it even better?"

The words eased a small part of Dominic's worry for Michael, but he'd been alone for so many centuries, he was neither able nor willing to believe that Michael would not come to resent him, as he did his own maker.

"Your life can't be as it was, Michael," Dominic persisted.

Michael dropped the spoon into his coffee and swirled it through the foam, not exactly sure why Dominic's words had pissed him off and not willing to admit they frightened him because they just might be true. "I think I figured that one out already, but fuck, it doesn't have to be all doom and gloom. I have you, my friends at Ink…."

"You will watch them die."

"Fuck." Michael groaned and pulled an expression of utter frustration. "You are determined, aren't you? Yes, they will grow old and die, or have babies and move to the suburbs. That's part of life I would have had to deal with anyway. The only difference is, I'll still be around to make new friends or look after their kids or something."

Dominic couldn't deny a gentle smile at Michael's optimism, despite his mood. "Have you ever met the elderly lady next door?"

"Um, yeah, well, I've seen her but never really chatted."

"Her name is Violet Thompson. I knew her parents and held her the night she was born. Her introduction to the world frightened her, and she cried bitterly until I sent a message that her new life might not be as warm and safe as her old one, but it would be full of challenge and days of sunshine. Violet grew fast, and it seemed no time at all before she married a handsome accountant and moved away to start her own family. When she returned, it was as an old woman. She knew me as my own son and frequently remarked on my likeness to the man who used to read her books in the veranda chairs on summer nights."

The story dispelled any anger Michael felt, and he was sorry for losing his temper, but he still didn't agree. "I think that proves my point, not yours."

"I will watch her die soon."

"But you watched her live and were part of that life. Days of sunshine, remember?"

"I remember," Dominic whispered and reached across the table to straighten a dark curl, only to watch it spring back against Michael's cheek. "Do you really think you can go back to Ink?"

"Don't see why not." Michael nodded. "Abby knows what I am."

"Does she know what you can become?"

Michael frowned for a moment until he deciphered the real meaning of the question. "I told her why I had to leave Hunters, what happened when I was with Scott."

"If she can forgive you for what you are, she is a rare person."

"I know it scared her at first, but she sees more than the average person. Abby sees what's below the surface, underneath all the crap."

"And yet she still likes you?"

Michael blinked, then threatened to flick his teaspoon at Dominic. "Shut up." He laughed and put the spoon between his lips instead. They were still smiling when Michael reassured him by confirming, "I feel safe around Abbs, and I don't think—no, I know—I would never hurt her." Michael thought a little more about what he'd just said and nodded his surety. "She's always had the ability to make me see sense, even when I didn't want to."

"You will need her if you go back to Ink. The place reeks of broken skin and blood."

Even though it had been after hours when Michael visited Abby, the pervading scent of humans had struck him. He knew it would be hard, but Ink was still the closest thing to home he'd experienced since leaving his suburban bedroom. He looked at Dominic. "I've wondered about that. Why you would put yourself through going into a place that you knew revolved around the artistry of ink and blood?"

You.

The word, and all the love that went with it, filled Michael's mind and spread warmth from fingertips to toes.

I remember it all now, Michael thought, looking into those pale eyes. *I remember the first time I touched your skin. How cool it felt, how smooth and flawless it was under my fingers.* He leaned over and kissed Dominic.

You had me then, even though you tried to make me forget.

I needed you to forget, Michael, because I knew I couldn't return.

But you did return, and I knew you.

Michael's lips teased over Dominic's. He knew logically that they were cool to the touch, but he couldn't deny the heat that radiated in his when they met. *I still have parts of my old life, but I also have this. I have you.*

CHAPEL STREET was bracing itself for the onslaught of another Saturday night. Extra tables had been added along the footpaths in readiness for the swell of café patrons. To Michael, it was the same as every weekend night he'd experienced before, but very different at the same time. He watched the passersby, catching some of their random emotions while reading their T-shirts or checking out their tattoos, but he soon noticed that, once again, they rarely met his eyes. Michael was used to flirty glances from groups of young girls and more than the occasional guy. He was not used to the way they actively looked away when he attempted to make eye contact. At first Michael was disconcerted, but that quickly turned to anger, and he purposely forced his presence into the personal space of a young man who was trying to read a tram timetable. Peering over his shoulder, Michael felt the man's surprise become fear, which escalated rapidly until the sharp stink of panicked sweat filled the vampire's nostrils. When the elevated thump of the human's heart penetrated Michael's temper, he realized what he'd done and muttered a breathless apology. The young man still refused to meet his eyes, so Michael just backed away.

The traffic lights changed, and the waiting pedestrians moved on, but Michael remained alone on the street corner. Bit by bit, his new realities had crept up on him, but Michael still refused to give in to them. He gritted his teeth and blurted out defiantly, "I'm still me, no matter what else happens to me!"

Two older women turned as they stepped off the crosswalk, and one said, "Good for you, love." Both smiled and continued on their way.

Michael watched them go, and his own smile slowly returned.

"HELLO, gorgeous," Abby beamed from behind the counter. "What brings you here?"

"I work here, don't I?" Michael said and leaned over the cabinet to give her a kiss.

"I didn't think... well... I assumed you didn't need to do this anymore."

Michael gave a little huffed laugh; he actually hadn't thought of the everyday logistics of his current life. "Yeah, I guess," he said thoughtfully. "Probably don't need my apartment anymore either, and hey, it's not as if I need to buy food anymore." Michael shook his head and flashed Abby a toothy grin.

"Should I be worried?" Abby laughed, then had to ask, "So you live totally on blood? You can't eat anything else?"

"Gray area. From what Dominic told me I can still eat and drink, but food can cause problems if I have too much because our bodies aren't built to process it anymore."

Abby wrinkled her nose. "Now that is bordering on too much information, but...." She narrowed her eyes and leaned a little closer. "But speaking of too much information, what about... you know? I mean if you aren't technically alive then your heart doesn't beat, and if your heart doesn't beat it won't pump blood, right?" Abby raised her eyebrows and glanced down to indicate where the conversation was going.

Taking her hand, Michael placed it on his chest so she could feel the slow, steady beat. "I'm not dead, Abbs, just changed. And yes, I can still get it up. Thanks for asking."

Abby wriggled her fingers against Michael's chest and winked. "So now I know."

"Yes, you do." Michael grinned back and looked down at the book that housed Scott's schedule for the night, noting that his own wasn't even on the counter. "Busy," he muttered. "How about I do the next one? It looks like a small job, a good one to get me back into it."

Abby had always been good at reading body language, so she knew Michael wasn't as confident as he was trying to make out but chose to let it go. Scott would be in there with him, and she'd already decided to close the shop door to keep the "walk-ins" out. Just in case. Although what she thought she could do to stop a vampire, Abby had no idea.

Michael registered both the chemical and human smells even before he went through to the workroom. He braced himself and walked in, smiling when Scott looked up from the design he was marking out on a newly shaven leg.

"Hey, man, what happened to you the other night?" Scott asked.

Michael knew he meant his hasty exit from Hunters and shrugged.

"You missed a great night," Scott mumbled, but the lure of the design process pulled his attention back to the partially drawn Celtic knot.

Michael watched for a while, then began to set up his workstation. His back was still turned to Scott when the whir of the tattoo gun started up and the acrid scent of blood tinged the air. Michael tensed. His fingers tightened around the frame of the equipment trolley he'd been loading. *Get a grip, Mikey*, he told himself and began a series of long slow breaths. The intake of air brought with it the promise of warm, fresh blood, but Michael tried not to concentrate on the thirst it triggered. Instead he focused on the movement of the ink. The varying speed of the gun gave off subtle changes in sound when it curled slowly around a spiraling curve or lifted from the skin to change direction at a corner. Michael expelled a breath with each change, and gradually, enough of his control returned so that when Abby walked in with his client he was ready to face them.

A quick exchange of glances and Abby led the teenage boy to Michael's station. Michael cleared his throat and said, "Hi, mate, take a seat and show me where you want it?" The small skull had already been drawn up and traced over, so it only needed positioning.

The teenager sat in the chair, but shifted uncomfortably and watched the tattooist. "Um, here," he said and pointed to the fine skin just below the crease of his elbow, although his eyes never left Michael's.

"Okay," Michael said calmly, even though it was a bluff for the benefit of both the boy and himself. "This won't take long, so just sit back and relax." After delivering his usual banter, Michael picked up a disposable razor. "Need to give the area a quick shave first, okay?"

The boy mumbled his understanding but flinched as soon as Michael touched him. He instantly flushed with embarrassment and apologized. Michael pretended it was simply a nervous response to a first tattoo, but he knew differently. *Block it all*, Michael warned himself, and he brought up every wall he could muster to separate him from the boy's fear.

With a sigh, Michael continued. He shaved the arm, applied the gel that allowed the ink of the image to be transferred to the skin, and applied the drawing. Michael was relieved it wasn't a freehand tat because it was very clear that the human was repelled by his touch.

"You doing okay?" Michael asked when he picked up the tattoo gun.

The teenager's hue had become an unpleasant shade of gray, but his pride forced him to answer that he was fine.

The gun buzzed into life, and Michael concentrated more than usual on the tip as it closed in on the virgin skin. He hesitated briefly, and then the first contact was made. A tiny bubble of black ink became a small line, and Michael focused on the dome of the skull. The chemical smells of the ink and antiseptic were strong but did nothing to mask the hot stink of the boy under his hand.

Michael ground his teeth, forcing down his interest in the red swirl that rose and mingled with the ink. The hunger was there, nibbling away at the edges of Michael's defenses. A light sheen of sweat broke out on his forehead, and he thanked whatever god or gods watched over him that the myth of sweating blood was just that: a myth.

With the outline finished, Michael glanced up to see Abby in the doorway watching him. She flashed him a quick smile, and its intent warmed him, even though it did nothing to quell the hunger that cramped his stomach. Michael nodded and attempted an unsuccessful smile, then returned to his work.

"How're you holding up?" he asked quietly, mostly out of habit, while wiping off the excess ink to check his progress.

"Okay," came the tense reply. "Doesn't hurt as bad as I thought it would."

"Good. The shading won't take long," Michael said and tried sending a message to soothe him, but the onslaught of the boy's fear forced Michael to block him again.

The gun kicked into life and moved skillfully over the already raw skin to render the delicate shading. Michael saw the tiny pin pricks of blood form in the gun's wake, but he kept himself on task, concentrating on the black rather than the red. Slowly under the smears of ink and blood, the skull became a reality, until the sunken hollows that replaced its eyes stared back at Michael. Carefully, he wiped the area clean and applied a thick layer of antiseptic cream.

His gut trembled with the effort of resisting as he mumbled through the aftercare routine, and as soon as the last word was uttered, Michael excused himself and fled to the bathroom.

Each wave of hunger-induced nausea rolled and pounded at Michael's resolve. He leaned heavily on the old-fashioned porcelain sink and fought to shut down his vampire's thirst. With eyes tightly closed and head hung low, Michael gulped a few lungs full of air, then slowly opened his eyes. They were still his, but a faint crimson hue warned him he was not totally back yet. Another breath, a splash of water on his face, and Michael waited.

"Mikey?" It was Abby. "Can I come in?"

Michael heard the doorknob turn and said quickly, "No. Not yet, Abbs." As much as he needed his friend, Michael didn't want her to see him until he was the person she'd always known.

"Not gonna happen, sweetheart," Abby said softly and cracked the door open to slip inside. When Michael didn't turn around, Abby stepped in behind him, leaned her head on his shoulder, and wound her arms around his waist.

"It's okay, Michael. I could see how hard that was for you, but you did it." She gave the fabric of his worn T-shirt a gentle kiss and squeezed him. "You proved it doesn't control you and that you're no monster."

"It was there, though, Abbs," he muttered and leaned back in her embrace. "I had to fight it every step of the way."

Slowly she released him and said, "Turn around and let me see you."

The face she saw wasn't threatening or scary; it was Michael. Abby smiled and pulled her sleeve down between her fingers to wipe his face. "How about you tell me what it's really like?"

Michael shook his head and looked up at the lilac ceiling. "Sometimes it's like nothing has changed, but then I can feel...." He grimaced at his inability to express his situation. "It's like there are two of me. The me I've always been, and this whole other person or thing that has a whole bunch of other needs and sees the world through different eyes."

Abby took both his hands in hers and asked, "Is there any part of you in this other person?"

"That's just it, Abbs, he *is* me, but a me who wants to do things that I know are wrong."

"Like?"

"Like tasting that kid's blood. Like lifting my gloved fingers to my lips and tasting him," Michael spat out. "I could hear his heart racing when I got near him. He was afraid of me, and all I could do was concentrate to stop myself from ripping his throat open."

"But isn't it *something* that you didn't do it? Listen, Michael, you sat in that room with two bleeding humans and finished a tattoo. Come on, cut yourself some slack."

Michael stared into her eyes as if searching for the truth in her words then said, "It was only a small tattoo."

Abby grinned. "Face it, Michael; you still rock."

ABBY watched Michael wander back along Chapel and sent him all the love and courage she could. He had a new journey to deal with, and as much as Abby wanted to help, she had to trust Michael could deal with it. And if he couldn't, then Dominic would see him through it.

"Would you trust your best friend to his vampire lover?" she mumbled, then laughed at how ridiculous that sounded. The laugh had barely left her lips when she shuddered. *Get off my grave, whoever you are.*

The CD had changed to her favorite Vast song when she walked through the door of Ink, and Abby began to hum along, singing every other word. She was just starting on the chorus when she came face to face with a young man watching her from his perch on her counter.

Abby stopped humming as she looked into the greenest eyes she had ever seen.

Chapter
FIFTEEN

MICHAEL wasn't a child; Dominic knew that. He'd lived a lot in his short life, but that life no longer existed. His new world consisted of darkness and blood and threats that the fledgling would not have even considered.

Dominic sighed. He was tempted to open their link and reach for Michael. "But is that for him or you?" he muttered to himself and looked down at the sandy soil of the small border garden, soil that trickled like water between his fingers. The daffodils were still in bloom, but a hint of rusty brown blemished and curled the edges of their golden petals. Dominic moved to pull a dandelion from between them, but paused. His fingertips gently caressed the closed flower bud. The faintest line of yellow peeped out from the green, and he knew the flower would only appear when warmed by the morning light.

"I'll never see you, flower," he said and brushed his thumb very lightly over the frilled top of the bud.

"Don't envy the weeds." Michael smiled from the footpath. "They're beautiful for such a short time. Not like us, huh?" He wandered slowly up the driveway to stand behind Dominic and run his fingers gently through the dark-blond hair, hoping to dispel the melancholy that still haunted his lover's moods. "Isn't it enough to know you left it there to flower where others, humans, would just rip it out?"

Dominic chuckled softly and looked up. "Ever the optimist."

Michael winked and lowered himself to the grass beside the garden. "Nah, just don't need to see things to know they exist." Michael took a handful of sand and let it filter through the bottom of his closed fist. "Why do you keep this part of the garden when you can't see all the flowers in full bloom?"

Dominic frowned and caught some of the sand before it fell to the garden bed. He looked at the fine gray granules on his palm and said, "Because I know the garden grows." He smiled and brushed off the sand.

"Yep." Michael grinned, then wiped his hand on his jeans before his smile slipped a little. "Before, when I said humans would pull out the dandelion, I said it without even thinking that that isn't me anymore, isn't us. We're not human, are we?"

"I still puzzle over that question, Michael," Dominic answered seriously. "How much of our humanity remains within, and what replaced it if it is gone?"

Thinking back to his conversation with Abby about his internal struggle, Michael asked, "Are we a different species now or, I dunno, have we changed or evolved into…?"

Dominic shook his head. "In the beginning, I believed it a sickness that would either pass, or I would die. But I endured with this affliction and came to believe I was overtaken by a demon. None of that is true, but I do not understand what the truth is."

"We are what we are. I guess." Michael shrugged. "Speaking of which, I went to Ink today." He let the sentence hang there, not totally sure he wanted a full discussion about his experience in the tattoo parlor.

"To see Abby?"

"Yeah, partly." Michael stopped and pulled up his knees in an almost defensive position.

"What happened, Michael?" Dominic pushed, understanding that Michael wanted to talk but needed an extra little shove to get him started.

"Nothing and everything, I guess," Michael mumbled. "I knew things had changed, but I couldn't get my head around stuff."

"Like we talked about earlier?"

"Uh huh. The other night at Hunters freaked me out, but I still need to see what… what my boundaries are, I guess, what I can still have and what I can't. Does that make sense? So I went to Ink because I believed that was something I could still do." Michael stopped and closed his eyes for a minute. "Okay, that's a lie. I went back to Ink *hoping* I could still have that part of my life. I'd almost convinced myself that I would walk in, and it would all be like it was before. Abbs and Scott would be the same; I'd have a heap of bookings; and I'd get to ink people and kid around like normal."

"But it wasn't like normal," Dominic said, knowing full well that Michael would have struggled.

"No," Michael mumbled against his knee. "I scare people, and I fuckin' scared myself in the process."

"Did you hurt anyone?"

Michael looked up quickly. The question was asked in an almost matter-of-fact tone that emphasized just how simple it would have been to inflict pain or worse. "I didn't. I could have, but I didn't."

"Good," Dominic said and grabbed at the sleeve of Michael's T-shirt to drag him closer. "Tell me what happened."

"My appointment book wasn't even on the counter," Michael said, as if that simple act spoke volumes about his current state.

Dominic just nodded and waited.

"Abbs was cool about it. She always is. But it was as if I'd been cut out of their life."

"She's a realist, Michael," Dominic explained. "But she didn't shut you out, did she?" Dominic had only met Abby twice, and both times he'd compelled her to allow him into the back room to be tattooed, but on each occasion, he'd sensed an awareness in her that was dormant in most humans.

"No, she didn't, but when she agreed to let me do one of Scott's small jobs, I could tell she was worried."

A tiny thread of fear shivered through Dominic that Michael had attempted to tattoo a human. "She had every right to worry." Dominic met Michael's eyes. *You are a fledging vampire, Michael. The hunger controls you, and you cannot put yourself in a situation where it can overtake you.*

"No," Michael said out loud, determined to hear his refusal spoken. "It tried. It tried fucking hard, but if there's to be anything of me to survive, I couldn't let it win. I did the tattoo, even though every fucking bit of me was screaming to take the kid. But I did it, and he walked out of there with fresh ink and a patch of cling film."

"You are stronger than I am, Michael," Dominic revealed, forcing down buried memories of early blood feasts lest they be passed on to Michael.

"I can't lose myself to this," Michael stated, admitting a desperate fear, and he reached over to close his hand around Dominic's. "You managed to get through it, and now I have to."

Dominic knew that wasn't totally true, but it was not the time to tell Michael the things he had done and why he had hidden from the world for so many centuries.

When there was no answer, Michael gave Dominic's fingers a gentle squeeze and said, "I know it wasn't easy for you. I shared some of your memories when you turned me, remember."

"What did you see, Michael?" Dominic asked quietly.

"Flashes of things. Mainly it was feelings and some images. Not a lot of it made sense to me, but maybe one night you can tell me?"

"Maybe."

"And maybe you can tell me about him? You can tell me about the one who turned you?"

At that Dominic shook his head and stood up. "You do not want to know about him, Michael. He is not part of my life now. *Cannot* be part of my life with you. He was a beast without humanity, and I will not talk of him."

Michael stood quickly and took Dominic's hand again. "It's okay; I'm sorry I brought it up. He's gone and we're together and nothing can hurt us when we're together, right?"

Dominic pulled Michael into an embrace but did not answer.

Chapter
S I X T E E N

HE WASN'T the usual type who sought out a vampire. Dominic watched the man approach his table with affected disinterest. This one carried none of the romance for death associated with the panda-eyed youths who begged to be turned after reading too many teen angst novels where eternal love was found in the embrace of a vampire lover. A smile almost quirked the corners of Dominic's lips at the irony of that thought. The smile didn't quite form because he needed all his attention for the man who had silently taken a seat at his table.

"What do you want from me?" Dominic asked.

A confused expression crossed the man's face, and he struggled to answer. He shook his head and started to stand, but Dominic quickly sensed the internal conflict, and when desire overcame fear, the man was forced back into the seat. With a blink and frown, he glanced from Dominic to the nearby bathroom and mumbled out the words, "I know what you are.... I need...."

Very different indeed. Dominic weighed up the situation. The human was tall, well built, and tanned, with fair hair clipped to barely half an inch in length. There was no trace of smudged eyeliner or gothic adornments, and the visible tattoos were modern displays of manhood rather than attempts to fit a social genre. But more interesting to the vampire, there was no plea for what the usual prey assumed to be gift. A gift that Dominic had never, and would never, grant them.

Dominic stood and smirked a little when the other all but leaped to his feet. Without further discussion, they walked to the bathroom and elicited only mildly curious glances when they entered the stall together.

Fear beaded on the man's skin, shining in the blue hue of the junkie light, but on Dominic's tongue, it also held the sharp tang of desire. With a single lick of his lips, Dominic looked into the now panicked blue eyes and asked, "Is this what you need?"

"Yes." The hissed answer expressed all the desperation of the young Goths who found him, but none of their melancholy. That was all Dominic needed to hear. This one came for other reasons, but was still willing.

The strong vein throbbed rapidly against his lips, and Dominic gave the vulnerable throat a gentle kiss. He was tempted to send the image to Michael, but he hesitated, preferring to share and savor it with him later when the blood was passed between them.

"Do it," the man grunted and shoved his hand down between them, where he began to fumble at his jeans.

With little care taken, Dominic drove his fangs into the vulnerable neck. He knew the pain his victim would feel, but he also knew that was exactly why they were together in the cramped cubicle. A hint of unease briefly irritated the edges of Dominic's thoughts, but the copper taste was already on his lips, and any hesitation was quickly buried under the compulsion to feed. The first trickle of blood dribbled down Dominic's throat, and he heard the man gasp. *Touch yourself if you need to*, Dominic sent the thought, and the gasp transformed to a moan.

The unfettered flow of blood clouded Dominic's senses until all he knew was the hot pulse of the other invading his body and the urgent grunts of the man as he brought himself to completion.

Dominic had taken more than he should. The blue light of the bathroom vibrated with each flicker of the fluorescent tube as Dominic drew back to lean against the wall of the toilet stall. He stared at his prey, disconcerted to find that he was staring back. Although the pallid skin shone a sickly gray under the junkie lights, the man sported what could only be described as a feral grin. Lifting sticky fingers, he offered them to Dominic, only to place them between his own lips when the offer was refused.

Dominic watched with some curiosity until a sickening realization began to dawn. He was aware that this was not his usual prey, yet the man had found him. Yes, there had been apprehension, but there was also an awareness that the others never displayed.

"This is not new to you," Dominic stated. It was not a question. "You have been with my kind before."

The man smiled around his wet fingers and nodded.

Tell me, human, or you will die where you stand.

Fingers slipped from his slack lips at the silent command, and the large man seemed to visibly shrink.

"Another like you," he stuttered, glancing at the closed door debating if he could make it through to the relative safety of the club before the vampire snapped his neck.

"When…? Where?" Dominic growled, pushing down the terror the disclosure brought. Vampires had been known to share territories and hunting grounds, but Dominic had Michael to consider, and fledgling vampires were often treated with the same disdain as human prey, many not surviving their first season.

"He said I should tell you something," the man offered, as if the information might be a possible escape route.

He said…. Two simple words that froze Dominic's heart. He shoved his prey harder against the scarred, graffiti-scrawled wall and held him pinned there. *Not him, not now*, he silently pleaded before forcing himself to take action.

"What did he tell you?" Dominic demanded and reached out to close strong fingers around the still weeping throat.

"Hide-and-seek is over. Time to come home," came the choked reply.

Dominic's fingers tightened, and the man began to struggle. Fear and rage almost spelled his death, but Dominic stopped and pulled back his grip. The neck would bruise, but given the human's choice of recreational activities, that would cause no alarm. When he made to move, Dominic held up his hand in warning. The vampire needed a moment to calm himself and clarify his thoughts, but one realization overrode all others: *He has found me, and if he knows this haunt, he knows about Michael.*

"What else did he say?" Dominic hissed between gritted teeth and returned his hand to the vulnerable throat.

The man tried to respond and failed. However, it was no longer simply the fingers that constricted his air, but another obstruction that took control and halted any more discussion of "the other."

They stood in this deadly embrace until the whimper of desperate gurgles penetrated Dominic's terror. He looked at the glassy eyes rolling back as the human began to breathe his last and released him. The near-lifeless body slid down the wall to form a crumpled heap on the concrete floor. Dominic looked down at the mess of a man: gray, bruised flesh, vacant eyes, flaccid cock hanging from gaping jeans. Within the knot of anxiety was a brief second of relief that he had not formed the connection with Michael while he fed.

Dominic crouched in the claustrophobic confines of the stall and methodically straightened the man's clothes. "This is not how it should be," he said, partly to the blank face in front of him, but mainly reinforcing a long-recited oath. "This is how he would have it, but I am not him."

Dominic paused and held the man's face between his palms while he whispered, "Do you understand what I'm saying?"

There was a blink of consciousness, followed by a hoarse, "No."

The man knew this could be his end, but ultimately, he was too exhausted to actually care.

I will leave you here, Dominic sent silently. *Rest until you can stand, then remember only what you need to: you got off with a stranger. It was rough and it was good, but it took its toll on your body. You need to go home and sleep. You will sleep for a long time; then you will not remember me or the other like me, and you will no longer desire our kind.* Dominic stroked a gentle hand over the short hair, the surprisingly soft buzz cut yielding easily under his touch. "Do you understand me?" he asked quietly.

That time the question was met with an exhausted nod and the hint of a satisfied smile. Bile threatened the back of Dominic's throat at the compliant look and the way the man lovingly fingered the blossoming bruises on his throat.

The vampire fled his prey and pushed through the throng of dancers who were not given time to sense the predator and part for him.

When the relative fresh air of Chapel Street touched Dominic's face, he gulped a breath and walked quickly away from the entrance to where the pedestrian traffic thinned enough that he could scan his surroundings. It was a difficult and somewhat dangerous process because to do so meant revealing himself to others near him. The instant cacophony of minds jolted him, but Dominic sensed only the human confusion of thought, emotion, and desire.

His walls went up as quickly as they had been dropped. Dominic turned away from the Windsor end of Chapel and walked toward South Yarra. It was a futile ploy and he knew it, but if he was being watched, Dominic would not walk back to Michael.

Chapter
SEVENTEEN

MICHAEL stared into the dim space of the living room, not really seeing the dark wood that formed the skeleton of the floor-to-ceiling bookshelves or the mismatched patchwork of book spines they housed. The curtains were open, so the glow of the street light filtered in, illuminating the cultured, but disordered, room.

A distant car horn startled Michael from his reverie, and he blinked until his eyes finally focused on the intersection of the window frame. Dominic had gone out earlier to feed, leaving Michael to wander around a house that contained the collected belongings of several lifetimes. He'd assured Dominic that he had things to do, but the reality had been at least an hour of flopping on the armchair navel gazing. Michael filled the room with a frustrated groan and muttered several expletives into the silence. Even though he'd left home at seventeen, Michael had rarely been alone, and he was only just beginning to realize how much of his time was filled with combinations of friends, alcohol, and a variety of technologies. Dominic's house had none of the above.

Michael hauled himself to his feet and flicked through a few books. He grimaced at the orange- and white-covered novels that looked far too much like school texts before finally admitting that he was not in the mood to be caged in the old house and needed to get out.

The front door sounded a satisfying clunk when it closed behind him, and Michael gave the little row of daffodils a departing nod before walking happily toward Chapel Street.

He heard the hum of traffic and buzz of people mere seconds before their scent tickled his nose. Dominic had told him he'd get used to the smells of humanity, but each time he encountered them, Michael doubted that very much.

He toyed with the idea of going back to Ink to try again with a bigger tattoo. Maybe the more he did, the better he'd get at ignoring the lure of the blood? But Michael couldn't deny the near-constant gnawing in his belly and craving for the warmth of the fresh blood he'd spilled with the needle. *A couple more days... nights*, he corrected himself. *Dominic said it'd be easier in time.* Michael rubbed a palm over his belly and hoped like hell that was true.

Michael stood on the edges of the bustling street silently debating where to go, then turned his back on Chapel Street and walked the familiar path to his apartment.

Been a while, Michael thought as he fished around in his pocket for his door key. He chuckled quietly, thinking perhaps Scott wasn't so dumb for sewing his key onto the end of one of his dreadlocks. There wasn't a key among the debris that always seemed to litter Michael's pockets, which was no surprise considering he'd slept in Dominic's bed since before his turning, borrowing clothes from Dominic or Ink when his own could almost walk without him.

"No problem," he mumbled and made his way to the back of the building and his bedroom window, where the lock had been broken since he moved in.

The window easily pushed open, and Michael climbed in. Not the first time he'd had to do that. Michael looked around the dark room, and even though it had been his room for almost a year, he couldn't see a lot of things he'd want to take with him despite how important they'd seemed only weeks before.

He grabbed his old duffle bag, shoved in jeans, underwear, shirts, T-shirts, and a couple of hoodies. Michael briefly debated if he'd need more, but he decided what was in the small bag would get him through until his next visit. Michael straightened and scanned his shelves: not much amassed in his twenty-six years of life. The DVDs weren't of much use when there was nothing to play them on. "Ah, Dominic, I'm going to have to drag you into the twenty-first century." He chuckled at the thought, but his smile slipped when he saw the photographs pinned on his cluttered notice board. The first was of Michael, Scott, and Abby all mugging for the camera on the day he started at Ink. The second picture was the Chapman clan: grandparents, parents, and Bob the dog, taken last Christmas. Only his sister Jess was missing because she had taken the photo. They were all holding up burnt sausages, except for Michael's dad, who was standing behind them brandishing a pair of barbecue tongs as if threatening the photographer. The whole family was laughing. It was a good day.

For the first time, Michael really felt the impact of what Dominic had tried to tell him. Sure, Abby knew, but what was he supposed to say to his parents. Trevor Chapman had only just come to terms with his son being gay. A sad smile twitched at the corners of Michael's mouth. "See, Dad, it could be worse. Your one and only son could be a vampire."

None of the other things around the room mattered anymore. His beloved CD collection, his autographed poster of Trent Reznor from before he became a Golden Globe winner, even his vast array of graphic novels; none of it meant anything anymore.

"I'm sorry," he whispered and sat on the edge of his bed, not sure if he was apologizing to his family, to Dominic, or even to himself for not really listening to the warnings.

Time passed swiftly without Michael noticing until he realized he hadn't heard Dominic's gentle voice calling him home. The glass of the window still reflected his confused image against the darkness outside, but dawn was coming; he could feel it. The approaching sun tugged at Michael's body with an urgency that masked even the ever-present hunger, and he understood that he must get home or find sanctuary in his room. Looking at the wide, unsecured window, Michael knew home with Dominic was his only option. He opened himself up to his lover and sent out a call: *Dominic, I'm on my way.*

Grabbing the duffle bag, he slung it over his shoulder and moved rapidly through the door and out onto the street, all the while struggling to find Dominic in his mind.

I can't find you, Michael sent, the desperation clear in his inner voice as only silence rebounded. There was no reason Dominic would be blocking him unless he was feeding, but that would have been earlier in the night. Afterward, they always sent light tendrils of thought to each other, a gentle caress to reassure that they would be together again soon.

Something was wrong.

It wasn't that Michael could sense Dominic was in trouble. Quite the opposite. The complete blanket of silence seemed deliberate and left Michael completely unnerved. "Don't do this to me again. Please," he muttered while sending out another call.

Nothing.

Not a murmur. Not the mental touches Michael had grown so accustomed to that he felt empty in their absence.

He increased his pace along the road, desperate to get home, but Michael was brought to an abrupt halt. The path stretched before him, long and straight, with regular circles of light created by the street lamps. At the end of the road, Michael made out a figure swinging languidly around the lamppost. Michael watched him as he swung, hand on the pole and feet dancing lightly around its base. His first thought would normally have been that it was a drunken teenager, but there was something about the figure that prickled the hair at the back of his neck.

Another circle completed, and then, while Michael watched, the figure was a pole closer. Michael blinked, and in that blink, he'd moved closer again. Only three poles separated them. The figure's lithe frame spun fluidly, his long pale hair floating out from his shoulders.

He was only two poles away.

Michael could make out his almost serene expression, eyes closed in his bizarre dance. Michael didn't move or run. Instinct compelled him to turn and take off as fast as his legs could take him, but Michael remained still.

One pole away, and the figure opened his eyes. Each swing around the circumference of the light, and those eyes met Michael's. The green of a deep forest clearing lit by a sliver of light, Michael decided without actually thinking, as they caught then released him in the loop of the circle.

Then the images began—of blood and flesh, of Dominic and places Michael couldn't identify.

On and on it went, with more and more flashes, as if Michael was trapped in the spin of an antique zoetrope. His head ached with the rapid onslaught of images, but still Michael could not look away.

"Stop," he whispered, and instantly, it did.

The other leaned against the nearest pole and smiled.

Child of my child.

The thought crept into Michael's awareness. A mere tickle, at first, until the words became clear. Michael shook his head because the voice had no right to be in there. "Who are you?" he asked fearfully.

The figure continued to smile, although the rest of his features were untouched by the curve of his lips.

Michael shifted from one foot to the other in an attempt to reactivate his body in readiness for escape; then the familiarity of those eyes struck him.

"Are you him?" Michael asked. "Are you the one I feel in Dominic's memory?" The question was asked, and Michael cursed that he'd uttered Dominic's name in front of this creature.

Child of my child. The words came again.

"Get the fuck out of my head and speak to me," Michael hissed and dropped his duffle bag to the path. His gut was filled with ice water, but Michael stood his ground. "You are his, ah, maker, aren't you?"

"As he is yours." The words were stilted and deliberate, as if the speaker had not needed them in a very long time.

Michael nodded. "He is mine." But the other's smile broadened so that Michael could see the array of sharp teeth behind the full lips, and he took an involuntary step back. That the man was beautiful there was no doubt. He stood a little shorter than Michael, with a fine build that contradicted the deadly power Michael could feel radiating from him. His hair fell in delicate waves that were so fair as to be almost white, except that it held a yellow hint of winter sun. The face it framed would have been feminine, except that the high cheekbones narrowed to a strong jaw. But those eyes....

"What do you want from me?" Michael asked, a lot less sure of himself under the gaze of those eyes.

"Knowledge."

"There's nothing I can tell you," Michael replied, confused by the answer.

The other tilted his head in an action that looked frighteningly like that of a reptile waiting to strike. "I can give you knowledge."

That was not what Michael expected to hear, and he found himself moving closer. "Start with your name."

The vampire emitted a small laugh that sounded as disused as his voice. "Many names I have known, but I am Galen."

"Galen," Michael repeated, noting how different it sounded on his own tongue.

Tomorrow. The word ghosted through Michael's mind, and before he had a chance to respond, Galen was gone.

Michael blinked and looked at the now empty air in front of him. It was several moments before he could even begin to process what had just occurred. Slowly, his feet began to move along the path, and with each step, his sense of foreboding increased. *Child of my child. He knows me. He knows Dominic turned me. Fuck.*

Michael glanced around, sure the vampire had not gone far, and walked a little faster. He knew his speed would be no match for the other's, but the sky was already changing, compelling Michael to find sanctuary before dawn.

"DOMINIC?" Michael tentatively called into a house he already knew was empty. After dumping the bag in their bedroom, he pulled the heavy curtains tightly together and sat in the chair beside the window. Being alone had never spooked Michael, but he knew the rising sun would force sleep on him, and there was no Dominic to share his bed. Michael scrubbed his hands over his face. He wanted to call for his lover but finally understood the silence. Dominic was trying to keep them safe. At least, that's what Michael hoped was causing the silence.

Chapter
EIGHTEEN

A HUMAN would not have picked up his soft breaths, but in Dominic's vampire ears they rasped harshly against the concrete walls of the stairwell.

For years he'd kept at least one bolt hole in reserve that he did not own, so it could not be connected to him. After leaving Hunters, Dominic looped his way around the back streets of South Yarra in what he hoped was a confusing path, then finally made for a small derelict house. However, Dominic had become complacent in recent times, and rather than a safe haven, he was faced with a construction site.

Dawn approached with deadly speed, and Dominic needed to find somewhere to wait out the long summer day. The looming shape of a tower block caught his attention. There might not be any vacant rooms in which he could hide, but a windowless underground car park or storeroom would suffice until he had more time to search.

Outside sounds of the human world waking into life were muted by the thick concrete, but the occasional bang of doors and footsteps on lower levels echoed up to Dominic's resting place. He huddled in a corner with the knowledge that he would awaken if disturbed by a hapless human, yet he was safe from natural sunlight should an internal door be opened.

Dominic had slept in more uncomfortable and dangerous places in his long "life," but sleep did not come immediately with the rising sun. He'd always known that Galen would eventually find him. In fact,

Dominic had often thought that his maker knew where he was and was simply waiting until the time was right for him to make his presence known. This was not the first time he had run from Galen, but it was the longest he'd been left alone, long enough that Dominic had begun to believe he could lead some kind of life of his own. A foolish belief. Galen claimed him from the start, and there was no escaping their monstrous coupling.

Dominic's head fell back against the hard concrete wall, and he stared blankly at the gray light of the stairwell. The fluorescent tube flickered briefly in a failed attempt to illuminate the space, then emitted a final sickly hum before shutting down. Dominic was tempted to question why Galen had chosen now to resurrect their deadly game of cat and mouse, but he already knew the answer. Michael. Dominic had unwittingly found someone who allowed him to love, and to give life to a humanity he'd long thought dead. There was no way Galen would permit that.

Dominic's one hope was that Galen had no real interest in Michael, that if Dominic stayed away, he would lure Galen away with him. But what of Michael? Dominic's chest tightened with the knowledge that the young vampire would find himself abandoned and unprepared to survive alone.

"I'm sorry, Michael," he whispered, only to have the sibilant sounds bounce off the walls and back to him. He had to push that image out of his mind and pray that Michael would remain silent and hidden in their home. *Better you learn alone than the way I did.*

At some stage of the morning, sleep claimed Dominic.

IN HIS dream, Dominic searched a house that wasn't his, yet it felt familiar. Room to room he traveled along seemingly endless corridors. As he wandered, Dominic began to notice small ornaments secreted in compartments of the floor-to-ceiling bookshelves and cabinets. They came from many and varied eras. Some were so broken that only fragments remained, but Dominic recognized them and the memories they sparked.

A painting that had never been painted adorned a wall at the distant end of the hallway. Dominic squinted to make out the features of the portrait; they were his, but not the ones he saw in the mirror. As he walked closer, the image faded until he wasn't sure the picture had been there at all.

A door clicked behind him. Dominic turned to watch it slowly swing open. Part of him knew he needed to walk away, toward where the painting had once been, but he couldn't resist the compulsion to go through the open doorway.

The room it revealed was his or one of the many he'd inhabited throughout his long years. His bed was empty, but from the doorway he could make out Michael sitting in a chair by the closed curtains.

"Michael?" he said, only to have his words swallowed by an unnatural silence.

Michael didn't move.

"I'm sorry, Michael," Dominic whispered and walked over to crouch in front of the sleeping figure. He slid his hands slowly over Michael's thighs. *Please understand that I couldn't risk contacting you.*

I couldn't find you. Dominic looked up to see Michael's deep brown eyes looking into his. *I called for you, but you didn't answer.*

Please forgive me, Michael. Dominic stretched up and cupped Michael's face in his hands. *You need to stay here and be very quiet.*

Michael looked at him, not understanding what he was being told. *I came home and you weren't here.*

I know, Dominic sighed and stood up to lead Michael to the bed where they lay together. *I can't be here with you. Not because I don't want to be. I want to be very much. I just can't.*

I'm so hungry. Can you feed me? There was a lost expression in Michael's eyes that Dominic had never seen in his waking hours.

This is not real, my love. It's just a dream. Dominic eased him closer and closed his eyes against what he needed to say. *The pain of hunger will be great, but you must stay in this room. I will come to you when I can.*

Michael blinked once, then closed his eyes to rest his head against Dominic's chest.

If I don't come back... if I can't come back, then you must go to your friends. Dominic knew even in sleep that the hunger would overtake Michael, with a fatal outcome for any human he came into contact with, including the two tattooists, and as monstrous as that was, Michael had to survive.

Dominic stroked the soft curls, his fingers gently straightening them to let them spiral back. But something wasn't right. The fine strands did not return to their original shape and simply lay in his grasp. Tentatively, Dominic followed the length of the hair well past Michael's shoulder. There was the barest kink of a wave under his touch. It was then Dominic registered that the body against his had none of Michael's substance and was deceptively delicate despite well-defined muscles.

Long fingers crept over Dominic's torso, demonstrating their knowledge of where to touch him. The body moved, and soft full lips brushed along his jawline, imparting gentle kisses that could not conceal the needle points behind them. A fleeting kiss on Dominic's lips, and they disappeared, only to be felt against the vulnerable skin of his throat. Dominic's moan broke through the pall of silence, and his palm settled against the back of the other vampire's head, increasing the pressure while he waited for what he knew would come.

It was all too easy to sink into the familiarity of the bite, losing himself under the ministrations of the knowing hands.

Together.

The word floated between them until Dominic bolted upright to stare at the concrete walls of the stairwell.

Chapter
NINETEEN

DOMINIC? No response. Michael rolled onto his back and released the pillow he'd been clutching.

The dream had been all too real, but what else did Michael expect, lying in the big bed they usually shared surrounded by Dominic's belongings. His scent filled every corner of the room, so much so that if Michael closed his eyes he could almost see his lover sitting by the window watching him or sharing his reflection in the dresser mirror. *Almost.* When Michael's eyes opened, the old-fashioned bedroom was as empty as when he had been forced into his daylight sleep.

Michael shuffled higher in the bed and looked at the duffle bag where it sat unopened on the floor from the morning before. He dragged himself up, unzipped the bag, and tipped its contents on the bed. A quick poke among the clothes, and Michael decided he'd rather pull on one of Dominic's old shirts than anything he'd brought with him. Somehow, he knew Dominic wouldn't be home that night and that he, Michael, needed to remain quiet and not call for him. That was okay; he could do that for now. But the other command that echoed around his thoughts after the dream, Michael couldn't obey. *You need to stay home and be very quiet.* He could hear the desperation in Dominic's voice, but it was easily dismissed as a manifestation of his own fear of what he was about to do.

"I have to do this, Dominic," he muttered to the lingering voice in his head. "If he's the reason you're gone, I have to find out why, and anyway, if you won't tell me about your past, then I guess I have to hear it from him, right?"

They were reasonable excuses for leaving the house, but something told Michael it wasn't the safe haven Dominic hoped it would be in any case. If Galen wanted to hurt him, the old terrace house wouldn't stop him.

A mixture of hunger and trepidation bit at his stomach, and Michael winced against the unexpected sharp pain, but he wasn't going to let it stop him because he was determined to prove that side of this new life couldn't control him. "Prove it to whom?" he sighed and walked down the stairs to the front door. Michael hesitated at the threshold, wondering briefly if it could protect him from a vampire intruder, but he doubted it. Like almost all the other things he thought he knew about vampires, that, too, would be relegated to the stuff of Victorian novels and primetime TV.

With the door pulled tightly shut behind him, Michael strode down the driveway and instantly turned right when he reached the path. It didn't occur to him until he was halfway along the street that he knew where he was going. Another couple of corners, and Michael stood in front of the small park where he'd spent that first night talking to Dominic. The connection to his lover tickled at his senses and was almost forged until Michael saw the figure lying on the wooden picnic table.

Galen lay stretched out, long legs dangling over one end as if bathing in the sun's rays, except it was the cool light of the moon that shone on his pale skin. As Michael watched, Galen turned his face toward him. There was no smile of recognition. In fact, the face remained impassive, but Michael knew he was being summoned closer.

"Okay, I'm here," Michael said, a little startled at how his voice rang in the night air. However, the only indication that Galen had heard was a slow blink, until he caught the whisper in his mind. *Come sit with me, Michael.*

"I'm here for information and nothing more, got that?" Michael said defiantly and stood his ground.

Galen remained silent and waited because he knew Michael would eventually come to him. They always did.

A few more minutes of indecision was all Galen had to endure before Michael stood beside the picnic table looking down at the prone figure. The unwelcome recognition of the vampire's beauty combined with a twinge of doubt, and Michael wondered absently if it was jealousy or insecurity at the sight of Dominic's maker.

Galen smiled, and his fingers played lightly over white skin where his T-shirt had ridden up to expose his flat belly. Michael watched, almost entranced by the path of those fingers following the line of what looked to be a primitive tattoo, before catching himself with an abrupt shake of his head.

"What were you going to tell me?" he demanded, although his voice sounded much stronger before it left his lips.

Sit so we may talk.

Michael lowered himself to sit on the wooden bench, far too aware of his close proximity to the vampire.

Galen's hand slowly left his own skin and very gently brushed over Michael's hair. It barely made contact, but every fiber of Michael's body responded to the power Galen emanated. *I feel my child in you, fledgling—just as you "know" me.*

Michael wanted to deny it, but what Galen told him was true; there was a recognition within him that was more primal than conscious thought.

"Tell me about that," Michael murmured softly. "Tell me about him."

The fingertips made contact with Michael's skin. *All in good time. You hunger, young one.*

"I am stronger than that, stronger than the hunger," Michael lied and pulled away from the touch.

Galen's smile grew a little broader, but he let his hand return to rest on his belly. *I can tell you about him, or I can show you.*

Michael remembered the vivid, intimate images Dominic shared with him on the pier and had to wonder if he wanted that with Galen. Michael feared letting Galen even further into his mind, but more than that, he was afraid of what he might see in the memories. "I guess that's why I'm here, right?" He looked directly into the forest green eyes and asked silently, *Can you lie in a memory?*

Galen laughed and sat up, swinging his legs to either side of Michael. *I can show you only truth.*

It was as if a trap was being set, and Michael could only proceed into its jaws. *Okay, you can show me truth, but will it only be your truth?*

My child and I shared much; both flesh and blood linked us. I can only give you an honest recollection with both his truth and mine. Let me in, Michael, and you will feel us both.

As he listened, Michael felt arms encircle him, and he knew he had no choice but to lean back into the cold embrace.

Michael closed his eyes and accepted Dominic's maker.

WINTER had receded, but the warmth of the thin sunlight had only begun to spread the new life of spring in the northern land. Dominic kicked at a stone and watched it fly across the road earlier legions had built both for their troops and for trade with the local tribes. The leather at his toe was wearing through, but he knew it would have to wait until he returned home, or at least until his cohort of legionaries reached the eastern seaport of Arbeia.

"Did you need something, Sir?" a young soldier asked.

Dominic shook his head. "What I need is not to be found on these shores."

The soldier gave him a curious look, but put it down to the melancholy his commander had suffered in the passing months of winter. But Dominic smiled and said, "Ignore my moods, Roman. I have felt the distance from home of late." The young man nodded his understanding, for they had been in this land building his Emperor's wall for the turn of several seasons.

"This land holds its own beauty, but it is not home," Dominic said and turned away from the soldier to scan the surrounding landscape. The local tribes had already called the man of green to bring on their spring, and summer would surely follow, but Dominic's body ached for the warm sun of his homeland. He had already summered west of here, supervising the seemingly eternal construction of the wall dividing the tribes of north and south, and although this sun shone brightly, it cast a yellow hue rather than the golden glow he felt in his fields at home.

"Enough," he grumbled and caught up to a fellow officer. He grinned and pointed to the troops ahead of them. "I fear the men fret for a skirmish to occupy their time," he commented.

"The long winter took its toll on their patience," Marcus agreed.

"Bremenium kept them warm, and for the most part entertained, but men of battle need more than a full belly and company in their beds."

Marcus chuckled. "I believe the Brigante women had had enough of them too." He looked at Dominic and grinned. "And I believe the young men of the tribe understood little of seduction? Or so I have been told."

"You were told correctly," Dominic agreed. The nights he sought company in the fortifications were generally spent with the young men who accompanied them rather than those of the native tribe.

"Ah, my friend, when we return home, my wife had better be prepared to birth many sons, for I miss the heat of her thighs."

Dominic shot his friend a look and teased, "And what of your spawn here, Marcus?"

"Merely playing my part to improve the local stock." Marcus laughed and shouted an order to the men behind them to hurry lest they be left to feed the Brigante spirits.

"Do not put those notions in their heads, for we make camp under the stars tonight," Dominic said, again looking out across the roll of the low hills on the horizon.

THE mist of their warm breath floated up into the clear night sky as Dominic walked away from the circle of men around the fire. He signaled he would not be long, but in truth, the meal they had shared sat heavily in his stomach, and Dominic felt the need to walk it off.

The land the Emperor's advisor had chosen for his wall shone brightly under the light of the full moon, and Dominic soon found that he'd wandered far from their temporary encampment. The call of a night bird kept him company as his curiosity took him to a small grove of trees just beginning to sprout their spring foliage. Hidden at their center was a dark pool of water, touched in parts by the illumination of the moonlight. Dominic walked a little closer, only to discover that he was no longer alone.

Stepping quickly behind the trunk of an ancient oak, Dominic watched what he assumed to be the lithe body of a young woman wading through the water. The slim back was pale enough to shine white beneath the moon, but shadows played over its surface to create a series of lines and markings. Although women were not to Dominic's taste, he could not pull his eyes from the path of the water that ran down from long fair hair to rejoin the pond at the small of the bather's back.

Slowly, the figure turned and moved closer to the bank, allowing Dominic to see that she, in fact, was no woman. Water trickled down over a well-formed chest and flat stomach. The bather stopped and looked in Dominic's direction. Neither moved, and then Dominic heard a quiet voice that spoke in the language of the natives, but it held an inflection not known to him.

"I knew you would come to me this night," the young man said and continued his path out of the water. "I have followed and waited."

"Followed me? Why?" Dominic asked and stepped further into view.

The other stood calf deep at the edge of the pond, and Dominic could see that he was indeed a man. The slender body glistened with rivulets of the icy water, yet he seemed not to notice the cold. He smiled and stepped onto the bank, where he took hold of Dominic's hand and placed the palm against his chilled torso. When Dominic made to look down, cool lips met his in a brief, yet intimate, kiss before he flinched away.

"What are you that you feel like ice yet do not tremble under my hand?"

"I am Galen," he replied as his fingers traced over one of the crude, yet lyrical, markings tattooed near Dominic's hand.

The Roman's fingers itched to follow in turn the path of ink that extended the length of the pale body—over belly and hips and down until it touched his thighs. Slowly, the centurion's fingers moved to brush over what looked like the symbol of a full moon crowned with a crescent before he pulled them away.

"What do they mean?" he whispered.

"I am beloved of my gods," Galen responded simply and moved forward until Dominic was again touching him. "I was offered and was accepted."

The cold of the skin crept through Dominic's palm, and he glanced up to search for meaning in Galen's eyes. "Your gods are not my gods," he said quietly. "I do not understand."

Galen nodded.

You understand enough to know I need your warmth to fill me.

Dominic heard the voice, even though it had not been spoken, and lifted his hand to the still lips.

Galen did not waver under Dominic's touch even when he was asked, "How can I hear you when your soft lips do not move?"

Do you want me, Roman? Will you have what was shared with the gods?

Dominic's warm breath hung briefly between them when he whispered, "Yes."

Galen smiled, and Dominic felt the stretch of the chilled lips beneath his fingers. Without hesitation, Dominic let his fingers slip away and replaced them with a kiss. He felt the cool tongue against his, but rather than repelling him, it only heightened his desire for the ethereal man.

When Galen's mouth moved to his throat, Dominic's hands slid down the naked back to clutch the firm cheeks and press their bodies hard against each other. His eyes closed, and he gulped in a breath of the cold night air, tasting the smells of the forest rather than the grime and sweat of the young men who usually frequented his bed. Galen began a slow, sensual roll of his hips while he mouthed and kissed the heated surface of Dominic's neck. Sensual images of them coupling invaded Dominic's thoughts. The Roman was all but paralyzed by his seemingly unnatural desire for the youth and clung to him, gasping each tortured breath.

Finally, two sharp fangs broke the surface, and Galen tasted the first drops of Dominic's blood. He had watched the men march through his land in their well-ordered formations as many suns set. He had watched them battle the tribesmen and stack block upon block, building their wall and fortifications. He had listened with curiosity when they uttered prayers to their gods to keep them safe throughout the night, and grinned when their gods abandoned them in his embrace. But Galen had lingered over none of them. Not until this one.

He drank a bare sip, as if prolonging and savoring the moment. The warm blood sparked on his tongue with a life he'd thought had left him. He swallowed a longer drink, and the heat of it flowed down his throat to surge through every vein and nerve ending, eliciting a low moan against the tortured skin of his prey.

Then Galen stopped, and with lips still bloody, he gently kissed a closed eye, leaving the faintest smear of red on the delicate lid.

"You taste of summer," he whispered and stepped away.

"I… you…." Dominic stumbled over his words, not yet understanding what had just occurred. Traces of his blood colored the stranger's lips, and Dominic cautiously touched the tiny wounds on his neck. His lips were again covered by Galen's, and Dominic heard the command in his thoughts: *Look for me, centurion. When the sun sleeps, you will find me near.*

The lips vanished from his, and the pale young man vanished as well. It was only then that Dominic realized he had come with the stranger's bite.

"FUCK!" Michael jolted forward. A thin trickle of sweat threaded its way from his hairline down his neck, and Michael wiped his fingers through it to reassure himself that Galen had only fed in the vision.

"That was real?" Michael asked, shaking out his arms in an attempt to banish the imprint it had left in him.

It was real, Galen confirmed.

"But… shit." Michael shook his head and pulled at his shirt, hating the hard flesh he hid in his jeans from witnessing his lover's seduction. He took a breath and stood up, refusing to give Galen the satisfaction of his arousal. "So," he started in a calmer voice. "So, did you turn him the next night?"

Not the next night or the many nights after.

The smile wasn't lost on Michael, and his eyes narrowed. "Why are you showing me like this?"

You wanted to know.

"But it's different to the way it was with Dominic. We were there. We were together in his memory."

You were not there when I took my child.

"I know, but…."

He chose to let you be part of a memory. I do not. It was our time.

Michael felt Galen's possessive nature, but also something else: love. "I'm sorry, Galen. I think I understand," Michael said quietly.

Do you want to know more?

The green eyes did not blink while he waited for a response, and it left Michael more than a little unnerved. *Did* he want more? Michael had wanted to know it all until he'd felt Dominic's desire for Galen, but what he'd seen had created more questions than answers. "I want to know if he agreed to be turned by you." Michael also wanted to know how long they had stayed together, and why Dominic had run from him, but he kept those questions to himself.

There was a soft touch of cold fingertips on the back his hand, but this time, like Dominic in the vision, Michael did not flinch. He knew Galen was part of him, just as much as Dominic, and felt no imminent threat; however, that was not to say that he felt no threat at all.

THE cohort had divided at the next fort when a runner met them with word that the savages from the north were stirring trouble, which needed to be dispelled before others joined them. Dominic volunteered to remain at the fort, much to Marcus's surprise, knowing how much his friend fed on the adrenaline of a fight. Marcus teased him mercilessly that he was growing complacent in his old age, preferring the pleasures of the bathhouse within the fortifications to a good battle with the Pictish savages. Dominic had laughed and taken it with seeming good nature because he could not divulge the truth—that he stayed behind to feel the intoxicating caress of a night spirit.

Dominic stood watching for Galen as soon as night patrols had been inspected, unaware of the vampire's presence until he felt surprisingly soft lips on the nape of his neck. His head tipped forward, but his hands reached back for the slender body, no longer wondering at the cool smoothness of the white skin.

"How long have you waited for me?" Dominic murmured, coaxing Galen around to face him.

I have endured centuries alone. The green of Galen's eyes caught a sliver of moonlight shimmering like dew on a newly opened spring leaf, and Dominic did not doubt the statement.

"Are you real, Galen? Or are you a spirit of this land, sent to drive me mad?" he whispered, running a battle-scarred hand through the silken hair.

I am formed of flesh and blood like any man, but my maker has changed them in his image.

Dominic had no real understanding of what Galen was telling him, but he plucked at the coarse tunic that covered the light frame. "But your needs are of a man?"

Galen smiled and pulled the tunic over his head to let it drop to the grass at his feet, so he once again stood naked in front of the centurion.

Dominic laughed. "That wasn't exactly what I meant."

But it is what you want, Galen stated simply.

"It is what I want," Dominic answered, without hesitating to quickly remove his own tunic and loosen the ties of his pants. Cool fingers passed over Dominic's chest, catching a taut nipple in their path. He watched their progress and couldn't deny the power of the young man before him. *What power do you hold over me, night spirit?* Although it was merely a thought, he was not surprised when an answer sounded in his mind.

You will see, Roman; we will taste of each other, and I will no longer endure this eternity alone.

A slight frown creased Dominic's brow, for he did not understand Galen's intent, but he knew that as long as he stayed in this land, Galen would spend no night alone.

Again, Galen smiled on hearing Dominic's silent vow, exposing the deadly points of his fangs. Yet Dominic did not back away from the sight of them. Instead there was anticipation of the vampire's bite and the pull on his blood that had his cock aching within his pants.

Without pause, Galen dropped fluidly to his knees and pressed his cheek to the bulge still confined in the woolen pants. The heat of the swelling flesh warmed him through the fabric, and Galen moaned lightly at the scent and throb of new blood.

Dominic tentatively touched the fair head and pressed him a little closer, his desire mounting with each nuzzle against his crotch. Still holding Galen close, Dominic reached down to ease his cock through the opening in his pants, and although he knew the damage those teeth could inflict, Dominic rubbed his flesh against that dangerous mouth.

Slowly, Galen's full lips closed over the swollen head, where he teased and tasted the heated skin while exploring the full vein with his tongue. The blood was there, just below the surface, and Galen could feel each beat of the human's heart through the pulsations of the hot fluid.

"More…," Dominic pleaded and urged Galen to take more of the hard flesh into his mouth. The threat of those teeth only heightened his excitement. With a slight rock of his hips, Dominic gasped at the drag of sharp points so close to breaking his vulnerable skin. He repeated the action, almost willing his blood to flow.

But Galen stopped, and before Dominic could fathom what had happened to that lethal mouth, there was a sharp pain in the tender flesh of his thigh. Dominic emitted a guttural curse, but when he looked down at the beautiful creature looking back at him while sucking on the bloodied thigh, Dominic gripped his cock and tugged hard and fast with each pull of his blood. His release followed quickly, and he watched Galen move from his torn thigh to gently lick the last drips of come.

Galen stood, and although his smile was bloody, it did not deter Dominic, and his hands cupped Galen's face and drew him into a tender kiss. Traces of blood and come played over Dominic's tongue, but neither repulsed him.

What have you done to me, Galen? He did not expect an answer, but the thought was returned.

I have shared desires that are more than human.

The kiss ended, and Dominic stared into the depths of Galen's eyes and finally understood that this was no spirit, but was definitely no longer human.

"Will I live if I leave you?" he whispered.

"You will live," Galen said aloud, the physical voice ringing strangely in Dominic's ears. "But would you want to?"

At that moment, Dominic could not imagine an existence without Galen, yet surely he could not be real and was a conjured dream of these shores?

Do you think of me when the sun shines warm on your shoulders? The voice had shifted back into Dominic's head, and he wondered at the change.

Do you long for the pull of your blood as it leaves your flesh?

Dominic closed his eyes and listened. As much as he wanted to say no, he knew it would be a lie.

Do you dream of tasting me, Dominic?

The last question was unexpected and shook Dominic's resolve. His answer to this of all questions needed to be a lie. "No. Your lips, your skin, and your manhood, yes, but I am no monster to desire your blood."

Galen remained still and silent until Dominic believed there would be no answer. Then the tip of the vampire's tongue passed over his bottom lip, clearing all traces of crimson, and he said, "We are all monsters, Dominic." With that, Galen backed away and faded into a moon shadow.

A chill shivered through the centurion, but he did not search for Galen. He needed to clear his head and sort through what had occurred that night; at least, that's what Dominic told himself to reason with the crushing loneliness that echoed in him. Dominic looked down and watched a fine trickle of blood escape from the bite mark and meander through the hair on his thigh until he halted it with an abrupt swipe of his fingers. But the blood glistened darkly on his fingertips, tempting and taunting him, and he raised his eyes to the moonlit countryside in search of the vampire as the wet fingers slipped between his lips.

THE sun shone with a warmth that promised an end to the long nights of darkness and hinted at fruitful summer months, but Dominic sat silently with his morning meal untouched. Several nights had passed, and Galen had not returned.

"Is this what you wanted? You created a desire for you then left me wanting?" he muttered, just loud enough that the men within earshot exchanged looks of amusement at the grumblings of their superior. Having no answer for his questions, Dominic abruptly pushed the plate aside and sat back in disgust.

"The food isn't that bad, is it?" the voice came from the other side of the food hall, and Dominic looked up to see Marcus striding toward him.

"I did not expect you back so soon, Marcus. Did the battle bore you?"

"The skirmish was little more than a dance," Marcus said, chuckling, and pulled Dominic's plate toward him to stuff a large chunk of bread into his mouth. Still chewing, he described in detail the fight and how the natives had fled their encampment overnight for no discernible reason. When the plate was empty, Marcus slapped Dominic's shoulder, grabbed a cup, and led him out into the sun. Together they walked while Marcus oversaw the feeding of his men, but it soon became obvious that the conversation was one sided. Finally

Marcus stopped and turned to Dominic. "What bothers you, my friend? And don't tell me nothing, for despite the fact you have always been a miserable bastard, something weighs heavily on your thoughts."

Dominic attempted to dismiss the concerns with a wave of his hand. "I have not slept well without your snoring as my lullaby," he joked, but he knew he must look like hell for that was how he felt.

"Ah, if that were the truth." Marcus laughed before his tone turned serious. "Sleep does not come easily in this part of the land. Many of my men have suffered a type of night terror, as if sensing unseen predators hunting in the night. Guards posted against marauding wolf packs did nothing to calm their fears."

"Did you feel it, my friend?" Dominic asked uneasily.

Marcus nodded. "This land reeks of the otherworld, and the sooner we set out for Arbeia, the better our nights will be."

"One more night," Dominic said quietly, then added quickly on seeing Marcus's expression. "One more night to rest and ready your men for the march."

It was an anxious wait until nightfall, but Dominic knew Galen would return. In the final light of dusk, the dogs began to growl and snap at each other in their unease until their handlers were forced to separate them. The guards acknowledged Dominic as he walked past them, but the dogs simply followed his path with black, fearful eyes.

"I know you are near," Dominic uttered, once he was a good distance from the fort. He could feel Galen's presence like a swelling of his heart and was not surprised when he heard an answer.

You are leaving.

"We leave at first light to reach the port, but we still have this night," Dominic replied, looking around for the man he'd come to understand was his lover.

We will have more.

The dark intent of the statement was not lost on Dominic, but he did not have time to ponder it, for Galen was quickly on him. No kisses or caresses, just fingers and fangs tearing at his throat. Fear surged through Dominic, and he grabbed at Galen, attempting to halt the onslaught, but the seemingly fragile frame belied Galen's unyielding strength. Galen's fingers held like a metal trap while Dominic felt his blood flow from him, but he no longer feared the vampire's kiss and held Galen in a lover's embrace.

Take all you need.

Galen slowed, and his bite became a kiss, then a gentle lick to clean and heal the wound. *You offer me much, Dominic.* Galen met the Roman's gray eyes and gently stroked cool fingers over the fine beads of sweat shining on Dominic's brow. *But this night will only give you a taste of what I am.*

While Dominic watched, Galen bit himself lightly on the wrist, not a deep bite, but enough that two points of blood welled in the tiny puncture wounds. Staring as the red bubbles grew, Dominic murmured fearfully, "I cannot…. I'm not like you."

Not a monster? The thought caught only the edges of Dominic's mind when Galen said, "You will not become as me, but we will be forever entwined."

The understanding that he would soon leave those shores hung heavily between them, and Dominic lowered his lips to the offered wrist. It was to be just a taste, nothing more. Galen's blood seemed no different to his own; it was slightly bitter with a hint of copper that tingled at the edges of his tongue. With his lips still on the vampire's skin, Dominic glanced up, and although Galen's expression had not changed, his eyes danced with a light that was very new.

They lay together in the spring grass throughout the night, and when the dawn approached, they parted with a shared promise that Galen would follow the march as far as he was able toward the mouth of the great river, and each night Dominic would find him.

"HE LOVED you," Michael said softly, finding himself once again in Galen's embrace. The ancient vampire did not reply other than tightening his arms. The image of Dominic in those arms was difficult for Michael to shake until a fresh wave of hunger-induced nausea rushed through his system, forcing a sudden intake of air.

Your hunger grows.

"It can wait," Michael hissed, through another gut wrenching cramp that all but took his breath away.

It will soon take you, fledgling. Galen's message was pure fact, but for an instant, Michael heard a hint of satisfaction in the vampire's thoughts.

"I can control it," Michael stated fiercely, but he already knew it was a losing battle, and each hour was hard fought. The hunger rippled below his skin, it stretched and knotted every nerve, muscle, and tendon until the ability to remain still became an impossibility.

You need to hunt. The insidious whisper echoed through his mind. *It is what you are now, and it will take you.*

"No…. No, that isn't me. Dominic doesn't kill to survive," Michael insisted. He clung desperately to the idea that he could feed without killing and make it pleasurable for his victims. No, not victims. Those who offered.

Galen leaned forward over Michael's shoulder and said quietly next to his ear, "My child killed many and bathed in their blood, as will you when the hunger takes you."

Chapter
T W E N T Y

INDECISION warred in Dominic. Every fiber of his being ached to go to Michael to hold him and feed him, to ease the pain he knew his lover would be suffering, but Dominic knew Galen was close and would be watching. As he sat on the bare boards of a derelict room, another thought insinuated its way into the mix: What if Galen had already found Michael? Dominic quickly leaped to his feet ready to... ready to what? He stood, unsure how to proceed, and took a long breath.

"My maker hunts me and panic will only hinder my ability to elude him," Dominic muttered in an attempt at reason to quell his new bout of anxiety.

Little light penetrated the boards covering the window of the condemned house, although Dominic already knew night loomed. Sliding the loose boards aside, he left in the same way he had arrived, jumping effortlessly to the weed-filled garden below. Though the sun had fallen below the horizon, the evening glow of its departure still illuminated the court of vacated houses that had once bustled with children trying to fit in one last game or a final ride of their bicycles before their mothers called them in for the night. The world continued to change around Dominic, even though he remained the same.

A vague twinge of hunger reminded the vampire that he had not fed since discovering Galen's arrival. He made to push it aside, but he knew the distraction of hunger would weaken his awareness and could leave him disadvantaged in Galen's game. "Whatever game it is we play now that hide-and-seek is over," Dominic grumbled, repeating the words told to him by the man in the club as he waded through the knee-high weeds until he reached the path.

Then why do I continue to hide? The thought niggled. One that Dominic had no real answer to, except it had been his salvation for long centuries and was all he knew.

Dominic was sure Galen had been around well before he revealed himself through his prey, but why the subterfuge? If the ancient vampire knew Dominic's hunting ground, he would also know where....

"Damn," Dominic groaned at the knowledge of what came next in that train of thought. Galen would know where he lived, and more importantly, he would know that Dominic had taken a lover.

At the corner of the deserted street, Dominic stood torn between his need to lead Galen away and the terror that he had already found Michael.

"Ink," Dominic said to the empty air, hoping he could get some indication that Michael was safe without leading Galen straight to their home—in the vain hope that it was still unknown to him.

STEPPING onto Chapel Street posed its own problems. Dominic attempted to avoid contact with passing humans which, given their natural survival instincts, proved not to be a challenge, but their smell was still a distraction. With each that passed, Dominic forced himself to ignore their heat and the thrum of their blood to concentrate, lest he overlook scents or thoughts that would alert him to his maker's presence. With his senses open as much as he dared, Dominic moved purposefully through the pedestrian traffic until he saw the painted window of the tattoo parlor. Without hesitation he walked straight past it and stood as if looking in the window of a retro clothes shop a few door down, but every sense was attuned to his immediate surroundings, listening and searching for any vampire presence. It was only when he was sure he was alone that Dominic returned to Ink.

Though it was still early, the parlor would usually have been open, but not a single light shone out through the window. Dominic peered through the glass, between the painted demons into the dark store front. There was no sign of life within. He moved further along the window in an attempt to catch any movement at the rear of the shop near the workroom, but neither the woman with the crimson hair nor her lover were anywhere to be seen. Dominic frowned. Even though he could not see them, their scent was strong.

Dominic glanced up at a small window to the apartment where they lived over the shop and wondered if the scent was simply the residue of their belongings, for even if they had left the apartment, there would still be a lingering marker. No, it was more than that; Dominic could almost feel Abby near him.

A quick look over the front of the shop revealed no access to the apartment above, and scaling the wall with that many witnesses was definitely out of the question. Instead, Dominic walked quickly to the nearest side street, where he could access the back alley. He climbed swiftly over the high gate, then, with unnatural speed, clambered up the brick wall and in through an expertly broken window.

The darkness of the apartment was no deterrent to the vampire, and he moved stealthily from the small bathroom along the hallway.

"Abby?" he said quietly, letting it bounce around the still apartment and return to him without answer. Dominic paused; it was quiet, but not silent. The soft sound of frightened breathing came from a room to his left. At his slow turn of the doorknob, there was a sharp intake of breath and shift in the breathing.

"Abby?" Dominic whispered before pushing the door open. "It's Dominic. Michael's Dominic, and I won't hurt you."

"I know," Abby said, and for some unfathomable reason, she knew he wouldn't.

Dominic stepped into the bedroom, and although her smell surrounded him, all he could see was a large unmade bed and a dresser with a mirror adorned with concert tickets and Polaroids of people he assumed were friends and family. The sight of it saddened him. "You're safe with me, Abby," he said and attempted to color his words with silent reassurances, although he knew he failed to make them convincing. Moving further into the room, Dominic saw her huddled between the bed and the far wall. Walking slowly and quietly, Dominic made his way around the bed and crouched in the tiny space in front of her. Abby looked up, and for the first time since she had walked back into Ink and been confronted by Galen, Abby allowed herself to cry. Knowing his touch would not be welcome, Dominic lowered himself completely to the floor next to her and waited.

He didn't have long to wait until the pressure of the past couple of days was released and Abby pulled out a tissue and blew her nose. "He was in the shop waiting for me after Michael left," Abby stated, sure that Dominic would know who "he" was.

Even though Dominic's instant impulse was to ask about Michael, he held that back. "Did he hurt you?"

Abby shook her head. "I think he was going to. I mean, he glared at me with those strange green eyes and then moved so fast, but as soon as he touched me, he backed away."

Dominic felt her revulsion at the memory of Galen's touch, but her words puzzled him. His maker rarely left his prey alive.

"Have you seen Scott?" she asked, tears welling again despite her resolve to remain strong.

"No," Dominic replied simply, needing to block the pain he felt radiate from her. "Was he here that night?"

Abby nodded. "He was out back in the workroom, clearing up. I don't know what happened or where he is. It's like everything after *he* spoke to me is gone. And so is Scott."

"What did he say to you, Abby? What did he tell you?"

Abby concentrated to clear her head and remember before she said, "He didn't speak in words, but I still heard him. He said something like 'you are like her, the one who offered me'. I dunno. It didn't make much sense, just a jumble of crazy stuff and weird tattoos." Abby stopped and thought about what she had just said and emitted a small mirthless laugh. "Nothing about what has happened lately has made any sense. I feel like I'm inside a late-night TV show and can't get out."

Dominic smiled sadly and asked if she wanted to get up from her hiding place on the floor, but she shook her head and tugged on the candlewick bedspread. "Just gonna stay here a little longer, okay? I haven't been here the whole time, and, hey, I know it isn't really going to stop him if he wants to get to me, but when it gets dark...." Abby shrugged and smiled. "It's like a kid thing, I guess, and I just need to get my head around everything first and figure out how to find Scott."

"Can I ask you about Michael? Did Galen follow him?"

"So that's his name. Galen." Abby repeated it slowly as if tasting its sound, then frowned. "I don't think so. He didn't mention Michael and couldn't have followed him because... because he didn't leave, not right away. Do you think... I mean... did he take my blood?"

It was Dominic's turn to shake his head. There was no aura of the ancient vampire around the woman to indicate that he had fed from her. Yes, it could have faded in the day or so since, but Galen was powerful, and Dominic doubted he would leave no trace. "He did not feed from you, Abby."

Lifting her hand to her neck, Abby asked, "Are you sure? I don't remember what he did, and that scares me more."

Her fear of violation pervaded Dominic thoughts, but he knew she hadn't been touched.

"I'm sure," he assured her. "Why he came here, though, I cannot be sure."

Abby sat quietly and stared into the room. Try as she might, she could not remember everything that had happened after she saw those beautiful eyes watching her. "I've felt him here before," Abby said very quietly. "But I didn't recognize it as a person, or whatever the fuck he is."

"He was a person once." Dominic sighed. "He was a young man who believed he was a gift for the gods and was offered to them by his people. Galen told me that, and I think he still believes it, or has chosen to believe it to make this all easier."

"I'm not sure I could feel much of that person left in him."

"Galen is older that the written word and has existed in this form for so long, I think he's forgotten what it's like to be human."

Abby's hand slowly reached over and closed over Dominic's. There was still some fear in her touch, but she knew Michael loved this man. "You haven't forgotten, though."

The warmth of her hand seeped into Dominic's skin, and he whispered, "I haven't forgotten, and Michael helps me hold on to that."

"Is that why Galen is here now?"

Dominic nodded. "I fear so."

Silence again filled the bedroom, until Abby asked, "Did he take Scott?"

"Perhaps," Dominic muttered, although he could not fathom why Galen would take the young tattooist rather than simply drain and kill him where he worked.

Despite the heat in the small bedroom, Abby pulled the bedspread a little closer and murmured, "Even if he has him, I know Scott's alive." She looked at Dominic, suddenly very sure of what she'd said. "He's alive and I *will* see him again."

Dominic was not so sure, although he couldn't deny that the woman had an insight not tapped by most humans. "Do you want to come with me? I have somewhere to hide not yet known to Galen."

"I don't think so," Abby replied quietly, but with a tiny trace of a smile. "Something tells me I need to stay here at Ink."

"Perhaps you do," Dominic agreed, the memory of his dream still strong, as was the advice he had given to Michael to find Abby if it proved impossible for Dominic to return to him. After tucking an edge of the bedspread under Abby's toes, Dominic looked at their still clasped hands and gave her fingers a gentle kiss. "Please take care of Michael if he returns here, and I will try to lead Galen away."

"Could he hurt you?" Abby asked.

"He is my maker."

Although he did not directly answer Abby's question, his tone spoke volumes. "Please, be careful, Dominic," Abby said, surprising

Dominic with her sincerity, and it pained him that he could not offer any hope for her lost lover.

Dominic exited the way he had arrived and walked rapidly down Chapel Street toward Hunters. It was well after midnight, and not a night that would attract his usual prey, but none of that mattered because Chapel buzzed with activity, and he rarely struggled to find a willing volunteer to feel his "vampire kiss," as one lost soul had called it. Even amid the techno beat, Dominic knew he would be sought out.

The strobe lights and the relentless thump of the music assaulted the vampire's senses even before he made it past the crowded bar of the club, and the stench of chemical-tainted sweat almost overpowered the scent of heated blood. Almost, but not completely, because Dominic was hungry, and the blood shone through it all. Casting his gaze around the edges of the room, Dominic soon let it rest on a young man standing away from the main dance area. He nursed a drink in which the ice had long since melted, and he emanated a loneliness that Dominic could use.

Dominic walked slowly past his prey, giving him the briefest look, yet it was enough that the young man followed him into the bathroom without question. The violent memory of his last feed was still raw, so Dominic held his hand out to the nervous youth and said quietly, "I will not harm you and will give you the choice to leave untouched if that is what you desire."

"I want to be with you. My name's Ricky," he said, with a tremor he hoped went unnoticed when he took Dominic's hand.

"Thank you, Ricky," Dominic whispered and locked the door of the stall.

Dominic did not take much of Ricky's blood, just enough that his hunger was sated and his strength returned. The young clubber bought a new drink and sat at a table with the belief that he'd just had an encounter with a handsome man who would usually be way out of his league. Ricky's smile held a new confidence, and he decided it was a good night.

Crowds of twentysomethings spilled from the packed club to congregate outside, where they smoked and bitched about both friends and enemies. Many laughed and posed, happily jostling for the prime real estate under the light of the neon signs. However, they quieted uncomfortably and created a pathway when Dominic moved through them, each pretending he was not among them and only a few casting furtive glances in his direction.

Galen had used this club and one of its patrons to get a message to Dominic, so he knew he didn't have to protect his hunting ground; however, Dominic still moved far enough away so that no human would be endangered when his maker answered his call.

Standing beneath the light of a street lamp Dominic opened his thoughts to Galen and invited him to come.

Chapter
TWENTY-ONE

GALEN'S grip on Michael loosened. He cocked his head to the side as if listening. "My child calls me to him," he whispered. "Can you hear him?"

The question startled Michael, but he listened and caught a hint of Dominic's call. None of the message reached him, though. It was the faintest echo of Dominic, yet it infused him with the scent of his lover when they woke together and the taste of his skin before they shared blood. Michael ached for him, even if it was just to goad those moody lips into a smile before they kissed. But Dominic had left him alone for a reason, so Michael shook his head and said sadly, "No, I can't, because the message is for you."

"I know you can, Michael. I can feel the change in you," Galen said, then fell silent as if he was again listening to the distant call.

"Why didn't you go to him at the start?" Michael asked abruptly in an attempt to distract Galen.

I have told you of our beginning. Galen blinked and focused once again on Michael.

"No, I mean here," Michael said and turned his face so their lips were very close, hoping to keep Galen's attention on him.

Why? Have you not guessed? Galen smiled in a way that chilled Michael's blood. *I have watched and waited for so many turns of the moon, wondering how long it would take Dominic to return to what he is.* Galen quieted briefly and pressed his lips to Michael's in a soft kiss. *Return to what we all are… and what we are no longer.*

Although the kiss surprised him, Michael did not pull away.

I felt him find you, and that awakening drew me back to him. Galen shifted a little and closed his eyes. *It was then you gave him my mark, and I knew it was time.*

"Your mark? What does that mean?" Michael asked and flinched when unexpected fingers roamed down his belly to slip under his shirt and into the waistband of his jeans, where it caressed his hip bone. The image of the interlocking knots in the crescent moon on Dominic's pale skin passed to him through the touch, and Michael frowned.

"The tattoo was just a design I used because he came to me at night and… and it made a pair with my sun tattoo. It had nothing to do with you."

It had all to do with me. I was adorned with the mark of the moon to prepare me for my sacrifice, and now Dominic wears it.

An alarm bell sounded in Michael's mind, and he wrenched himself out of Galen's hold. "Dominic is no sacrifice," he snapped, only to see Galen's calm eyes open.

You misunderstand me. He shares my mark, but not my fate. It merely shows we are forever bound.

Michael's eyes narrowed. It was true he had begun doing this to discover Dominic's past, and then to keep the vampire away from his lover, but the mention of Galen's own story had him intrigued. "What exactly do you mean when you say you were a sacrifice?"

Galen's fingers had returned to his own T-shirt and traced over the fabric beneath which were his own crude tattoos. *I was chosen, as were others. All young, all beautiful. We were kept pure of human touch, and each was marked before we became men so none would interfere with us. As our time grew closer, many in our tribe looked on us with pity, but we were revered above all others. When the long night came, we were stripped bare and taken to the sacred place, where we remained until the night spirit chose one.*

Although he kept his distance from Galen, the image the ancient vampire projected was so vivid that Michael could clearly see the naked youths standing in the forest clearing, trembling as they awaited their fate.

"He chose you," Michael said softly.

One by one the others' necks were snapped, until he stood in front of me. I was afraid. That was my fate, but I was very afraid.

Michael looked at Galen, and despite his ghostly visage, the frightened youth briefly shone through. Every instinct told Michael that Galen was no longer that sacrificial victim, but he still reached out to brush a fingertip along a tattooed curve that peeped out below the T-shirt's sleeve.

His bite was like fire, but I knew I had been created for that moment. He took my blood and body many times before his gift was given to me. My body was broken, and I was ready for my death, but I drank of his blood, and I healed. I was kept for the full cycle of the moon, enjoying all his pleasures, and then I knew my time was over.

Galen stopped and looked down to where Michael's fingers lingered near his arm.

It was to be the time I would die as both human and spirit to join my brothers already slain, but I was not ready to give up what I had become.

"What did you do?" Michael asked quietly, trying to find any emotional response in the vampire at such horrific acts, and failing.

I destroyed my God and took his place. Any trace of Galen's human persona vanished into his past. *What will I do now, Michael? Stay here and tell you the rest of my tale, or have you heard enough?*

There had been a brief glimpse of humanity before the beautiful monster returned, and Michael knew he was no longer there simply to distract Galen from his lover. Michael wanted to know how much of the human still existed.

"Tell me more," he said and took his place back on the wooden bench.

If they were witnessed by any passerby, the pair could easily have been mistaken for two young lovers in an amorous embrace. Michael leaned back into Galen's arms and felt the cool breath on his cheek.

THE march to Arbeia took many nights, on each of which the Roman sought out his lover. The first gray hours of darkness were spent in anticipation of the vampire's arrival and the rest in bloodletting and lust, leaving Dominic a scant few hours before the birdsong of false dawn when his men marched in unison to the next encampment.

"What ails you, my friend?" Marcus finally asked, after Dominic's second stumble of the morning.

"A simple fever," Dominic lied and concentrated on the road ahead.

"That will not wash with me. I am no fool, so do not treat me like one," Marcus disputed. "True, your skin carries the signs of sickness in its pallor, but your eyes are of one haunted by something other than a simple fever."

Dominic began to speak, but Marcus stopped him with an abrupt hand gesture. "Before you continue with your excuses, I must warn you the talk among the men is that your strength is being stolen by the nightly visitations of an incubus spirit. Now, I prefer to believe that your nighttime wanderings are to spend your cock in flesh, not fantasy, but either way, I have decided that we will not push on after the midday meal, and you will eat a full meal, then sleep."

Dominic did not even attempt to argue, for his limbs were heavy, and his joints ached with the effort of each step. Feeding Galen every night was destroying him, but he could not stop.

Although there was discussion of why the men made camp early when the port was so close, the legionaries soon took advantage of the break in routine by indulging in games of chance and bawdy tales of how they planned to squander their pay when they reached their homeland. Marcus sat close and watched Dominic until he fell into an exhausted sleep.

Dominic's dreams were of home and childhood, when he played barefoot with the warm grass tickling between his toes. He turned from his game to the nearby fringe of the woods, where he saw a small white wolf watching him. With ears pricked, it cocked its head, then stood up and loped into the tree line. The child followed, but as he entered the woods, the wolf shed its fur and Dominic shed his youth. Both were men and the sun was gone. *This will be our last night, unless you make your choice and stay with me*, Galen said across a distance that seemed to grow between them until it took the form of a river. Dominic watched the water swell and began to wade into the icy flow that rapidly rose into a torrent. Further and further it took him away from the beautiful man on the far bank.

Dominic bolted upright, waking Marcus from his doze. "Shit, you put the fear in me." He laughed, then saw the look of real fear in his friend's eyes.

"I have to go to him," Dominic muttered and stumbled awkwardly to his feet.

"What you need is sleep, centurion," Marcus said and attempted to get Dominic to return to his bedding.

"No," Dominic said firmly. "The sun is down and I feel him near. It is our final night, and I will not be stopped from spending it with him." As he spoke Dominic's hand rested on the hilt of his dagger. It was not yet drawn, but the threat was clear. He took a step backward.

The dogs howled their discontent, and Dominic looked into the gloom, where he saw the pale figure waiting outside the ring of light created by the campfires.

"You are bewitched, Dominic," Marcus said and held his hand out, beckoning him back. "Let me loose the dogs to chase him from us, and we will leave these shores before the sun sets another night."

Dominic shook his head and continued his backward steps. "I know my mind, and this is what I need, Marcus. Do not try to stop me, and I will return by first light."

It was clear there could be no argument. Dominic fled to where Galen waited, and together, they found sanctuary in the nearby woods.

"I cannot stay," Dominic whispered and ran his fingers through the fine blond hair, already feeling the waves of loneliness rolling off Galen. "Tomorrow I must sail to my homeland, and you will find another to sustain you; for if I stay, I will surely die, and my death is to be on a battlefield, not in the arms of a lover."

"I have endured long without you," Galen said in his strangely accented voice. "I can endure no more alone. You are not simply food to me." He struggled with his words, but his intent could not be mistaken. "My God changed me, and I will change you."

"There is no change in me, Galen. I must leave tomorrow because this is not my land and staying with you is not my fate," Dominic insisted, misunderstanding the meaning behind Galen's decree. "We have this night together, but it must be my last."

Galen remained passive while Dominic gently removed his threadbare tunic and planted a kiss on his cool white skin. Dominic's fingertips delicately traced a tattooed curve down the vampire's torso, following the motion with his tongue when he felt Galen's shallow breath falter. *You will leave me this night, Roman, but you will come back as I am.*

Strong fingers gripped Dominic's hair to haul his head back. Dominic stared up into Galen's predatory green eyes for only a moment before the vampire fell on his prey.

The force of the bite caught Dominic off guard, and he stumbled backward, but viselike hands held him steady.

The human in you will be taken. You will feel its death, and then we will be together.

The blood was dragged from Dominic's veins with a cold ferocity that brought both pain and panic, but each terrified beat of Dominic's heart only pumped the blood faster.

"Stop!" Dominic gasped in desperation, although the spreading numbness in his limbs made them ineffective against Galen's hold. His tortured veins screamed against the unnatural depletion of blood, and his unfelt blows weakened as the night blurred around him.

Galen stopped. Blood rendered black under the blue moonlight dripped from his lips, creating new and evolving lines down his chest.

It is almost done.

Dominic's vision faded. He fought the inevitable creep of death, but it was a battle he knew he would lose. Galen lowered him to the grass with surprising gentleness after his initial onslaught and lay next to him.

"I don't want to die like this," Dominic rasped.

Galen stroked back his hair and whispered, "You will die as I died and be reborn as much more than human."

It didn't make sense to Dominic, but none of what had happened in recent nights made sense to him. He forced himself to look at Galen, to focus on the bloody mouth, then up to witness the eyes that burned with green passion until they, too, faded from his sight. Dominic felt lips close once again over his broken skin, and there was only the briefest moment of panic when his heart slowed.

Galen swallowed, sensing the moment was right, and sat back to look down onto the still, expressionless face of the Roman. All fear had fled its features.

Your human life is leaving you, and you must drink of me now.

Sharp fangs rent the translucent skin of Galen's wrist, and he watched the red drops of his unnatural blood fall on Dominic's lips.

Taste of me.

Although hesitant at first, Dominic's tongue touched his lips and caught the next drop. Just a tiny drop, but it tingled, then burned, with promise, and Dominic knew he wanted more.

Galen smiled; their connection was forged. He lowered his wounded flesh to Dominic's mouth with soft, but insistent, pressure. There was no initial response until a dribble of blood trickled over Dominic's tongue. He swallowed, and small bursts of fire once again ignited within him. Dominic fought the deathly chill numbing his limbs and tried to reach for the offered wrist, but his fingers merely twitched before falling still.

Drink, Galen murmured in his foggy thoughts, and Dominic's lips made contact. His first attempt to draw the blood from Galen's vein failed, but steady drops of blood fell into his mouth, and his desire for the rich nourishment slowly increased. With each taste of the offered blood, Dominic's senses returned, and soon he was once again looking into Galen's eyes. Holding their intense stare, Dominic began to suck— slowly and ineffectively at first, then with a force that stole Galen's breath. Other than in the arms of his maker, Galen had not experienced the sensual pull of his blood being drawn.

Galen lowered his head until his lips rested on the tangled hair of his lover and whispered, "Does my blood please you?"

Dominic did not answer; he was lost in the passion of the blood that now surged through his veins and reasoned thought eluded him. His body, however, responded to the change, and his fingers once again found the strength to clutch fiercely at Galen. His nails bit into the white skin, creating small furrows of scarlet in the otherwise flawless surface. The pain was sharp, but rather than deterring Galen, it enflamed his desires, and he was barely able to contain his urge to bite and tear at the emerging vampire.

Galen groaned and mouthed the hair against his lips. Their connection grew stronger, and their fervor joined until their combined lust for blood and flesh became frenzied. Grabbing at Dominic's hair, Galen yanked him from the torn wrist, and they kissed with a bloody clash of teeth that split tender lips, while desperate fingers grabbed and clawed at each other lest their connection be broken.

It was Galen who sensed the intruder first. His hand closed over Dominic's throat to stop and pin him into the crushed grass beneath them. The smell and sound of humans were upon them mere seconds before the Romans emerged from the trees.

"Back away from him, demon," Marcus roared into the silence. The two legionaries who flanked him stood their ground despite their obvious terror.

Galen's face turned slowly to the group of humans, his eyes unblinking. The soldiers stepped a little closer to their commander, because although the talk around the camp had been of a night spirit, actually standing before a Roman officer lying, bloodied, with the ethereal specter froze the blood in their veins.

"Stand your ground," Marcus hissed, sensing their agitation. "Release him or die, demon."

Galen glanced down briefly into the blood-drunk gray eyes before running across the clearing with a speed that the humans would barely have registered as a blur. Sharp fingernails slashed a throat, leaving a startled soldier to fall to his knees, too shocked to stem the lethal flow. The other's neck was snapped with barely a pause, and Galen stood in front of Marcus.

Though he'd faced many enemies, the color visibly drained from the centurion's face.

Full lips parted in a bloody grin, and Galen spoke, "He is no longer yours, human."

"Back away or with the gods' help, you will not see the dawn," Marcus spat out, denying his primal instinct to drop his sword and run from the ghastly apparition.

"I killed my God," Galen said. "Understand that yours will not save you."

"Dominic," Marcus called, glancing past Galen in the hope that he could compel his friend to take action and aid him, but Dominic was facing his own fight. The new vampire's muscles cramped and cried out for fresh blood to fuel his transition, despite all he'd taken from his maker.

"He is *not* yours," Galen repeated coldly and took a step closer. "He notices only the scent of your blood. Do you need to see that he is gone from you, human?"

A chill surged through Marcus, threatening to weaken both his knees and his bladder, but Marcus's fingers tightened around the hilt of his sword, and he remained unmoved. "You do not frighten me, spirit," he lied and risked another glance at his friend, only to see that Dominic now watched, but made no move to aid him.

Unfortunately, Marcus's distraction proved fatal. Cruel teeth closed over his throat, and although Galen drank very little, the gaping hole pumped Marcus's life blood down his armored chest. With no thought of the dying man, Galen dragged him effortlessly to drop before Dominic as if presenting a gift. Galen smiled and gave his newborn child a tender kiss; it was fleeting, but enough that Dominic tasted his first human blood. He rose onto his elbow and looked down at his dying friend with hunger rather than sorrow. Dominic leaned over Marcus and licked carefully at the trail of blood that ran from the savaged throat. It lacked the vibrant rush of vampire blood, but it was hot, fresh, and contained life the other didn't. It was the first time Dominic tasted the sweetness of a final heartbeat.

MICHAEL sat silently. That was not the Dominic he knew. Galen's mind still caressed his, and with an involuntary shudder, he forced up his barriers so that only a whisper could be heard: *I made him and he made you.*

Michael shook his head. "No. Okay, that may have been how you turned him, but he's not like that. Not like you. And it wasn't like that for me."

It will be.

The words were not what Michael wanted to hear; they frightened him more than any mental battles about holding on to his human side because the hunger cramped his stomach and the tightening of nerves grew with each hour he didn't feed.

You thirst, young one.

Michael shook his head again, as if denial could quell his growing desperation.

It will make you as I am.

"Not as long as some of my blood, even just a little bit, runs in my veins," Michael growled. "Yep, I'm a vampire, but I'm never going to forget that I was born a human, and a big chunk of that person is still in here."

You will kill and rejoice in their blood as did your maker, Galen persisted, as if Michael's protest was not even heard.

"Is that why Dominic ran from you?" Michael asked as realization dawned. "Fuck! Now I get it. He wasn't scared of you like I thought he must have been, but scared of turning into what you are." Michael glared at Galen and expected anger in return, but what he heard instead was an amused chuckle. *My Dominic has killed many when he could have let them live, and so will you. You cannot deny what you are. His denial made him run once again and left you to me.*

"Bullshit!" Michael shouted, loud enough that it seemed to echo around the deserted park. "He wants to keep me safe. That's why he left me, and that's why he called you."

Are you safe, Michael?

The question stopped Michael dead in his tracks because he knew Galen could take him anytime he wanted, so there had to be another reason he was still breathing, one that Dominic may not have considered. Michael's anger subsided, and he sighed. "I know I'm not safe, but that's not Dominic's fault, is it? He wanted me to hide from you, but I didn't. There were things I wanted to know."

Do you know them now?

"Not everything, and maybe not nearly enough," Michael admitted. "All I know is that right now I'm tired and fucking scared that you'll go to Dominic and try to change him."

Galen smiled. *That is not for this night. Eventually, we will reunite, and he will see what we all are and join me once more, but for what remains of this night, I have other plans. Go now, young one, and sleep. My needs are no longer here.*

Michael looked for the truth in those green eyes and found nothing. An argument flittered briefly through his mind, and part of him wanted to call Galen out on his intentions, but every part of Michael, mind and body, threatened to betray him.

The thirst will only grow. What you endure now is only the beginning. Galen stepped down from the picnic table and stood in front of Michael. *I hunger too and leave you to feed.*

Michael wanted to say something wise or profound, but his head swam with images of blood that he knew were placed there by Galen to reinforce his need and physical vulnerability.

"Will you leave him alone?" Michael asked, too exhausted to continue playing games.

"I will not answer his call. That is not for this night," Galen said clearly. Michael felt the words float in the night air and watched Galen walk down the footpath, tight jeans, dark T-shirt, and boot heels clicking on the concrete as if he was any other denizen of Chapel Street.

Michael's progress home was not so elegant. He walked purposely in the opposite direction, hands buried deep in his pockets, hoping like hell he didn't encounter a hapless human on the way.

He hungered and it hurt.

The house was in darkness, and, as before, there was no sign Dominic had been there while Michael had been out scratching through both Dominic's past and his lover's trust. At least, that was how it looked to Michael. He all but fell onto the steps of the porch and buried his face in his hands. "I'm sorry, Dominic," he wept quietly. "I shouldn't have pried… shouldn't have…." There weren't words for the misery Michael felt. He was hungry, lonely, and didn't understand a lot of what was happening to him.

Michael sat lost in his own thoughts until a flock of Rainbow Lorikeets flew noisily overhead and roused him with the warning to get inside and take refuge from the approaching sun. The stairs that he would normally have bounded up two at a time bordered on insurmountable, and it was only with a tight grip on the handrail that Michael was able to make his slow progress to the bedroom.

It was exactly how he'd left it.

Michael lowered himself onto the unmade bed, and his last thought before sleep took him was of the pain Dominic must have endured alone in this room, waiting for starvation and death.

Chapter
TWENTY-TWO

ANOTHER tray of tiny gingerbread men were lifted out of the oven and carefully slid onto the cooling tray, where a whole crowd was already lined up. Abby gently touched a biscuit torso and tested the first batch to see if they were cool enough to start decorating. "Not yet," she said to the little figures and nudged them over to make room for the newcomers. She glanced across the kitchen at the cat clock on the wall, steadily ticking the night away with a regular swish of its pendulum tail.

To anyone else, it might have seemed strange to be baking gingerbread men at four o'clock in the morning, but it gave Abby a mundane outlet and calmed her frayed nerves. She'd endured the previous night tucked away in the crevice between her bed and the wall, then slept a few hours once the sun was up. The rest of the day she spent calling friends or visiting Scott's favorite haunts, hoping someone had seen or heard from him. From the first call, she knew he wasn't going to be with any of them, but it kept her occupied and almost stopped the dark and terrifying thoughts about the pretty blond man who had smiled at her.

When night came around again, Abby was already bunkered down in their home above the tattoo parlor, with all the doors locked and a deadly looking carving knife at the ready.

She'd only just begun assembling her requirements for adding iced expressions to each of the figures when she heard a faint noise downstairs. It could have been a passing pedestrian or wayward dog, but it was followed by the unmistakable click of their apartment door being unlocked. There was no sound of the door being forced, and apart from the one on her key tag, only Scott and Michael had keys, but her nerves jangled anyway. Something was not right.

Her fingers curled around the handle of the knife she had kept within easy reach on the bench, and Abby edged to the entrance of the small kitchen. The door was slightly ajar, and it crossed her mind to slam it shut and wedge a chair under the handle, but then what? It had no lock, and she doubted her old furniture would keep anything out for long. Instead, she stood and listened. Light footsteps grew closer until she heard them pause momentarily at the junction of doors. Abby could feel him out there, waiting for her to make a move. She held her breath.

The door opened slowly, and Abby backed away, brandishing the knife in front of the pale figure who stepped into the room. For a split second, it occurred to her that a vampire should not be standing there amid the canisters and cookies of her kitchen. But when Galen smiled, those needle-like teeth made it all too real. Abby waved the knife in warning, but the vampire continued to smile. It was then she noticed the copper key hanging from his hand, or more to the point, she noticed the key chain it hung from. On first glance, it looked like a thick blue cord, but Abby knew better, and tears prickled her eyes.

"What've you done to him," she asked, bringing her gaze up from the disembodied hank of hair. "You better not have hurt him."

"He lives," Galen replied.

"He better be okay, you prick, or you'll suffer for it," Abby growled, giving the knife a twist so that the overhead light caught the highly polished stainless steel to show she would fight for Scott, and for herself. "So have you come for me now?"

"I have," he said calmly, yet didn't move closer.

"Do you really just think I'm going to let you—" Abby started but was quickly silenced by the vampire's stare. "What are you going to do with me?" she asked instead.

Galen held out the hand that gripped her boyfriend's hair and said nothing.

Abby frowned. She knew she had to move closer to take it, yet making her legs move was a big task when her knees felt like jelly. She swallowed, and her gaze flickered between Galen's face and the human keychain. Slowly Abby edged forward, her feet shuffling over the linoleum floor, until her fingertips brushed the key. It swung away from her then back to where she could grab it. Abby avoided touching the blue hair, even though she had spent many hours twisting loose hairs back into Scott's dreadlocks in an attempt to give them some semblance of order. Tears sprung into Abby's eyes when she remembered the night Scott announced his "great" idea to sew the key onto the long cord of hair. "That way I'll always have it with me, and there'll be no more banging on the door waking you up when I forget it," he'd proudly stated, sitting at their kitchen table hunting through the old biscuit tin that doubled for a sewing kit looking for thread that matched his hair. *It was more purple than blue then*, Abby thought sadly.

There was a tug on the key, and Abby looked up at Galen. "Will you take me to him?" she asked, allowing her fingers to travel a little way up the cord while keeping her distance from the vampire's slender white fingers. She had a tiny glimmer of hope. The hair was a link to Scott, and there was no way Galen was going to take it from her now without a fight.

"You must take another with you," Galen replied. "Come, he sleeps soon."

He began to lead her, but Abby pulled back to carefully replace the knife in its slot in the block and take a breath.

"Okay, let's go," she said, not exactly sure what Galen was asking her to do, but if it meant getting to Scott, she was determined to get it done.

Abby clutched the hair tightly in her hand and walked a pace behind Galen away from Chapel Street and down to the older residential streets. Her heartbeat thumped loudly in her ears, and it pissed her off that Galen's vampire ears might hear her fear. They walked along the path, not speaking or communicating in any way, until Galen stopped.

"We are here," he said, looking not at her, but at an immaculate old terrace house. Although she'd never been there before, it was strangely familiar to Abby. She listened to what Galen told her, then walked up the driveway where a row of daffodils was beginning to die down, leaving only one bright-yellow head with the petals still untouched by rust.

Chapter
TWENTY-THREE

DOMINIC stalked the length of the empty room only to turn and pace back again. Day was fading into dusk, and he knew he could escape his confinement soon, but time passed slowly, and he was anxious to get out and put an end to Galen's game. He stopped near the boarded-up window and leaned his forehead against the crumbling wall. There was no denying he'd messed up the whole situation and made a mistake leaving Michael, unprepared and uneducated, to deal with the cruelty of fledgling hunger. His first instinct had been to draw Galen away, and even that had failed. Dominic had panicked, but it made sense at the time that Galen would follow him away from the city and away from Michael. A grimace contorted his features because his plan hadn't actually gone beyond that point. What had he thought would happen to Michael? Young vampires were vulnerable to their thirst, and Michael hadn't even tasted his first human blood.

Dominic knew that he'd left Michael alone and in pain.

"What game are you playing with me, Galen?" Dominic gritted out and banged his head lightly against the peeling wallpaper. Frustration with his maker combined with the frustration he felt over his own bad choices, and Dominic struggled to see a way out of the box he'd nailed them in. He turned and slid down the wall amid a shower of brittle wallpaper shards and plaster dust to wait out the time until darkness.

Do you remember the rise of your own hunger?

Dominic tensed.

You left your child to that.

It took Dominic a moment to understand the voice was not a lingering remnant of his human conscience, but the sibilant whisper of an ancient vampire.

"It is me you are chasing," Dominic replied, with the knowledge that Galen would hear him. "He does not concern you."

That you will be mine is not in question, but what of your child?

Dominic was on his feet in an instant, and he stared impatiently at the fading light through a gap in the boards. "Stay away from him! Do not even speak of him."

His mortality is gone from him, yet his humanity haunts him. Is that what drew you, Dominic?

"I will not speak of him with you," Dominic muttered angrily, his fingers already on the boards, ready for Galen to appear in the window once dusk arrived.

It was a false dream, child of mine. The thing you cherish most you have taken from him.

That stopped Dominic short. He couldn't deny the truth of it. From the first moment he saw Michael, Dominic was drawn to his warmth and light. Yes, he had tried to fight the desire to be near the young tattooist, but even now an involuntary shiver of pleasure ran through him at the recollection of the first time Michael's fingers met his skin.

"I know," he admitted softly to Galen. "I took from him what you took from me."

Do not mourn its passing. We are more than human. Let our prey keep their petty mortality and even smaller dreams.

"I almost believed you, once, but we were born human, and part of us will always remain human until our time is over." When no reply came, Dominic parted the boards. The last of the light was gone, and he climbed through.

The air of the new night was still; there was no breeze to rustle the dried flower heads of the weeds in the garden, and even the night birds were silent. Dominic looked down the cracked concrete of the driveway and said, "We are not gods, Galen. We are merely changed."

Dominic pushed through the rusted gates and looked upon a face he had not seen for many long centuries. Galen sat cross-legged in the overgrown grass at the roadside, beneath the branches of an old plane tree. Even though Dominic knew age would not have touched him, the vampire's delicate beauty almost swayed him to remember the love he'd had for his maker. Despite the modern garb, Galen was still the ethereal night spirit who had seduced him in an ancient grove of trees.

Galen looked up at Dominic and spoke, "Does not the very change make us gods?"

"No," Dominic said wearily. "It simply makes us different."

"I was given as a gift to a god and accepted."

"And you killed him. Can gods be killed, Galen?"

Galen emitted a soft chuckle. "Gods can be immortal or gods can die. How many gods have simply ceased to exist because there is no one left to worship them?"

"Who worships you, Galen?"

"Everyone I look upon; everyone who feels my bite."

Dominic sighed. When not consumed with Galen's and his own bloodlust, they had indulged in many such endless, and frequently pointless, conversations.

"Why are you here, Galen?" he asked. "Why now after all this time?"

What is time to us? Galen replied, returning to thought rather than words.

"Oh, do not start that again," Dominic grumbled, his frustration returning. "You left me alone, without interference, until I began to believe I was free of you, and yet here you are again."

"Did it please you, being alone?" Galen asked, unmoved by Dominic's comment.

"That is not the point."

"You denied your true nature for solitude. Yet that solitude did not please you, either."

"I deny that *is* my true nature."

"Yet they sensed it in you?"

There was no way Dominic could refute that humans avoided being near him, never mind accepting his touch, because he had lived many more than one human lifetime without the comfort of human skin on his.

"Could they not feel the predator?" Galen persisted at Dominic's hesitation.

"Not all avoided me, Galen. One brought me back when I believed what you told me and chose to end things rather than kill or curse him." The words were barely uttered when Dominic understood another part of Galen's game. "That's why you're here, isn't it? Michael?"

"I slept after you left. My land was changed and my forest ravaged, so I retreated to the earth and slept. Many dreams came to me of when wolves still hunted among the trees, and I longed for those times. Then the dreams stopped and time passed unnoticed until I felt you again. You were far from me, but you were strong."

"When was it you woke?" Dominic asked, although he had already guessed the answer.

You know when.

Dominic *did* know when. His life was renewed when he met Michael, and his love for the young tattooist had to be what penetrated Galen's sleep. Dominic met Galen's eyes and said with cold clarity, "I do know, and you will not touch him."

Galen tilted his head in a manner that made him look deceptively young. *He is the child of my child, so why would I do him harm?*

"Because I loved you, Galen, and if you were capable of it, I believe you loved me."

He knew you were mine.

"You are talking in riddles, Galen," Dominic replied angrily. "How could he know? There was a slight glimpse of a memory long gone when we joined, perhaps, but other than that, he had no knowledge of you and what we were. I did not want him to know."

You went to him, and he gave you my mark. Galen touched his T-shirt-covered belly, then reached toward Dominic's hip.

It took Dominic a moment to understand what Galen was telling him. "It was his trade, nothing more. Mere coincidence that it matched your scratchings."

Galen's hand retreated to slip under the fabric of his T-shirt. *Is coincidence not fate?*

Dominic made to answer, then realized he was once again being drawn into Galen's word games. "You will leave him alone, Galen. I will come with you if you leave him alone."

You will return to me anyway, Dominic. His thirst grows and will overtake him soon. Then you will see what we are and will understand.

Dominic closed his eyes and sighed. He would not be baited by Galen's distractions. "So *why* are you here?" he asked, slowly and deliberately.

I am here for you when the humanity in your little "sun" fails. Galen grinned and held his hand over his bellybutton, where Dominic knew Michael had his own tattoo—the sun that matched his moon. *He is safe and will spend this night with the crimson one and her mate as told, but his undeniable need will soon surface, then together we will go to him.*

Galen had a plan, that much was obvious, and Dominic knew from so many years of experience that his maker would not be diverted from his path. Michael was safe, and Dominic could ignore the danger the humans were in—at least for now.

"When can we go to him?"

When the moon rises again.

Dominic turned and motioned for them to move. "Why not tonight? Why not now?"

We will spend this night together. Sit with me, and we will remember.

Dominic looked down at Galen and saw the face he'd once loved. He sighed because there was little else he could do.

"I remember much, Galen," he said. There was no point in arguing, so he took his place among the weeds beneath the branches of the tree and felt his maker's hand touch his.

THEY'D taken him while he slept. Dominic had not been gone from Galen for more than three nights when they took him.

You can no longer be among them, Galen had told him, but Dominic refused to believe and told his maker he would prove him wrong, so when the sun fell each night, Dominic steadily made his way south to what he knew was a major Roman settlement. There he could go relatively unnoticed by Romans and Britons alike, or so he'd hoped, but by the time he reached the first outpost, Dominic knew that would not happen. It wasn't simply that he was an outsider. Dominic quickly saw that anyone he encountered gave him a wide berth or invoked the protection of their gods within his hearing. What he didn't see were the knowing nods of legionaries as he passed.

Dominic was still a fledgling vampire and subject to the coma-like sleep of day, so when he woke, it was with confusion at his changed surroundings. He moved cautiously around the small chamber that housed him. There were no candles to illuminate the room, but that did not hinder Dominic's vision. At first, he could distinguish no doorway, and solid bars lined every wall. Then, a sound above caught his attention. A latch was thrown and a hatch opened over his head, momentarily blinding him with the blazing light of a flaming torch.

"It is true, then, demon? You do wake at night." The disembodied voice spoke in Dominic's native tongue, then laughed at an unspoken jest. "It disgusts me that you were once a noble man of arms and now...."

A stream of hot liquid rained down on Dominic's bare skin, and the claustrophobic cell filled with the stench of urine. The hatch was slammed shut, and the chamber was once again plunged into darkness. Dominic wiped his hand over his wet skin and realized he'd been stripped of his few remnants of Roman garb and stood naked. He circled the walls again, hunting for a means of escape.

Dominic could only judge from his involuntary periods of sleep how long he'd remained in his prison, but it amounted to many nights, broken only by the jeers of curious centurions who spied on him through the hatch in the ceiling. As each night passed, Dominic's hunger grew, until it clawed at his senses every time the hatch opened and the air filled with human stink. *I am to die here*, Dominic decided and lay on the dirt floor waiting for the temporary death of sleep.

Death, however, was not the sport Dominic's captors had in mind. The curses and shouts of a hostile crowd dragged him back to consciousness. When Dominic stood, he was no longer in his dark cell, but caged in the middle of an arena surrounded by a small crowd of Roman dignitaries. They fell silent when Dominic cast his gaze over them—not in fear, but in anticipation of the coming spectacle. It was a familiar environment to Dominic, having witnessed games of combat or animal baiting, though none that caged the combatants. *Built for monsters such as me*, he mused before being hit by a wave of nausea.

Adrenaline and sweat combined with the lure of blood to assault Dominic's senses. He stood, dazed and grasped for the logic of the situation. The Romans knew what they were doing when they'd locked him away: starve the monster, weaken him, then fire up his bloodlust to create savage sport for their arena.

With the collective pounding of heartbeats swamping any chance of reason, Dominic simply remained still while he watched the heavy gates open. The crowd rose to their feet in anticipation of the brutality to follow. Two heavily muscled men entered, each smeared with blood that may have been their own, though Dominic doubted it. Both men were armed with nothing more than a short-bladed swords, and Dominic quickly understood that they were not gladiators but victims chosen to see out their days for the entertainment of the waiting crowd.

Though they moved quickly to either side of him, their stances were not battle ready, and fear rose from them like a heat haze. Dominic simply stood, still and silent.

Curious glances were swapped between the men before they advanced under the mistaken assumption that their foe feared them. What they failed to understand was the internal battle Dominic was rapidly losing. His thirst raged, and each breath of the foul air heightened its hold over him.

"Stay back," Dominic warned through gritted teeth.

He heard one of the men laugh, relief rather than mirth coloring the tone, and Dominic knew they did not want to be there any more than he did, but that made no difference to the vampire.

Dominic stared miserably at one man and said clearly, "I am sorry for what I must now do."

Confusion barely crossed the man's face before Dominic was on him. The blade hung uselessly from his hand for a few more seconds, then fell unused to the sand beneath his feet. The other watched, frozen in his own terror, as Dominic ripped at the man's throat and drank the still steaming blood. Only a few spectators cheered; most sat in stony silence, not prepared for the brutality of the outcome.

Dominic gorged on the still living blood; its heat pumped throughout his body and fed more than his flesh. Sharp nails clawed in bloodlust, leaving the fresh corpse nearly flayed of its skin and the scarlet-stained sand decorated with shredded flesh. It left Dominic filled, but not sated, and his attention turned to the ashen man clinging desperately to his sword and his sanity. However, Dominic's focus shifted to another beyond the bars.

A young man dressed in the rags of a tunic walked slowly around the cage, unnoticed by all except the vampire within. He was as tall as the heavily armored centurions guarding the gate, but a fraction of their bulk. Dominic watched the wraith-like figure unchain the entrance and walk without challenge toward him.

"Look down at your prey," he said softly, as if unaware of the frantic activity that had broken out around the cage. "This was once a man who lived and breathed."

Dominic stared at the ruined body and listened to his maker.

"But what are they to us?" Galen continued and walked close enough to drag his fingers through the blood spattered over Dominic's chest then place them briefly between his lips. Galen smiled. An observer in another time and place might have been charmed by the illusion of innocence in Galen's smile, but his sharp fangs and bloodied lips chilled Dominic to the core.

Dominic knew what he was and reached out for Galen's hand.

THEY sat in silence beneath the tree in the street deserted of human life. Dominic looked down at their joined hands and remembered. "Why was *that* the memory we needed to share?" he eventually asked.

You understood, that night. Your child will understand, this night.

"What have you done, Galen?" Dominic muttered in a desperate attempt to contain his anger and fear. It was pointless raging against his maker, he knew that, but the need to remain while Michael was a pawn in one of Galen's plans ripped at his heart.

He will feed this night. It will overtake his human will, and he will feed as you did then. Your child will sleep with a full belly and the knowledge that he is more than his prey.

"He will not be harmed," Dominic stated, not as a question.

He will not be harmed, Galen repeated. *And we will spend this night together.*

Chapter
TWENTY-FOUR

LIVING blood, gingerbread, and the unmistakable scent of Abby....

Sleep had only begun to retreat, but the human smell had already woken something else in Michael. It was always there, lurking and whispering to him, although Michael could usually push it away as a dark mood or divert its insidious message with his lover. But the vampire in him wouldn't be silenced in the heat of his bedroom. It clawed for dominance and was winning.

"Get out of here, Abby," he muttered with his face still buried in his pillow.

The sudden voice startled Abby, even though she'd known Michael would soon wake. She quickly straightened in the chair and stared at the bed. It was Michael—she'd seen him crashed on their couch or snoring on their floor many times when he couldn't face the walk home after a night of drinking with Scott—but at the same time, the man under the bed sheet wasn't him. Apprehension surrounded her like a swarm of bees, buzzing and nipping at her nerves.

Abby took a slow breath and said, "I can't go, Michael. He brought me here and told me to take you to Scott. He said we have to go together."

Michael stirred a little, as if testing his control over his body. "I don't think I can," he murmured, clutching and twisting the sheet with the effort of functioning through his pain.

Abby stood up and walked to the bed. She'd seen enough people suffering dependencies to understand a little of Michael's agony, even though her junky friends were less likely to tear her throat out.

"Come on," she said softly. "I know you, and I know you're stronger than this." Abby reached out and touched the cold skin of his bare shoulder. "You're still my Mikey no matter what else is in there. And anyway, that sexy man of yours wants us to stick together."

Abby's touch jarred and soothed at the same time, but the mention of Dominic momentarily dragged Michael away from his vampire. He pulled himself up onto his elbow and looked at Abby. "You saw him? I'm so scared. I can't do this without him, Abbs."

"I know, sweetheart," she replied, more than a little relieved to feel Michael push away the "other" she knew was growing in strength and making its presence known in his hollow eyes and waxen skin. Michael *looked* wrong. "He came to see me to ask if you'd come to me."

A wince of guilt crossed Michael's features. "He told me—at least I think it was real—to stay here and then go to you if I needed help," he said quietly.

"Then why didn't you come to me, sweetie?" Abby asked. Michael's distress was palpable, and it sickened her that she would soon drag her friend into Galen's web.

"I didn't do anything I was supposed to because I had to know, and it took too long, then… then I couldn't come to you, Abbs, in case I hurt you. You can feel it, can't you? You can feel what I am now?"

Abby *could* feel it. Not only had the colors that usually surrounded him faded, but that primal sense of danger tugged at her gut the same as she had experienced it that night outside Ink. It held none of the malice of that night, but it was a warning that something lurked in her friend that could do her harm. Abby shook it off; she didn't have time to dwell on it. "You're still my sweet Michael," she said and stood up. "And we have to go and get Scott."

THE walk to Chapel Street was slow. Michael forced himself to concentrate on putting one foot in front of the other, even though the bulk of his strength was channeled into blocking the bloody images his hunger danced through his mind at Abby's close proximity. They crossed through a small car park a block from Chapel Street and stopped. "I can't get any closer," he muttered and leaned against a lamppost.

"I can help you," Abby offered and made to reach for him, only to pull her hand back. "That's not it, is it?"

Michael shook his head, keeping it down so his dark hair covered his face. "It hurts so much," he whispered. "And I can hear them already… so many hearts beating."

"We have to, Mikey. Please," Abby begged, but she kept her distance. "He said it was the only way I could get Scott back, and I know he would kill him without even blinking." A strange thought crossed Abby's mind: When Galen stood in front of her in her kitchen, she couldn't actually remember those cold green eyes blinking at all.

"What if I do the same?" Michael asked, giving voice to a fear he'd held onto since the night at Hunters. "What if I can't control it, and I kill Scott?"

Abby stood looking at Michael. As much as she wanted to flip the question off and simply reassure him, Abby knew Michael deserved more. "I don't know," she replied honestly. "But I don't think you will, Michael. You're not like Galen. Dominic's not like him, either, because he would have died for you, right? You told me what he was willing to do to protect you."

Michael knew that, but all he wanted to do was slide down to the asphalt of the car park and cry. Everything hurt—body, heart and soul—but he pushed away from the lamppost and took a step, and then another. Abby's hand slipped into his, and they made halting progress to Chapel Street.

Abby watched Michael closely as they stepped onto the main footpath. The Windsor end of Chapel was still quiet, but she could feel Michael's disorientation among the few pedestrians who passed them.

"Keep going, Michael," she whispered. "We'll be away from them soon."

Michael didn't respond but continued his slow, yet determined, steps across the street and toward a side alley. He didn't ask where Abby was leading him because at that moment he didn't care.

Abby muttered the address Galen had whispered to her while counting down the numbers of each building they passed. They'd walked several blocks from Chapel, and Abby heard the clanking of a train as it drew to a stop at Windsor Station. They were close. The numbers appeared further apart as the architecture changed from retail to industrial, and they stopped in front of what was once a printer's warehouse.

"This must be it," she said and pulled Michael gently to the door. Abby jiggled the door knob, but it wouldn't budge. She peered through a gap in the newspapers that had been pasted over the window. It was too dark for her to really see anything, and there was no movement to catch her attention. Crushing despair tightened her chest, but she knew Galen hadn't lied. "Scott's here somewhere, I know it. Can you feel him?"

Michael closed his eyes for a few brief seconds. It was hard to get past the rushing of Abby's blood, but he frowned upon hearing another. "I think so... maybe?" Michael whispered and looked helplessly at the locked door.

"Okay, then; there has to be another way in," Abby stated resolutely and walked them a little further down the road to a back alley entrance. "Makes sense, I guess," she mumbled to herself. "Wouldn't do to advertise a hiding place, would it?"

A push at the back door opened it, and a cocktail of smells hit them: ink, machine oil, and something darker... *much* darker.

Michael emitted a low moan, and Abby knew not to ask what he'd picked up in the stench that assaulted them. Positive thoughts of seeing Scott alive and unharmed were all that kept her going, and she couldn't let anything squash them.

Abby made slow progress through the dark room, stumbling occasionally on the debris that littered the floor. She stopped and fumbled briefly in her pocket to pull out her phone. The little screen illuminated the room just enough to allow them to safely navigate their way down a flight of stairs to the next door.

With a slight crunch, the rusted doorknob turned and the stink intensified. Abby couldn't identify all she smelled, but for Michael, each was painfully obvious, and in amongst the reek of old sweat and urine was the malicious sweetness of blood and decay.

The faint light of the phone cast an eerie glow over the windowless room. A couple of shapeless forms were barely distinguishable in a far corner, but Michael's sharper eyes caught what they were looking for. "Scott," he whispered, and the soft sibilant sound bounced off the bare walls until a huddled mass well away from the others stirred. He blinked a couple of times until his eyes grew accustomed to the tiny square of light and croaked, "Hey."

Abby was at his side in an instant, leaving Michael just inside the doorway. "Hey, yourself," she whispered and wiped her fingers through the grimy stubble on his cheek. Her phone lay on the floor, so she relied on touch to find his lips, and despite his fetid breath, it was the best kiss they'd ever shared.

"Did he hurt you?" she asked as her hand explored the unbroken skin of his throat.

"Dunno," Scott mumbled vaguely, trying to get his head around exactly what had happened to him. "Don't think so. He had them for that."

Although Abby couldn't see them, she remembered the two heaps of what looked to be discarded clothing thrown in the corner and realized that's where the worst of the smell came from.

"I could hear him with them. They cried and begged him to stop. One stopped making any noise first; then the other one went quiet. He was a fucking vampire, Abbs. A fucking *vampire*!" Scott clung to Abby in the hope she would deny it—tell him it hadn't really happened and vampires only existed in schlock movies, but she didn't, and his voice diminished when he said, "I thought I'd be next, and I waited for it to happen, but he left me alone."

Michael listened from near the door and glanced over at the bodies of the two girls. They looked like they could have been curled together in sleep except for the dried blood matted in their hair and the mottled decay hastened by the hot airless room. As much as it revolted him, the tableau stirred his vampire, and he groaned, "We have to get out of here now."

Scott flinched at the unexpected voice and looked in its direction. "Here to rescue me, Mikey?" he joked feebly, then broke into a coughing fit.

"Something like that," Michael replied, distracted by the desperate need to get away from the smell of human ruin.

"Come on, Scott," Abby said and straightened to help him up. "Let's get you home and figure out what to do next."

Together, they retraced Abby's steps to the doorway, not noticing in the darkness that Michael backed away when they approached. Abby reached out and felt for the door that had closed behind them, but her hand did not close over a doorknob. Her fingers scrambled over the metal door plate, but merely poked at the hole where the doorknob had once been. "Shit," she cursed and crouched to feel around the filthy floor in the futile hope she'd find the broken knob. "It's a fucking trap...."

"Of course it is," Michael whispered and backed further away. "He knew… that's why you had to bring me here."

"Knew what?" Scott asked, but Abby had already figured it out.

"He knew you'd be desperate for blood and chose us for that, right?"

"I'm trying to fight it, Abbs," Michael moaned miserably and slid down the wall as far from his friends as he could get.

"What's going on?" Scott asked in a private whisper, but Michael still heard it.

"I'm like him," he said. "And he knows I'm starving, and it will make me kill you. Then he'll have me."

"We won't let that happen, sweetheart," Abby chimed in.

"You won't be able to stop me."

"But *you* will, Michael." Abby sounded surprisingly calm, considering her grip on Scott's hand had him wincing.

"Can't you just bust down the door or something?" Scott asked.

Michael shook his head, unseen in the darkened room, then said, "Only if I feed, and you don't want that."

"Fuck, man," Scott grumbled, then went silent.

They sat quietly for some time until Abby asked, "What about Dominic? Can you call him?"

"Won't do that," Michael replied quickly. "We know it's a trap, and I won't drag him into it too."

Scott was about to say something, but Abby gave his hand another squeeze to silence him. "You're strong, Michael. Even here you're strong, and I know you won't hurt us. We'll stay over here, okay?"

Michael made a sound that might have been an okay. With his knees pulled up against his chest, he closed his eyes and tried to reconnect with how things were before—before Galen, and even before Dominic.

Abby quietly filled Scott in on what had been happening, and even with all he'd been through, he found it hard to take in. He passed a half-drunk bottle of water to Abby without telling her he'd retrieved it from one of the bodies.

Michael was silent for the majority of the night, although Abby heard very soft whimpers of pain close to morning. She checked her phone, and although there was no signal, the time told her the sun would be rising soon.

"How're you doing, Mikey?" Abby asked into the dark.

Michael was drifting through his pain and couldn't immediately answer. He opened his eyes and stared, almost unseeing, at his friends. "Not too good," he said and hugged his legs a little tighter. "But I'll sleep soon, and maybe I won't wake up, and you'll be okay."

"Don't you even think that, Michael Chapman, because we're gonna get out of here and kick that blond bastard's arse, and you'll still be around to play with our grandkids."

"I'll try," Michael whispered. "I love you, Abbs. Even you, Scotty."

"I know, baby," Abby said, trying her hardest not to break. "I love you too. Now go to sleep and dream good dreams."

Michael went silent.

It was almost impossible to figure out how much time had passed in the dark basement when Scott whispered, "Do you think he's asleep?"

"I think so," Abby replied and tried to stand, not able to until her second attempt. She rubbed at her legs to get her blood flowing again, then tried to wiggle the pins and needles out of her toes. "Man, I seriously need to pee," she grumbled.

"Don't think it matters much where you go in here. I just found a wall away from them," Scott said, waving an unseen hand in the direction of the two girls.

"I'll hold it a bit longer, I think," Abby said, already preoccupied with turning on her phone to see if her signal had returned. It still displayed the tiny red SOS that meant people could call her, but she couldn't call out. She hoped like hell someone had woken up with a sudden urge to talk to her. "These walls must be bloody thick," she muttered and turned the light of the phone toward Michael.

He was still at the far end of the room, but his hold on his knees had fallen away in sleep and one lay stretched out in front of him while the other was curled beneath it. Abby wandered over and kneeled cautiously beside him to peer at the expressionless face. She ran her fingers through his hair and murmured, "Sleep well, sweetheart."

"Can he hear you when he's like that?" Scott asked.

"Hey, I'm no expert on vampires, and this is new to me, too, but from what he told me, they have to sleep during the day. Don't have any choice. But somehow I think he knows I'm here and can hear me."

"What about the other one? Does that mean he's asleep too?"

"I think so. I know I felt safe looking for you when the sun was up, but as soon as it went down...."

Scott relaxed a little for the first in what could have been days. Sure, he knew they were still trapped, but it helped knowing that the monster couldn't get to him for a while. He felt Abby snuggle in beside him again and put his arm around her shoulders. "I got scared for a while that I'd never get to see you again. I was sure he'd come after me when he'd finished with them."

Abby searched for his other hand and held it tightly. "Any idea who they… were?"

"They were already in here. I heard them crying, and one might have said Julie, but… oh fuck, Abbs, it was totally fucked up. I knew he was hurting them, but I was too damn scared to do anything about it." Shame radiated through the words, and Abby turned to give him a kiss, missing his lips, but managing to find his cheek.

"I keep thinking about it. Maybe I could have stopped him and saved at least one of them."

"You couldn't, Scott. Not against him. Believe me."

Scott made a soft sound that could have been a stifled sob, then said, "How the fuck can there be vampires? They're made up for books and stuff. They're not real, so how the fuck can my best mate be over there, with us waiting for him to suck our fucking blood?"

"You know, when he told me what his boyfriend was, part of me didn't want to believe it, but it made sense. Seriously, think about it. We all have our fears, and some we can put down to the everyday stuff we have to journey through, but others… they have to come from somewhere."

"But vampires, Abby? This is Melbourne, not fucking Transylvania."

Abby couldn't help but chuckle at the tone in Scott's voice. "Yeah, I know."

Scott stirred a little and asked a question that had been bugging him for a while, "Why us? Why did he take me just to lure you here? I mean if he's as strong as I think, he could have just grabbed us both and killed Michael as an afterthought."

"He doesn't want to kill Michael; he wants Michael to kill us," Abby said sadly, glancing in the direction she knew hid her sleeping friend.

"That's fucked up," Scott grumbled in his usual eloquent style, but it did sum up how they felt. "So is that how it's going to happen? Michael will wake up and…." Rather than finishing the sentence, Scott gave a growl.

"He's trying hard not to, and it's hurting him so much," Abby said. Not that she wanted Michael to feed on them, but she hated seeing her sweet friend killing himself for them. "He's dying, Scott."

Chapter
TWENTY-FIVE

ANOTHER storm was brewing.

The heavy dark clouds blotted out the sunset, and the air hung heavy enough to squash the workers who made their journey along the side street with newspapers tucked under their arms and rancid stains of the day's sweat marking their grimy collars. Dominic kept his face down and walked with purpose toward Chapel Street.

Dominic had woken before Galen. He'd forced his thoughts away from their shared dreams of the past and back into the derelict room. He would see Michael, and though Galen wove stories to suit his purposes, he never lied. Dominic looked at the still sleeping vampire and wondered at his destructive determination to prove to Dominic the humans that once existed in them were long gone. *What were you like before?* he wondered, not for the first time. The gentle, unmarked features made it all too easy for him to see the young man taken in the early stages of adulthood, rather than the killer that followed.

Galen's eyes flicked open, and he smiled.

I was adored and nurtured, ready for my time.

"But what were you *like*, Galen? Did you have dreams of your own?" Dominic asked, refusing to fall back into their old way of communicating.

Galen's face darkened, and he waved the fingers of one hand in dismissal. *They were of no importance. The simple dreams of a child; nothing more. I was meant for a bigger purpose.*

It was hard to read Galen when he did not want to be read, but the echo was there, and Dominic felt a hint of regret that vanished even before he was sure it existed.

Your concern is not for me, Dominic, Galen whispered in Dominic's mind. *You search for your young child and hope to see an end to me.*

How could Dominic deny that? He stared long at Galen, looking for any sign of the feelings they once shared, but Galen's features revealed nothing.

He will be as us, Dominic. With a full belly and wearing the blood of the humans he once called friends.

Dominic ignored Galen's grandstanding and said, "You told me if I stayed with you, then you would tell me where he is. So tell me now."

Galen tilted his head and looked at Dominic as if assessing his next move, then pushed up until his lips were close to Dominic's ear and whispered a number and a name.

Chapter
TWENTY-SIX

"ABBY?" It was a soft sound, almost spoken like a plea.

Abby jolted out of her fitful doze and sat, confused and disoriented in the pitch-black environment. Slowly, her exhausted mind began to piece together the events of the night before... or was it day before? Time had lost meaning when she couldn't regulate her body clock by the changing light of the sky. Abby could hear Scott's heavy "sleep breathing" and feel his body tight against hers despite the smothering heat of the room. She sat still and listened. Perhaps it was simply a voice from her dream? Were the two dead girls still whispering to her as they had while she slept? Were they still begging her in their little, lost voices to free them from the stinking basement to be returned to their families and final rest?

Then she heard it again and knew it was Michael. "I'm here, sweetie. We're both here."

"I don't feel right, Abbs."

Abby cursed silently because Michael certainly didn't *sound* right.

"Can I come over to you?" she asked and was already disentangling herself from her sleeping partner.

"Yes, please," Michael responded, although every word took another piece of his fading strength. "I can't hurt you anymore."

Abby's eyes were already blurry with as yet unshed tears when she turned on her phone, ignoring its low battery chime, and crawled over to Michael.

"I'm here, baby," she said and quickly pocketed the phone when she saw Michael wince away from the artificial light, but the sight she saw in those short, few seconds chilled her heart. Her sweet Michael was only hinted at in his emaciated features, and little life shone in his hollow eyes. Abby searched for his hand and wrapped her fingers over his icy skin.

"I didn't think I would wake up again," he said. "I hoped I wouldn't. But it's okay now. I can't hurt you."

The long held tears finally rolled down Abby's cheek, and she lifted his hand to her lips. "You were so strong, Michael, and I'm so proud of you. You showed him that you're better than he thought."

"I'm still human, aren't I?"

Abby forced the tears away with a flick of her hand and said as clearly as she could, "You never stopped being human, sweetie, no matter what he told you or what else has changed in you. The man I knew is still there. Nothing's gonna change that." Abby sat with him a minute or two longer until all her anger and frustration bubbled up. "Oh fuck it, Michael! This isn't fair, and there is no way I'm letting you go like this." She shuffled a little closer and took a breath. "I know you can control it, so you're going to feed on me, okay?"

Michael didn't answer.

Abby squeezed his hand and asked, "Did you hear me, Michael? You're going to take some of my blood, and we'll get out of here together."

A hand gripped her shoulder.

"I heard it too," Scott said softly. "And I'm not letting you do that." He knelt down beside them. "What do I have to do?"

"It's okay, Scott. I can do this, and... and he'll feel me inside, talking him through it."

The whole situation terrified Scott, but he was determined. The thought of losing Abby was even more unbearable than dying in that stinking room, plus he had another reason why he needed to do it.

"No, Abby. I need to do this more than Michael needs my blood. Please understand, Abbs; I couldn't help them, and that keeps screwing with my head. Anyway, I think it would be better for me to do it so you can help us, you know, talk to him."

Abby hated the idea, but she knew Scott was right. He needed to do it, and she *could* help guide them. At least she hoped she could.

They carefully swapped positions, and Scott felt for Michael. "Fuck, you're cold, mate, but we'll warm you up," he said with false bravado, attempting to cover the absolute terror that threatened every ounce of his courage. "You better still be with us, Mikey boy, 'cause I'm making a pretty noble gesture here, and you're gonna owe me big time." When there was no response, he gave Michael a gentle shove. "Don't you fucking conk out on me now, mate."

Scott felt Abby move away from him, but her hand touched him almost immediately from the other side of Michael. Soothing fingers stroked down Scott's arm, then closed around his wrist. "We may need a patch up job on your tat after this, but Mikey can do that for you," she said and imparted as much positive energy into the room as she could muster. Slowly, Abby lifted Scott's wrist to Michael's mouth, then released it to wrap him in the cradle of her arms.

"You won't hurt him, Michael. We're here to get you through this, and we'll show Galen that we love you, and you want to stay with us," Abby said in a soft murmur.

Michael stirred. His lips mouthed the warm skin, but he didn't bite.

"Dominic knew you would be okay if you came to us, didn't he? He loves you so much, Michael, that he left to keep you safe, and now you have to prove that you can be strong enough for you two to be together again."

Abby felt a tickle at the edge of her mind. It grew and began to take form until she heard Michael clearly and without the limitations of his body. *I love him, Abby.*

I know you do, sweetheart, and that's why you have to do this. Drink just enough of Scott's blood to survive.

I'm scared, Abby.

Your vampire is there, Michael, but so are you.

I'll try not to hurt him.

I know you'll try.

Scott felt a little pressure on his wrist, then a scratch. He thought he was ready for what would come next, but if it weren't for Abby's quiet encouragement, he would have yanked his arm away at the first penetration. It wasn't so much that it hurt, although it *did* hurt, but Scott had to steel himself against the horror of the acts he'd heard committed by the other vampire against the two girls.

The pull on his blood was weak, and Scott lifted his other hand to Michael's head and pushed trembling fingers through the thick curls.

"It's good stuff, mate," he said, forcing out the words with a long breath. "Not exactly vintage, but chemical-free for a change."

Abby smiled, and the arm around Michael extended so her fingers tickled over Scott's arm.

The first drops of blood sat on Michael's lips. They burned. He sucked once, and it was enough for Scott's blood to reach his tongue. Michael pulled a little harder and swallowed his first mouthful of human blood, felt its fiery path sear down his throat and into his belly, warming and waking his body.

Michael became aware of the arms surrounding him, and the words spoken joined those in his thoughts, urging him to take more. He began to drink, and as the blood surged through him, it also woke his thirst. It crept out and expanded to ripple through his flesh, demanding more, demanding all.

It's taking me, Abby. I can't stop it.

Abby had felt his hunger seconds before the warning and was ready.

"Talk to him, Scott. Remind him of who you are and who he is," she said, calmly so Scott would understand this could be done if they worked together to help Michael fight, rather than fighting Michael.

Scott gasped at the increased pain, but listened to Abby. "Hey, Mikey," he rasped, then cleared his throat and tried again. "Hey, do you remember that night after Soundwave? The last band was done, and we'd had too many fucking beers. You'd lost your train ticket so we jumped the barriers together...."

Abby's fingers stroked Scott's arm, urging him to continue.

"We stumbled into Ink and fell up the stairs, laughing and trying to sing Rob Zombie songs, until we got to the bedroom where Abbs just shook her head and lifted the quilt so we could crawl into bed together, still wet from the rain. Do you remember that night? The three of us together under the quilt."

Michael only heard half the words through the rush of his friend's blood, but the image was clear in head. Their connection was forged. It didn't stop the cruel ripping of his hunger, but both Abby and Scott were there, sharing his thoughts under that quilt above Ink. He clung to the image and let his friends embrace him. The hunger was there, and Michael acknowledged his thirst as part of him, but it was not *all* of him.

I remember.

Both Abby and Scott heard and felt the change. Michael's mouth left Scott's wrist, and he gently licked the wounds.

"You had enough, kid?" Scott asked, even though he was more than a little relieved that Michael had stopped.

"No," Michael said honestly. "But it is enough for now." He tilted his head back to look at his friends, even though they couldn't see him in the dark, and whispered a thank you.

"Do you think he'll come back, now it's night?" Scott asked, rubbing his fingers carefully over his aching wrist.

Michael was about to answer when he sensed someone near and tried to sit up.

"What is it?" Scott hissed, startled by Michael's sudden movement. "It's him, isn't it? He's here for us."

Abby smoothed her hand over Scott's matted dreads and said, "I don't think so. Help Michael up."

With a tangle of exhausted legs, the trio made it to their feet and stood in a huddle facing what they knew to be the direction of the door.

"Dominic," Michael whispered and stumbled toward the entrance of the basement.

"Are you sure?" Scott asked, not yet willing to follow.

"He's sure," Abby answered with a small smile. "I can feel him, too, and so will you if you trust your instincts."

Dominic's step quickened. For so long, he'd either blocked or been blocked from Michael, but he felt him. He was close. Very close.

I hear you....

He scanned the buildings, not even considering the address he'd been given because it didn't matter; he didn't need it. Dominic could hear his love and feel him, and for the first time in many nights, he felt hope.

Michael scrabbled at the door, frustrated that he still lacked the strength to break it, to pull it from its hinges, but then his fingers halted. With his palm flat against the solid door, he knew Dominic was on the other side.

"Dominic?" he murmured, as if unwilling to believe what his heart and soul told him.

"I'm here, Michael," Dominic answered and turned the rusty doorknob.

Michael took a staggering step back when the door pushed open, and he stood in the filth of the basement looking at Dominic. Neither moved for several seconds until Dominic gently cupped Michael's cheek and whispered, "I'm sorry."

Michael leaned into the touch as if it fed him more than the blood he still craved.

"He was strong, Dominic," Abby said from behind Michael. "He fed just enough to keep going and no more."

I should not have left you.

Michael looked at Dominic and said, "I didn't understand why you left."

"I thought... no, I didn't think clearly," Dominic sighed and pulled Michael closer. "I have run from him many times, and he always found me."

You loved him once, Michael sent, not wanting the others to hear.

He was my maker.

But it was more than that, wasn't it?

It was impossible for Dominic to deny that he'd loved Galen, but that was past. Dominic looked at the couple clutching each other and had some inkling of what might have happened, and then his attention turned to the far corner. The girls had suffered at Galen's hands, and there was nothing more he could do for them, but he still grieved their passing in that anonymous place. "We need to leave this feeding ground."

There was no argument, and they fumbled their way up the stairs, not willing to release their holds on each other.

A bright line of lightning streaked through the swollen clouds, followed almost immediately by an ear-splitting crack of thunder. The storm was directly above them.

"Prophetic," Scott muttered and stepped out of the door into the back alley. He sucked in a gulp of the warm night air that pressed down, needing it to clear his lungs of the death that filled them. "So, what now?"

Dominic remained silent, simply holding Michael against him until they could find a private place to feed.

Abby linked her arm into Scott's, glanced briefly at the open door behind them then back to Scott. It was the first time she'd actually seen him in what seemed an eternity. His face was smeared with grime, broken only by trails of sweat, and blood edged the collar of his T-shirt, but what hurt her most was the lost expression in his exhausted eyes. Without looking at the others, she said, "I'm going home. I want to pee in a real toilet and take a long, very long shower."

"Simple as that is it, Abby?" Scott said, with a sharp edge to his voice that Abby had *never* heard before. He turned to the vampires. "It's not over, is it? He didn't get what he wanted down there, so he'll come after us and finish the job, won't he?"

"Scott," Abby said softly, trying to calm him, but Scott wouldn't be silenced.

"We have to know this, Abby, or we're just fucking kidding ourselves. As much as I love Michael, this was never our fight, and now we wait for that fucking monster to come back and finish what he started."

Abby began to speak, but Dominic held up his hand. "Scott is right. This should never have been your fight. It should never have been Michael's either. I brought this on you all, and I will have to end it, but for now I think we do what Abby suggests."

"You'll stay with us? At Ink?" Abby asked.

"No!" Scott interjected. "Haven't you heard anything that's just been said? They're gonna bring him straight to us."

"Scotty, listen to me, please," Abby said, well aware that Scott wasn't coping with their new reality, and why should he after the trauma he'd suffered? "Galen had planned for us to be dead by now, so do you really think he's going to let that go, even if Michael and Dominic leave right now? I want them to stay the night with us so at least we're all together. He's going to find us whether they're there or not, and, hey, I'd rather put up a fucking good fight than provide him with dinner."

Michael had listened to the exchange and reached out to Scott. He didn't say anything the others could hear, but a little of the tightness in Scott's chest eased, and he clutched his friend's hand.

Together they walked to the front of the empty warehouse, where Abby stopped.

"Come on, Abbs, we have to get away from here," Scott urged her.

"In a minute," she mumbled, distracted by her search for something. Abby unhooked her arm from Scott's and walked over to a construction dumpster, where she picked up a large chunk of concrete. She weighed it in her hands, then turned and, without hesitation, flung it through the window, leaving the newsprint-covered glass hanging in shards. Abby then retrieved another object, threw it through the window of the premises next door, and grinned when an alarm screeched loudly at them.

"That'll get people here, and they'll search the place. Then the girls can go home," she announced and pushed the others to hurry away from the wreckage of the windows.

"You're a fucking lunatic," Scott laughed and grabbed Abby's hand to follow her.

Chapter
TWENTY-SEVEN

THE rain finally broke by the time they made it to Chapel Street. What started as a few bloated drops quickly became a torrent, sending pedestrians scurrying for cover under shop canopies and into cafés. Four did not run from the rain, but let it wash over them, cleaning away days of filth.

When they reached the painted window of Ink, Scott looked at the demonic eyes staring back at them and muttered, "I'm gonna have to change those windows; been meaning to do it for a while anyway. Too old school, right?" He automatically reached for the dreadlock with his key, but his hand stopped moving midway, remembering his shock when it was brutally torn from his head.

Abby's fingers closed over his, and Scott felt the little key in his palm. He looked down to see his blue cord of hair hanging from it.

"You've got plenty of dreads, Scotty; we'll sew it on another one."

Scott nodded, opened the door, and walked into the place he loved, but no longer felt safe in. "I thought vampires had to be invited into your home?" he said and stood near the door as if waiting for Galen to appear.

"Sorry, man, it doesn't work that way," Michael said as he made his way to the overstuffed sofa and eased himself down. "But he's not here."

Dominic followed Michael to the sofa and sat next to him. "Michael's right. I felt him near the warehouse, watching and listening to us, but he's not here."

"But he knows we're here," Scott said.

"He knows, and when he comes, I need you both to leave this to me. One way or another, it will finish."

"One way or another," Scott said sadly, not liking the sound of that, but he knew there was little he could do. He nodded and rubbed his hand over Abby's back. "Let's go have that shower, Abbs."

Michael waited until his friends had gone upstairs to their apartment before he asked, "What did you mean when you said one way or another it'll finish, Dominic?"

Dominic sat forward on the sofa, not able to look at Michael. "I need to make amends, Michael. What I did to you was unforgivable."

"I'm okay," Michael said, staring at Dominic's back, not sure if he'd welcome his touch. "You told me to stay in our house, and I didn't. I knew he was dangerous. Fuck, the first time I saw him it was like I was in a Marilyn Manson video or something. I wanted to know about you, and instead of waiting for you to tell me, I went to him when he offered. I messed up. I should have trusted you, but I messed up."

Dominic finally turned to face Michael. "I didn't tell you because I didn't want you to know what I was. What we all are."

"But that's the point; *we're* not like him."

"We're *all* like him, Michael."

"Then maybe he's not what we thought."

Dominic frowned and shook his head. He couldn't entertain any other thought except that Galen was a killer with no humanity left to temper his hunger. "Do not be fooled, Michael. He wanted you to starve until your thirst forced you to do inhuman acts on those you love. It *is* his way."

Despite what had happened to him, or maybe because of it, Michael couldn't believe there was no human self left in Galen. "Think about it, Dominic. Galen was human, and all his human life he was fed shit about how special he was and what vampires were. He was turned and still believed it, but, I dunno, just because he believes it doesn't make it true."

Dominic could see where Michael was heading with his speech and stopped him. "All I know is that I believed I could keep you out of all this and keep him away from you," Dominic mumbled and turned away to stare at the dizzying array of tattoo designs that covered the opposite wall rather than face the questions in Michael's eyes.

Michael's hand finally found its way to Dominic's back and rested there. "I know you did," he replied, moving his fingertips just enough to show Dominic he was okay with it.

Dominic's head hung low, and he gave a small shake. "It's not okay, though. All along, right from the very start, I knew I shouldn't get involved with you and drag you into this shadow of a life." He sneered at the very idea that what he had lived was a life. "I knew it, Michael, but I couldn't stop needing you."

Michael curled his fingers again and said softly, "I don't think people are meant to be alone."

"That's part of the problem, if not all of it," Dominic said, with a disgusted grimace, and slid back into the sofa. "Did I give up that right when I turned? Do we still deserve to be with another soul?"

"Hell, yeah, how can you even question that?" Michael said with a tired smile. "Do you love me, Dominic?"

"Don't ever doubt that." There was no argument to Dominic's love, and he drew Michael to him with a gentle kiss. The taste of the blue-haired tattooist lingered on Michael's lips, and so did his terrified protests that Galen would follow them.

Scott had been correct. Galen was close, very close. Dominic felt his presence even while he held Michael in his arms, and he knew, one way or another, it would end for them that night.

"Stop, Dominic, I don't want him with us right now," Michael murmured, having sensed Dominic's thoughts. "Just you and me right now, okay?"

Another soft kiss before Dominic gently pushed Michael's mouth from his lips down to the slowly pulsing vein in his neck. The offer didn't have to be spoken, and Michael didn't hesitate. Michael pierced the unblemished skin swallowed the heady richness of Dominic's blood, but only a mouthful before he eased back and looked into his lover's eyes. Michael smiled.

"See," he whispered. "It didn't take over. It might be part of us, but it isn't all of us."

Dominic nodded and stroked his thumb over Michael's cheek, where the short stubble had grown into a sparse beard. Michael looked tired, and his olive skin had paled a shade, but beneath all that, he was still Michael. "You are stronger than I gave you credit for," Dominic murmured.

"I don't know if it's strength," Michael said and licked at the fine dribble of blood meandering down Dominic's neck. "I just know who I am now." With a brief smile, he sank back to feeding, drinking with an insistent, but not desperate, pull.

Dominic closed his eyes and pushed his fingers through Michael's hair. They didn't share images or memories, simply intimate touches and thoughts. Time to reacquaint and reassure each other that they were together again and forgiveness was not necessary.

When Michael's lips stilled and his body warmed, he simply held on to Dominic and said, "I don't think he ever planned to kill me. He called me the child of his child."

Dominic sat in silence, pondering that thought, then turned to look through the store toward the tattoo workroom. "I am his child, but not what he is, and you are my child and not what I am," he muttered and tightened his grip on Michael.

"He was human like us too," Michael said softly and glanced at the curtained doorway. "I think he's just forgotten that."

Dominic slowly released Michael and stood. He held up a cautionary hand and bid Michael to stay where he was.

"I don't think so," Michael stated and stood up beside him. Dominic's blood added to Scott's and pumped through his body like a shot of adrenaline. Although he wasn't at full strength, Michael was determined they would face whatever happened next together.

Dominic cast a warning look that Michael chose to ignore. Small sounds drifted through from the back room: drawers opening and their contents being shuffled and searched, followed by what sounded like an ink trolley being shoved across the floor. Dominic frowned and walked slowly, cautiously, toward the curtain. Galen was distracted; Dominic could feel it.

With Michael a step behind him, Dominic's fingers closed on the edge of the curtain and drew it back.

Beneath the harsh neon lights, Galen's skin shone white, like it had that first night under the moonlight. He stood naked in the center of the room with only the ink trolley beside him. Slowly the figure looked toward the doorway and held his hands away from his sides. The long slender fingers were stained dark with black and blue ink that dripped into small murky pools next to his bare feet. Tiny spatters marked his pale legs. Galen's smile was childlike when he gazed back at the daubs he'd drawn on his skin.

Dominic edged a little closer, but motioned for Michael to stay behind him.

"Why are you here, Galen?" he asked quietly, with a forced calm. Something had changed in his maker that Dominic couldn't yet fathom.

The startlingly green eyes met his for barely a moment before once again focusing on his exposed skin. "My story isn't finished," he replied cryptically and pressed a blackened fingertip lightly against one of his original tattoos. "This tells of when I was born." Galen's touch slid to another image. "This told all *why* I was born."

Michael had seen the tattoos in the tale he witnessed, but watching Galen's loving caress over the crude image elicited an uneasy shiver.

"This told all I was not to be touched by any but the night spirit. It was for him alone to take my purity." Galen looked up. "I never knew an embrace until that night, but my skin ached for it. Can we miss what we never had?"

Michael pressed closer to Dominic's back and sought out his hand.

Galen didn't wait for an answer before his stained finger moved over his skin, smearing thin trails of ink in their wake. They circled the circumference of the moon symbol. "I was his. All others offered to him were rejected, and they died still pure from touch. One by one, I watched as they fell to the forest floor, necks broken. But then he looked upon me, and I was his."

Galen smiled again, but this time his lethal fangs shone under the raw white light.

"We know this story, Galen, and it does not answer my question," Dominic said while he tried unsuccessfully to read Galen's mood.

The smile faded, but Galen continued to run his finger down the line of symbols. "Each one explains who I am, where I come from, and finally, where I was supposed to find an end."

His hand stopped.

"But I did not end."

"No, you didn't end," Dominic repeated and watched the ancient vampire distracted with smoothing his hand over his bare skin.

"There were no more pictures," Galen said softly. "So I knew I had to become him. The god I believed him to be ended by my hand, and I knew I was no longer human."

Galen dipped his fingers back into the ink he'd poured all over the top tray of the trolley and added another off-center swirl to his freehand drawings until they resembled a crude crescent moon.

"Then you found me," Dominic said, entranced by the care Galen was putting into such artless images.

A brief glance at his child, then Galen drew a series of indecipherable symbols, not concerned with the fine trails of ink that trickled down his leg. "I showed you what he had taught me to be so you could become like us."

"But you did *not* show me that *I* still exist too," Dominic murmured and felt Michael squeeze his hand when he moved another step closer, only to see Galen take a single step back.

"What do they mean? The new symbols?" Michael asked, seeing Galen's hesitation and confusion at Dominic's advance.

"My children," Galen said and pushed his fingers back through the ink.

"Children? Does that include me?" Michael released Dominic's hand and stepped up beside him.

Galen's head tilted to one side, and he looked at Michael with an unreadable expression. "I had thought so."

When Michael moved a little closer, Dominic touched his hand to stop him, but Michael continued very slowly toward the elder vampire. "Why only thought so? Am I not the child of your child?"

"The apple has fallen far," Galen muttered.

Michael frowned. "Is that because I'm different from you?"

Galen stared at Michael until the young tattooist found it difficult to stand his ground, but he was determined to get an answer. Finally, Galen removed his fingers from the ink and held them in front of his face, watching the dark ink run down between his fingers and find their path through the creases of his palm, then down his arm.

"Draw your mark on me," he murmured, and his focus shifted from his stained fingers to Michael.

"Stay away from him," Dominic growled under his breath, and it could have been directed at either vampire, but Michael reached back and gave Dominic a reassuring touch before taking the few steps to the ink trolley.

He looked at the mess of murky ink spread across the top tray and was tempted to discard it altogether and find a marker. But Michael wouldn't deny Galen his touch. He stood directly in front of the pale body and looked over the smooth planes of Galen's skin. The ancient vampire's apprehension was almost palpable. "Why do you fear this?" he asked softly.

"I do not fear it."

Michael's hand rested lightly on Galen's chest despite the silent warnings that radiated sharply from Dominic. They stood for several seconds, until Michael nodded and stepped away. He turned to the ink tray and lifted a small bottle of scarlet ink, poured some of its contents into his cupped hand. Slowly it swirled around his palm, until he clenched his fist over it. Bubbles of red seeped between his fingers, but Michael only smiled at it and opened his hand to show Galen.

The red palm pressed against Galen's left breast and was held there while Michael looked into those green eyes and said, "This is my mark. It is not the sun on my belly, but a human hand print to show I was here, and I am still here. Just as you are still here."

Galen looked down at the hand on his skin. The scarlet ink pooled under the fingernails and formed little wells at the cuticles that used to be bitten and raw. The hand was as slender as his, but it still held the hint of sunlight and, despite its cool touch, Michael's hand warmed him.

"This will remind you that we remain," Michael murmured and eased the hand away, leaving the almost luminescent handprint.

Galen stared sadly at the mark and whispered, "Too far from the tree. He was all I should be, but I am not. I was not meant to survive beyond my time because I was his offering, not his equal."

"You talk in riddles, Galen," Dominic said quietly, uneasy at the direction Galen was taking.

"I was his child, but he was to end me," Galen said and looked at Michael's red-stained palm. "Is this why?"

At first Michael didn't understand what he was being asked, but then he felt the whisper of Galen's memory of his maker: waves of fear and awe, but below that was an undercurrent of need and....

Michael frowned. "You wanted him to love you."

"I was his lamb to be sacrificed. I would give pleasure, then join the others on their funeral pyre to leave this earth in flames."

"Abby and Scott were to be my 'sacrifice', weren't they?"

Galen glanced up to the peeling lilac ceiling, above which he knew the two humans held each other against their terrors. He nodded.

"And I didn't kill them," Michael continued.

"You should have."

"But I couldn't kill them because I love them, and I understand now that no matter what you believe and want *us* to believe, we are all still human," Michael said, determined to ignore Dominic's silent warning not to pursue that line of thought.

"I was wrong," Galen admitted and looked past Michael to Dominic. "My child was to be a god like mine, but can the shoot be as strong as the tree? Does the purity of the blood falter with each making?"

Michael turned and glanced briefly at Dominic, but answered the questions himself. "I don't think *you* were ever like your night spirit, Galen."

"Michael!" Dominic warned quickly, as Galen's fearful rage erupted, but it was too late for Michael to react. Galen's fingers clamped around his throat and stopped any possibility of escape.

"Do not do this, Galen," Dominic hissed but didn't advance on them when he saw that the murderous gleam in Galen's eyes was fueled by fear and misery. "He is young and doesn't understand."

"You could never deceive me, child, and yet you lie to save his life," Galen muttered and tightened his fingers.

"I would do *anything* to save him," Dominic said, with such conviction that Galen broke his deadly grip on Michael for a bare second, but it was enough for the young vampire to pull back, leaving Galen with only skin beneath his nails.

Dominic leaped forward, and the hold was reversed. With fingers wound tightly around Galen's throat, he slammed his maker back across the small room until the pair hit the shelves with a force that rained assorted jars, bottles, and boxes down over then. Glass shattered on the floor, and the stench of paint thinners filled the air and burned their nostrils.

Michael leaned against the bench of his workstation and coughed until his lungs were filled with the acrid air. "Dominic, don't. Please don't," he pleaded. "Galen could have killed me the instant he touched me, but he didn't."

Dominic heard the words, but didn't relax his hold.

"Even now," Michael said softly, "you know he could brush you away and slaughter us all if he wanted. He's stronger than both of us."

A voice came from behind, and Michael felt Abby's gentle touch. "Listen to him, Dominic," she said. "As much as I might want you to just close your fingers and finish all of this, I don't think he'd stop you."

Dominic frowned and held his maker's gaze. "Is that what you want, Galen? Do you want me to kill my maker like you killed yours?"

Galen didn't respond, but he couldn't hide the truth in his eyes.

Abby moved up beside Michael, where she stood still encircled by Scott's protective arm. "He's afraid, Dominic. Can't you feel it? He's afraid that everything he thought and believed he was is a lie."

Dominic *could* feel it hanging between them. Galen had lived his centuries fighting heart and soul, only to have it all crash in on him in the space of a single night. Dominic loosened his grip, knowing full well it had never really controlled the ancient.

"All those years of blood," Dominic whispered. "All those years, did you honestly believe your humanity had died with his bite?"

Galen blinked, and his eyes lost their focus. *What else could I believe?* he asked silently. *My marks tell of who I am and when I was to end, but when the time came I could not fulfill my destiny. I fought him, and through his arrogance, I defeated him. Who kills a god, Dominic?*

"He was no more a god than we are," Dominic said almost sadly, watching the crushing realization seep into Galen's thoughts.

One by one, those who bore the marks I was given died. Each saw their fate and accepted it, knowing they would return to their family and be honored in the funeral flames.

"You wanted to live, Galen, but you didn't know how."

Galen's eyes regained their focus, and he looked at Dominic. "Your child chose to die for them," he said, and his gaze wandered to the couple standing with Michael, looking incongruous in their rumpled pajamas and faded T-shirts.

Abby smiled sadly and said, "And we couldn't let that happen, any more than Michael could let Dominic go."

"It's true," Michael jumped in. "Dominic chose to die rather than inflicting what he thought was a curse on me, but it's not that at all. He didn't make me a monster."

Galen's pain filled the room and enveloped them when he asked, "Would you have died for me?"

Michael stared in confusion, but Dominic knew the question was for him. "I loved you, Galen, despite what you made me do. I loved you then and would have done anything to protect you, even though you never needed my protection."

"We all need protection," Galen whispered.

"Even those who believe they are gods?"

"Even those."

Dominic turned away and walked toward Michael. He could feel Galen's eyes on his back, but more than that, Dominic felt his emptiness. Michael's expression told him he felt it too. When Dominic stood beside his lover to face his maker, Galen once again looked very young. He stood alone at the back of the workroom, his naked skin marred with trails of dark ink and his long fair hair stained where it touched the crude finger paintings. Galen's attention fell to the red handprint, and he covered it with his palm, only to taint the pristine ink with dark smears.

"You loved me then, and I love you still," Galen said in a hushed tone, without looking up.

"Then leave me in peace," Dominic answered with equal quiet and felt Michael press a little closer.

Galen stood very still. His hand slipped down his body, smudging the newly drawn "tattoos." He crouched close to the floor and placed his palm over the pieces of broken jar and paint thinners. The ink swirled from his hand and marbled through the clear fluid. He watched it for a moment, then reached for a fallen bottle of turpentine, only to crush it between his fingers. Its contents spilled from his hand to swell the pool around his feet. Galen watched it spread for a while, then reached for an unseen object tucked under the nearby workstation. He stood up.

"Just leave, Galen. Please," Dominic whispered and held his hand out behind him to force the others back toward the curtained doorway.

"Do you believe I would die for you?" Galen asked, his hand wrapped tightly around something small and shiny.

"Galen...," Dominic murmured, "I would never ask that of you." After a quick glance of warning at Abby, Dominic continued. "This should be between you and me. Allow the others to leave, and we will talk."

Abby tugged on the loop of Michael's jeans. "Come on, Mikey, they need to talk, and we need to give them some space."

"I'm not going anywhere," Michael stated defiantly and stood his ground.

"Please, Michael, I need you to go," Dominic said without turning his attention away from Galen.

"It's okay. Dominic knows what he's doing," Abby muttered, hoping like hell that was true.

Michael moved reluctantly, but went with Abby and Scott through the curtain into the front of the store.

"It's just you and me again, Galen. Are we to end this together?" Dominic asked and made to cross the floor toward Galen, only to be forced back with a silent command to stay away.

"This is *my* end, Dominic. There are no more pictures to be drawn." Galen spoke quietly, but his hand caressed Michael's palm print. "This is my last, and your child gave it back to me."

"The child of your child," Dominic said sadly as he tried to push through the mental barrier to be by Galen's side.

Galen smiled, and his ever-present fangs looked out of place against his serene expression.

Always love him.

The message was sent, but Dominic knew it was not meant for him. It was a final message to Michael. Yet it distracted Dominic long enough that he didn't see Galen flick the lid of the gold cigarette lighter he'd had hidden in his hand until it fell to ignite hungry flames around Galen's feet.

They started low, but grew rapidly with the fuel of fluid-soaked T-shirts and cleaning cloths, and Dominic watched in horror as the orange flames licked at the thinner splashed on Galen's legs.

Galen's fear invaded Dominic's mind, but his maker held him back with sheer force of will. A bottle in the path of the flames exploded to send sparks that ignited the nearby curtains. Galen was surrounded.

It was only then that he released Dominic.

Dominic could hear Michael's panic, but lingered a little longer. He held Galen's eyes with his own and sent the message, *I love you still, Galen.*

A fine blond hair floated through the heat haze and glowed orange-red before burning to nothing.

Michael was on him as soon as Dominic ran through the smoldering curtain that separated the rooms.

"I couldn't get back in. He wouldn't let me," Michael said as he tried to see through the flames that engulfed the workroom.

Dominic shook his head and pushed Michael through the front door, where they joined the others on the footpath. An explosion crashed through the night sounds of Chapel Street, and the small group grew with onlookers as the flames rushed into the storefront, catching clothing and melting vinyl in their wake.

A siren sounded behind them, and two fire trucks came to an abrupt halt immediately in front of Ink. The onlookers were herded off the path and into the safety of the road, where they watched hoses being unfurled in an already futile attempt to save the store. Scott wrapped his arms around Abby while they watched both their home and their livelihood burn.

"Everything's gone," Scott muttered and tightened his hold.

Abby leaned back into him and shook her head. "Not everything. It's just stuff that's gone, Scotty," she whispered, barely heard above the clamor of the fireman shouting orders as their apartment floor crashed through and sent shards of painted glass, puzzle pieces of demons and dragons, spraying over the path. "It's just stuff that can be replaced."

INK was gutted. Only charcoal and the skeletons of blackened tattoo chairs remained to pay witness to what had been there before—nothing worth saving.

The four sat quietly on the steps of Dominic's veranda, lost in their own thoughts, until Scott finally asked the question, "So, that's it? Is he gone?"

"I think so," Dominic whispered, surprised that after all his years of running and hiding, he mourned the loss of his maker.

"You saw him burn, right?" Scott persisted, only to have Abby slap him lightly on the thigh as she stood up.

"Not tonight, Scotty," she said and held her hand out to him. "For what's left of tonight, you're going to take me upstairs, where we'll cuddle and talk about the cool stuff we're gonna do next, and then we'll fall asleep and start again tomorrow."

Michael looked up at his friends and smiled. They looked a strange pair: Abby with her crimson hair, star-covered, mauve pajamas and faded Fear Factory T-shirt, and the blue-dreadlocked Scott standing beside her in his old Batman boxers. A strange pair, but they were family.

"Tomorrow, I'll look for the key to my apartment, and you're welcome to stay there until the lease runs out and help yourself to anything in it, okay?" Michael offered.

"Thank you, sweetheart," Abby said and bent to kiss him. "I'll call the bank tomorrow to get things sorted so I can buy a few things to see me through, because something tells me I'm not going to find too many bras or frilly undies at your place." She gave him a wink then turned to Dominic. "Thank you for letting us stay here tonight."

Dominic nodded, but sent her a thought he knew she would hear. *I am sorry I brought him into your life, and I will never forget what you and Scott did for Michael.*

Abby's smile broadened, and much to Scott's confusion, she placed a gentle kiss on Dominic's cool forehead.

"What was that all about?" Scott mumbled as they wandered through the front door and up to their bed for the night.

"I heard the policeman tell Abby that the back door of the workroom was open when they got there," Michael said once his friends were out of earshot. "Was that how he got in?" *Or out?* Michael wanted to add, but thought it best not to.

Dominic didn't reply. He'd watched the flames lick around Galen until they caught and singed the ends of his fine hair, but when the ink-patterned skin of his legs began to scorch, Galen forced him out. He'd fought the command, not wanting Galen to die alone, but his maker's will was strong. Galen would not allow Dominic to die with him.

The last Dominic saw was the green eyes of a young man who finally knew who he was.

Michael heard a low rumble from nearby that steadily grew in intensity until out of the corner of his eye he saw the figure of an old woman trundling down her driveway, pushing a big green rubbish bin. Its wheels bounced and caught on the broken concrete of the drive, and she cursed.

Dominic was at her side in an instant. "Here, Violet, let me do that," he offered with a gentle smile.

"I was watching the news and fell asleep in my chair," she explained. "When I woke up, I realized I'd totally forgotten it was bin night until right now." She eyed Michael sitting on the step watching them and said cheekily, "He's very handsome, your young man."

Dominic chuckled, glancing in Michael's direction. "He is, isn't he?"

"It's about time you found a nice someone to share your time," she continued as they walked down to the curb, her fuzzy slippers scuffing over the path. "I used to wonder when I was a little girl why you were always alone. I worried about you, and I'd imagine I would grow up, and we would get married just like in that movie; you know, the one about the little girl who waited for her love to reach her age. Then you wouldn't be so lonely."

Dominic smiled indulgently and made to correct what he assumed was her failing grasp of time, but she quickly stopped him. "Don't give me that nonsense about being your father's son. I always knew it was you."

"And you never said anything?" Dominic asked, understanding it was pointless to argue.

"We all have our secrets," Violet said with a sly smile. "Besides, I decided you were my guardian angel because you were there when I was born, and you'll be here when I die."

"I'm no angel," Dominic whispered, but Violet simply gave him a dismissive wave of her hand.

There was nothing more he could say, so Dominic just walked her back to her door and promised that each week he would remember to put her bins out on the curb. He was still smiling when he returned to the step and enfolded Michael's hand in his own. With a long sigh, Dominic let his shoulders sag, and he leaned against Michael. He wanted to go up to their room, but the effort seemed a little too much.

Michael smiled and lifted their hands. "Violet has good taste in men," he whispered.

"Well, she thinks you're handsome," Dominic said with a tired grin.

"That's what I mean." Michael chuckled. "I like that she sees you as her guardian angel."

"She's old and her mind wanders."

"Seemed pretty sharp to me," Michael said and lifted his face to feel the cool breeze caress his skin. The rain had cleared the air and offered the hint of a cool change. A faint smell of smoke still lingered, but beneath that was the salt and seaweed of the bay. A tired smile twitched at the corners of his mouth, and a distant strain of violin music teased his memory.

We'll dance again.

When thought touched him, Michael nodded.

We'll dance many times together.

Epilogue

SHE lifted her nose to the stars, scenting something unfamiliar, something that didn't belong. The little red fox had lived all her life roaming the eucalypt forest, unaware that the humans believed *she* didn't belong—an introduced species, vermin to be eradicated. But their views did not color her world. Humans were merely providers of discarded snacks and twin lights that had to be avoided when she left the boundaries of her forest.

The vixen snorted delicately and trotted further into the grove of tree ferns, curious about the newcomer. He didn't smell like the ones who burned their meat on the barbeques or tramped through the tall trees. He smelled of smoke, fire, and blood. He smelled of old distant lands that part of her knew, though she didn't know why.

She sat with her head low and eyes wide open, staring at the pale man who stood among the ferns until he looked back at her. A small smile of recognition crossed his lips, and he crouched low over the soft earth. He sent a silent greeting to the vixen before he lay on the ground and curled elegantly as if to sleep, only to sink and fade into the soil.

The little fox trotted closer, but stopped before reaching the ferns. His scent lingered, although he was gone from her sight. She cocked her head as if to listen, then gave a single bark and trotted away to resume her scavenging.

The pale man who slept in the earth did not inhabit her world, so she would simply leave him to his dreams.

A black cat for a witch may be a cliché, but add a whole bunch of tribal tattoos and an intolerance to garlic (seriously), and you have ISABELLE ROWAN.

Having moved to Australia from England as a small child, Isabelle now lives in a seaside suburb of Melbourne where she teaches film making and English. She is a movie addict who spends far too much money on traveling… but then again, life is to be lived.

Visit Isabelle's blog at http://isabelle-rowan.livejournal.com/.

Also from ISABELLE ROWAN

ISABELLE ROWAN

MARGINS

OPEN

A Note
IN THE
MARGIN

There is more to life than the main story ...
check out the notes in the margins.

http://www.dreamspinnerpress.com

For more of the
best M/M romance,
visit

Dreamspinner Press

www.dreamspinnerpress.com

www.ingramcontent.com/pod-product-compliance
Lightning Source LLC
Chambersburg PA
CBHW071328250626
47159CB00004B/1507